FORGET ME NOT

BY

TERRI MOLINA

Decadent Publishing Company

www.decadentpublishing.com

Forget Me Not
Copyright 2011 by Terri Molina
ISBN: 978-1-61333-170-5
Cover design by Fiona Jayde and Cribley Designs

Published by Decadent Publishing Company
www.decadentpublishing.com

Printed in the United States of America

~DEDICATION~

This book is dedicated to my sister Becky, who has always believed in me.

~*Author's Note*~

This book would not be possible were it not for the support and encouragement of my husband and children. I also can't overlook my dear friends and critique partners for their valuable input in making this book better: Helen King, Kelly Armstrong, Marina Agostinelli, and Stacey Goita. Thank you to Rhonda Morrow who is always there when I need her. A special thank you to Lauren Baratz-Logsted for her encouragement and confidence in me and the story and to my initial readers Pam Mellor, Hermina Castillo, Michelle Bellot, Anna and Peter Salomon, and Christie Craig. There are many more I owe my gratitude to and I hope you know who you are.

CHAPTER ONE

The suits gave them away. Standard black linen. Crisp white shirt. Dependable black tie. FBI agents. At her front door. At eight o'clock in the morning.

This can't be good.

Casey adjusted the thin robe covering her even thinner teddy and pasted on a bright smile. "Good morning," she said, resisting the urge to cringe at the overly perky tone in her voice.

"Casey Martinez?" The older of the two men spoke, his gaze looking her over as if committing her to memory.

"Yes, I'm Casey Martinez." Although there was nothing sexual in his perusal, she rechecked her robe to make sure it was closed.

"I'm Special Agent John Simms. This is Special Agent Darryl Hawthorne." In unison they removed their wallets and opened them to reveal a gold badge and picture ID.

She blinked at the stoic men blocking her doorway, her mind spinning with reasons for their visit. Her latest novel had been set at the FBI academy in Quantico, Virginia, but she was sure she didn't write anything in the book that would offend the government. It was romance fiction, not a tell-all.

"May we come in, please?" Agent Simms asked, though it sounded more like an order than a request.

"Oh. Of course. I'm sorry." She stepped back, motioning them through the door. She wished she'd taken the time to get dressed. Or at least brushed her teeth.

The agents stepped into her apartment, scrutinizing the layout with keen eyes. It was a moderate sized room, sparsely furnished with an overstuffed sofa and matching loveseat that had come with the lease. A roll-top desk sat tucked against the wall next to the terrace, the surface hidden by a computer, several piles of paper and an overflowing ashtray. A week's worth of empty pizza boxes and cartons of Chinese food contributed to more of the clutter. Stacked against the plain white walls were various-sized packing boxes, most of which contained books. A few of the cartons were opened and rummaged through, while the others remained sealed. She had never placed any pictures on the walls, even the mantel above the fireplace sat bare. Looking at the apartment through their eyes, Casey realized she had never tried to make it a home.

After another check of her belt, she waved toward the couch. "Please, have a seat." She scooped up a basket of clothes from the sofa and placed it on the floor, mentally chastising herself for not cleaning the room sooner.

The younger agent, Hawthorne, nodded and sat on the rust-colored sofa while his partner wandered to the terrace doors and studied the skyline with feigned interest. A soft breeze drifted in, rippling the drapes into a delicate dance around him.

Casey skirted around the sofa and sat in the loveseat. "So, what can I do for you?"

"We have a few questions we need to ask you. Don't worry, you won't need a lawyer," Agent Hawthorne said offering her a reassuring smile.

"Sure, okay. What is it you need to know?" She settled back in the loveseat and tried to make herself comfortable. "Oh, wait. This doesn't have anything to do with the packages I've been getting, does it? I mean, I didn't think the FBI looked into that sort of thing."

"Packages?" Agent Simms asked. He turned away from the city view to face her.

"Every now and then I'll get some sermonizing rants and Bibles from a holier-than-thou fanatic who thinks I need to repent for my sinful lifestyle or something ridiculous like that. I guess they don't like my love scenes," she said with a smile.

They both gave her a blank stare.

She swallowed her sigh and added, "They're just harmless books and a few notes. After the third one came in, Jo insisted I turn them over to the police."

"Joe? And he would be…?" Agent Hawthorne took a small notepad from his jacket and scribbled the name on the page.

"*She*, actually. Josephine Landry. She's my agent." At the continued blank looks, she added, "I'm a writer. Paranormal romances. But not your typical vampire or werewolf story, more like witches and demons, which, I guess annoys enough of the zealots out there that they want to try and save my soul. Hence the Bibles. I'll admit when the first one came in all highlighted and dog-eared, it made me nervous because some of my readers are incarcerated, which isn't surprising since a small number of romance fans are convicted felons because our novels are mostly what the prison libraries are sent." Casey stopped and mentally kicked herself. She was babbling. *Geez.* She didn't intimidate easy, but there was something disconcerting about the men in her living room. She offered them a smile and shrugged. "Anyway, they really weren't threatening, but Jo wanted the police to look into it."

"How long ago did you get your first package?" Agent Hawthorne asked. He continued to scribble in his notebook as if he were writing his own great American novel.

"The first one came about six years ago, after my first book came out then another one two years later. I ended up donating them to a used bookstore. The third one came in a year after that, and Jo gave it to the police. But, like I said, since they weren't the least bit threatening, they decided it didn't warrant looking into." She waved her hand in dismissal. "These things just come with the territory. Sometimes readers will confuse the characters with the author or the author with the story. Believe me, the Bibles are the last thing I have to worry about from a fan."

"Have you received any of these notes or packages recently?" Agent Simms asked.

Casey heard the annoyance in his voice and looked at each of the men, fighting against the sudden knot of anxiety coiling up to her chest.

"I don't know. I keep a box at the post office and only picked up my mail yesterday. I haven't had a chance to go through it yet." She waited. Then, because Agent Simms seemed to expect it, she rose from her chair and moved to the desk and the mound of papers on top. She moved the stacks aside, trying not to make the mess any worse.

"So, did you find out who the guy is? Did he do something?" Although she wasn't really sure she wanted to know the answer. If the Feds were at her home this early, it had to be bad.

"We just want to cover all our bases, ma'am," Agent Hawthorne said. He rose from the sofa and stepped forward to join her at the desk.

Before she could ask him what he meant, Agent Simms grabbed her attention.

"Do you do a lot of traveling, Ms. Martinez?" He stole a look at her Simpson's desk calendar. She hadn't changed the date in over a month.

"Yes, some. I do the occasional book tour or writing conference. I also tend to relocate when I'm writing. But something tells me you already know that, Agent Simms." She sent him a sidelong glance. He stood just over six feet tall with a broad chest and wide shoulders that filled his dark suit. His once-black hair was nearly taken over by gray, and she guessed him to be in his mid-fifties. Hard lines etched his face, giving him a gruff look. Piercing dark-brown eyes watched her with a tense patience that told her she didn't move fast enough for him. If they were planning to do the 'good cop-bad cop' game, she would have no problem determining who was who.

"Do you generally travel alone or do you have an assistant or …someone?" Agent Simms asked.

Casey slowed her search and looked up, arching her brow. "Sometimes I travel with Jo, but most of the time I'm alone. But I haven't traveled in a while. My last few book signings were local."

"Did you have one of these signings recently?"

Casey grabbed a handful of letters and sifted through them. "Yes. A couple of nights ago in Manhattan. Why?"

"Do you generally get a lot of people at these? Men, perhaps?" Agent Hawthorne asked.

"There are always a few men, yes. They claim they're getting signatures for their wives or girlfriends. I guess no man would admit to reading romances, even if they are suspenseful," she said with short laugh. When they didn't respond, she stopped sifting and placed the mail back on the table. "I'm sorry, gentlemen, but I'm a little pressed for time this morning. If you're not here about the notes or Bibles, then could you please tell me what this is all about?"

"A young woman was found murdered in her apartment last week," Agent Simms said.

The words hit Casey like a sledgehammer and made her heart stop. "Oh my God. Who?" Her mind raced with names. She didn't have many close friends, but she knew a lot of people in the writing community. The fact that the agents were at her house told her she must know the victim.

"Her name was Catherine Flores. She was a school teacher from New Rochelle."

Casey blinked, processing the name in her mind. The weight eased slightly from her chest. "I'm sorry. I don't know her."

"No ma'am, we didn't think you would," Agent Hawthorne said.

"You didn't? Then why—? I don't understand."

Agent Hawthorne tucked his notebook in his jacket and motioned toward the desk. "May I?"

She nodded and stepped back, shoving her hands in her pockets while the agent rooted through her chaos.

"The person who murdered Ms. Flores left one of your books next to the body," Agent Simms said. "Initially, we thought the woman was you because of the picture on the back cover. We couldn't be sure because the guy did quite a number on her face. Until the dental records confirmed her ID, we believed the victim to be you."

Casey looked at the agent as if he had just sprouted wings. "So, what exactly are you saying? You think this guy was after *me?*" She shook her head, as if she could erase the words from her mind. They couldn't be serious. Sure, she was an up and coming name in the romance business, but she was hardly a big enough celebrity for someone to fixate on, much less want to kill.

"It's something we aren't ruling out at the moment," Agent Hawthorne said with a subtle shake of his head at his partner. He motioned Casey back to the armchair and returned to his place on the sofa. "Do the months April or June have any significance for you?" he asked as she returned to her chair.

"No," she said, her voice harder than she'd intended. She shrugged. "My birthday is April twenty-first. But there's nothing about the month of

June I find important." She rolled her shoulders to ease the tension in her muscles. She was not going to think about *him*. She shifted in her seat and tried to relax. "Why do you think this has anything to do with me? I mean, I didn't know Ms. Flores, so why would anyone want to kill her if they were after me?"

Agent Simms joined his partner on the sofa, his expression stoic. "Maybe he made a mistake."

Casey glared at him. "Made a mistake? A woman is murdered and you want to call it a mistake?"

There was a slight shift in the agent's expression, as if he'd been pleased by her anger. Maybe it made his job easier if he didn't have to control a hysterical female. Not that she'd ever been hysterical about anything, at least, not in the last twenty years.

"If you've been getting unwanted mail then you may have a stalker. He could be anyone," Agent Hawthorne cut in, shooting a look at his partner. "Maybe he's a crazed fan or a jilted lover. We were hoping you could tell us. Is there anyone you can think of who has any hostilities toward you?"

"No, of course not."

"Have you dated anyone recently or in the past that maybe didn't like how the relationship ended?"

"Not really. Well, there was Aaron. But our breakup was …fairly amicable," she said.

"What do you mean?" Agent Hawthorne asked.

She sent him a direct look. "He was cheating on me, so I dumped him. But Aaron is no woman killer. He loves them entirely too much."

"Just the same, we'd like to speak with him," Agent Simms countered.

Casey shot him a look that he returned with more authority. She mentally shook her head and rose from the chair. "Fine. I think I still have his number somewhere."

Returning to the desk, she inhaled a calming breath before sliding the top drawer open. It was pointless to get angry with the agents. They were only trying to find a killer and believed she could help. But they had to be off the mark if they thought she was the intended target. She'd been invisible her whole life and didn't attract attention from anyone, much less a psychotic killer.

The doorbell chimed as she grabbed her address book. Agent Simms stood, his hand shooting into his jacket as if he planned to pull out his gun. Casey sent him a dry look and moved to the door. "Don't shoot. It's just the messenger."

A young man in faded jeans and a red t-shirt stood at the door, his hand resting on the worn satchel strapped across his chest. "Good morning, Ms. Martinez. Sorry, I'm late. Do you have a pick-up for me?" he asked with a toothy grin. His smile wavered when he noticed the two men inside her living room.

"Good morning, Tommy. Hold on a minute. I have it right here."

She stepped back to the desk and grabbed a large padded envelope. Beside her laptop was a mug in the shape of a frog. She dug her hand inside and pulled out some money and handed it to Tommy along with the package.

"Thank you, Ms. Martinez," he said, shoving the money in his pocket with a wide smile. "Oh, wait. I have a package for you, too. Mr. DeAngelo said it was left in the mailroom and asked me to bring it up." He withdrew a manila envelope from his bag and handed it to her.

"Thanks. You be careful out there." She tucked the envelope under her arm and closed the door behind him before turning back to the men. "These are just the copy edits for my next book. Sometimes the letter carrier can't fit them in my mailbox so he gives them to the landlord for me," she said to ease their visible concern over the envelope. She grabbed her cigarettes from the desk and lit one up, dropping the pack into the pocket of her robe.

"Ms. Martinez," Agent Simms said, his voice strained with impatience. "Is there anyone else you can think of? An ex-husband, maybe?"

Casey paced to the terrace and blew out the first lungful of smoke through the open doors. The sky was overcast, the temperature unseasonably warm for the beginning of May. In the distance a school bell rang, the laughter of children catching on the breeze. She closed her eyes and tried to focus on someone, anyone that she'd had contact with over the years. But the sad truth was she didn't have any jilted lovers or a husband. In fact, she didn't have any lovers at all—not since Aaron—and that was three years ago. She preferred to spend her time working on her books instead of working on a relationship. It was much less exhausting, and she didn't risk losing more than her heart. As far as she was concerned, love was beyond the bottom of her list of priorities.

She turned back to the men and shook her head. "I'm sorry, Agent Simms. There's no one, really. I've never been married, and I don't date much. My work takes up most of my time." She tamped her cigarette out in the ashtray on the desk and set the stick in the groove before moving back to the armchair. "I really wish I could help you, but I just don't think this has anything to do with me."

Sliding a finger under the seal, she opened the envelope and poured the contents onto her lap. Several photographs of a bloodied, nude body spilled out. The eyes of the victim were scratched out and thick red streaks were smeared across her image like rivers of blood. Casey's new book, *Unholy Alliance—Dancing with the Devil*, had been placed in the extended, bloodstained hand of the poor woman, as if showing who was responsible. The letters had been intricately edited out of the title to read *U Die*.

She shot up from the chair, her chest expanding with the sharp intake of air. Her stomach pitched. The pictures scattered onto the floor.

Agent Simms vaulted from his seat, breaking the stunned silence. "Get that messenger back in here, now!" He pulled a handkerchief from his pocket and covered the pictures as Agent Hawthorne ran from the room.

"I'm sorry you had to see those," he said through clenched teeth, using a pen he'd pulled from his inside pocket to push the photos back in the envelope.

Casey pressed a hand to her chest, working to slow her rapid breaths. She staggered back to the open terrace and gulped in the warm spring air. At least she could be grateful she hadn't eaten breakfast yet. Gripping the sliding door, she closed her eyes and tried to erase the pictures from her mind. In most of the photos the features were unrecognizable. But in one, *her* face had been pasted onto the picture.

Casey filled her lungs with air and squeezed her eyes tighter, biting into her bottom lip. Her heart pounded against her breastbone as the unwanted memory of another murder filled her mind. The eerie silence of the bedroom. The rich copper odor of blood. Her mother's butchered body draped over the bed. The lifeless eyes staring at Casey, accusing. She pushed it all away and focused on breathing. Emotions rained down on her like ice water, but she wasn't sure what she was supposed to feel. Fear? Panic? Guilt? She closed her arms around her waist and stared blindly at the still waters of the Hudson River.

It had to be a mistake. Why would someone want to kill her? She never did anything to anyone. She didn't have any friends and rarely socialized outside of the writing community. The pictures were just a joke. A very horrible joke. They had to be. Catherine Flores' murder has nothing to do with her. *But the agents think it does. She mentally shook herself. No, they have to be wrong! They're reaching and trying to find a connection because they're desperate. Ms. Flores was killed because she was at the wrong place at the wrong time* It was New York, after all. People were murdered every day with no rhyme or reason to it. Okay, so maybe there was a resemblance between her and the murdered woman, but that was a coincidence, too. *Everyone has a twin or two in the world, it doesn't mean anything!*

She pressed her fingers to her eyes and saw the picture again. *U die.*

Forcing the image from her mind, she swallowed hard. Determined to keep her panic in check, she turned around to face Agent Simms. He stood at the foot of the sofa, waiting and watching with the same blank expression all federal agents seemed to master. "Okay. You have my attention. What is it you aren't telling me?"

The agent motioned her back to the sofa and waited for her to sit. "We believe we have a serial killer on our hands, Ms. Martinez, and we think he may have fixated on you." He paused as if waiting to see if she would react. When she didn't, he continued. "Three years ago I was assigned a case involving the murder of a young woman named Michelle Castillo. She was the only daughter of an attorney in Manhattan. She'd been raped, her body mutilated. Within a week several more cases with the same MO started pouring in. Each of the women was between the ages of twenty and twenty-five. All Hispanic and all who …all who looked a lot like you."

Casey swallowed. He'd spoken the words gently but she couldn't help feeling as if he blamed her. "How long has this been happening?" she asked, her voice barely audible.

"As far as we can tell, the first murder happened five years ago."

"Five years?" Casey stared at him. The words struck her like a punch. "You've let this happen for five years? How could you have let this go on for so long?"

"It's a bit more complicated than that," Agent Simms said, his voice tight. "The first two murders were two months apart and in two different states. The trails on both went cold fast, and the local officials pushed them to the back burner. The third murder didn't occur until ten months after that. No connections were made to any of the victims until Ms. Castillo's case landed on my desk three years ago. It wasn't until then that we realized we had a serial killer on our hands, and I've been playing catch-up ever since."

Casey paused. A part of her wanted to apologize for offending him, but she knew he wasn't telling her everything and would keep her as much in the dark as the rest of the public.

"How many?" she asked. "How many has he killed?"

"The murder of Ms. Flores makes thirteen." The annoyance in his voice eased, but his expression stayed grim. "So far the only connection we had was that each of the victims was found with shredded pages of a book. We're still trying to piece together enough of the pages to know what type of books they are, but we're almost certain they were all written by you."

Casey took the pack of cigarettes from her pocket and tapped one out. Her hand shook as she lit it, and she inhaled deeply. The smoke tightened the air in her already constricted chest. She'd spent the last twenty years trying to forget everything she'd come from, everything she'd been. But now, because of her, women were being murdered. Just like her mother.

Her gaze moved to the spot where the pictures had fallen. She could still see them there.

"Are you okay, Ms. Martinez?" Agent Simms asked. "Is there something I can get you?"

Casey blew out a slow stream of smoke and fixed her eyes on him. "I'm fine. Please finish. I know there's more." She'd managed to keep her voice cool and calm, showing no trace of the shock or panic racing through her. She would not be that hysterical female; no matter how much she wanted to scream.

"You asked us before if we thought this man was going to come after you." Agent Simms paused and returned her steady gaze. "We think that answer is yes, Ms. Martinez. This last murder, the one in those pictures you just received, leads us to believe he's coming for you next."

CHAPTER TWO

Four hours later Casey had been ushered into Agent Simms's box-sized office in Manhattan. She stalked the meager space, her arms locked across her chest, her fingers scratching an imaginary itch on her arm. Wandering to the picture window, she slid her hand into the wide pocket of her blazer and curled her fingers around the soft pack of cigarettes. She wished they had kept the meeting at her apartment. At least then she'd have been able to smoke.

Twenty-three stories below, the sidewalks swarmed with pedestrians weaving in and out of the crosswalk. Was there a killer down there? Was he watching her now, waiting for her to be alone? She imagined someone looking up to catch her staring and suppressed a shudder.

Rolling her shoulders to push the thought away, she shifted and resumed her pacing. She hated that she was scared; not that she would admit it to anyone. She'd worked too damn hard to become someone else, someone better. She wasn't going to let anyone or anything ruin it for her.

She rubbed her fist against the tightness in her chest. She needed air.

"Casey, sit down. You're making me nervous."

She slid a look at the older woman sitting in the armchair near the desk. She had called Jo after the agents left her apartment that morning, and though she hadn't asked her friend to accompany her to the Federal Building, Jo had been waiting in the lobby when Casey arrived.

"Sorry." She sat in the chair next to her friend and took out the cigarettes, playing with the pack in her hands. "I hate waiting. I mean, if he wasn't going to be here, why bother telling me to come in?"

Jo didn't answer, her attention focused on her iPhone as her fingers stroked the screen. Casey locked her arms across her chest and used the silence to take in the box-sized room. The white walls were adorned with various plaques, commendations and a framed American flag that took up half of one wall. An executive desk housing a computer monitor and office phone sat two feet from the wall and faced the office door behind her. On the corner of the desk was a mug that read *World's Greatest Grandpa*, along with several neatly arranged photos of a young woman cradling a child.

Tucked into the far corner of the room was an easel supporting a large, flat board. A white sheet had been draped over it and she could barely make out the corner of a photograph peeking through. A part of her wanted to look under the sheet at the evidence board, but she'd seen enough of the grisly crime scene that morning.

"What's taking him so damn long?" Casey pushed out of the chair and wandered back to the window, searching for a latch. She didn't consider herself claustrophobic, but the walls felt as if they were starting to close in on her.

"It's only been ten minutes," Jo said.

"I don't know why he couldn't just tell me at my apartment that he'd made a mistake. Why drag me all the way to the city?"

Jo looked up from her phone, her green eyes alert. "He said he'd made a mistake?"

Casey shrugged. "He said the killer *might* have made a mistake." She tapped the pack of cigarettes against her palm until one of the sticks slid out.

"Sorry, there's no smoking in the building," Agent Simms said from behind her as he stepped into the office.

"I know," Casey snapped, shoving the cigarette back into her pocket. *Stupid law.*

"You must be Ms. Landry." Agent Simms extended his hand to Jo. "I'm sorry to keep you waiting." He moved behind his desk and motioned Casey to the empty chair. "Thank you both for coming in."

Casey nodded. It wasn't as if he'd given her a choice. After dropping his bombshell that morning, Agent Simms ended their meeting and told her to meet him at his office at noon. Not asked, *told.* It had irritated the hell out of her. She hated to be told what to do.

"Casey." Jo nodded subtly toward the empty chair next to her.

Casey glanced at Agent Simms and noticed he was still standing beside his chair. He wasn't going to sit down until she did. She bit back a sigh and returned to her seat.

Agent Simms settled in his chair and leaned forward, folding his hands on the desk. "I'm sure you have a lot of questions, and I'll do my best to answer them."

"What's happening right now? Do you have any idea who this person is?" Jo asked.

"Unfortunately, no. The young man who delivered the package to Ms. Martinez didn't know where it came from. The building manager found it in the mailroom and doesn't know how long it had been there," Agent Simms said. "The photos were clean of prints but we're hoping we'll get some DNA off the seal of the envelope." He looked at Casey. "We canvassed the area around your neighborhood but so far no one has reported seeing anyone suspicious hanging around. However, that doesn't mean whoever left the pictures isn't still watching you. We'll be placing surveillance on your building for the next few weeks. If we're lucky, he'll return."

Casey swallowed against the unease growing in her chest. "So, what are you saying? You want to use me as bait to draw him out?"

"No, not at all. The plan is to move you into a safe house and place an agent in your apartment instead."

"A safe house? You want to lock me away in some one-room broken-down cabin in the middle of nowhere? I don't think so," she said.

"It's not as dramatic as that. We have an apartment over in Jersey. You'll be very comfortable, and you'll have 'round the clock protection."

New Jersey? Great, even worse. "For how long?"

The agent's pause held a second longer than it should have.

Casey crossed her arms and glared at him. "You don't know, do you?"

"It's hard to say how long this could take," he answered.

"Forget it!" Casey pushed up from the chair to pace.

"Casey—" Jo said.

"I'm not going to let them lock me up in some fleabag apartment for God knows how long because they *think* a killer is after me. Forget it."

"Ms. Martinez, I'm afraid you don't have much of a choice."

She whirled around to face the agent. "I don't what?"

Jo rose from her chair to stand next to Casey. "Agent Simms, what if she leaves the area? Goes somewhere farther away?"

"Jo—"

Jo pinned her with a firm look. "Quiet." Her voice was low but the order was there. Casey stalked to the window and scowled at the blue sky.

"She has a brother in Texas," Jo continued. "She could go visit with him and his wife for a while. That would take her out of harm's way while you do what you do to find the person who's after her."

"I don't think that's a good idea," the agent said. "If this person has been watching Ms. Martinez, then he'll know she has family in Texas and that could put them in danger as well."

"There's no reason he should know. It's a very small town, and she and her brother have different names," Jo replied.

Casey turned to look at the agent. "My legal name is Casey Martinez. I changed it after my first book sold," she said. It was the first thing she did with the advance money.

"Even the bio on the book jackets are fiction," Jo added. "Her hometown is listed as Yonkers."

Agent Simms tapped his fingers on the desk as he considered Jo's suggestion. After a moment he nodded. "Okay, it might work. But I still want to make sure you're protected. I'll contact the local bureau and see if there's anyone they can put on security detail."

"A bodyguard? Are you kidding me?" Casey said.

Jo sent a pleasant smile to Agent Simms. "Would you give us a minute, please?"

The agent looked at both of them then nodded. "I'll go make some calls."

"No!" Casey said as soon as the agent left the room. "You're not getting rid of me, and you're not going to stick me in the middle of nowhere with a bunch of rednecks and a robot in a *suit*."

Jo placed her hand on Casey's shoulder. "Casey, you know how much I admire your tenacity, but this is one time you need to do as you're told."

"You can't tell me you believe this? That someone wants me dead because of my books? That's crazy!"

"All that matters is the FBI believes it. If this person is as dangerous as they think he is, then I want you out of harm's way and somewhere safe. And what better place than a town that's barely even on the map?"

"I can think of better places," Casey muttered.

"I know you said you'd never go back there, but I think it'll be good for you. It's time to face your past. It can't hurt you unless you let it."

"Who are you, Dr. Phil?" Casey growled, moving away to stand next to the window. She took the cigarette from her pocket and played it through her fingers.

Jo eased out a sigh. "Casey, I know how hard you worked to build a new life, become this new identity, but you have a lot of unfinished business there. You need to find closure or you'll never be able to move on."

Casey squared her shoulders, her fingers tightening around the cigarette and sending flakes of tobacco over the windowsill. "I don't need closure. And I've been moving on just fine."

"Sweetie, I've read your work. You're suppressing a lot of pain and anger from your childhood. It isn't healthy." Jo moved beside her and placed a hand on Casey's shoulder. "I know you don't like to talk about your past, and I've always respected that. But sweetie, you need to talk to someone so you can find some inner peace. I know these murders are going to bring up memories—"

"You don't know anything; and stop acting like you're my fucking shrink," Casey snapped, shoving the mangled cigarette in her pocket. She turned and grabbed on to Jo's arm. Guilt and regret burned like acid in her stomach. "Oh God, I'm sorry. I didn't mean that."

Jo offered her a smile and squeezed her hand. "I know," she said. "And I know it won't be easy for you. You don't have to be afraid anymore. You're a much stronger person than you give yourself credit for."

Casey pressed her fingers to her eyes and eased out a tired breath. Jo was the closest thing to a mother she'd ever had. She hated herself for hurting her. "If it's that important to you, I'll go."

"*You're* important to me," Jo said. "I'm going to be traveling for the next two weeks, and I'll sleep better at night knowing you're safe and with people who love you."

Casey frowned. Guilt was a great motivator, and Jo knew how to use it better than anyone. "Okay, okay," she said, dropping into the chair. "I said I'd go."

Jo sent her a benign smile. "It doesn't have to be that bad," she said. "Look at it this way, at least you'll have more freedom to go out and do things. You'll be able to clear your head. Maybe even meet new people. You can't do that locked away in an apartment in Jersey."

Casey sent her a sidelong glance. "Is that your way of telling me I need to get laid?"

"That's not exactly my point," Jo replied.

Casey held up her hand. "I got your point, and that was a joke."

"All I meant was maybe you can start your next book while you're there. You said you wanted to have a story take place in the south. Texas is as good a place as any to write about."

"Right. Rednecks and rice farmers. Sounds like a bestseller to me," Casey said. She caught the disapproving look from Jo and shrank back against her chair, the guilt a ten-ton weight on her chest. Damn, the woman was good. She eased out a resigned sigh. "Look, I'll go to Texas, I'll think about the new book, and I'll promise not to be a hermit. But I'm *not* going to get a bodyguard."

"For goodness sakes, it's not like you have to hire Mr. Universe," Jo said, waving her words away. "I'll talk to Agent Simms and see if he can find you someone discreet."

"It's the FBI. I don't think they know how to be discreet," she said dryly.

"Then we'll contact the local police department and see if they have someone willing to moonlight. We can say he's your assistant."

"I don't need an assistant. I don't want anyone at all. I like my privacy," Casey said. "And what about my brother? I don't want him to know about this."

"There's no reason he should. Discreet, remember?"

Casey pushed up from the chair and moved to the window, locking her arms across her chest. It wasn't that she didn't want to see her brother and sister-in-law again. She just didn't know if she was ready to face a town that had always made her feel worthless.

"I think you're all worried for nothing," she growled. "You said it yourself it's not like the guy is going to follow me across the country, much less to some little hick town in Texas." She grabbed the pack of cigarettes from her pocket, flakes of tobacco floating onto the floor. "What if I—"

"Great," Jo said. "Then it's settled. Do you want to make the arrangements for your trip or shall I?"

Casey exhaled a world-weary sigh and shoved the cigarettes back in her pocket. "I'll do it."

"Good. I'll speak to Agent Simms and let him know what we've decided," Jo said, with a bright smile.

Casey frowned and turned to look out the window. She hated to admit it, but Jo and the federal agent were right. Unless she left town for a while the psycho would make her one of his victims. And after what happened to their mother ...she couldn't put Alex through a loss like that again.

Maybe Jo was right, and she should try to look on the bright side. She would get to see Alex and Jennifer again and spend some much needed time with them. They hadn't been together as a family since Alex's wedding seven years earlier. Plus, the lease was coming up on her apartment soon, and that was as good an excuse as any to relocate for a while. She'd been back in New York for almost three years and could feel the restlessness settling in. But a bodyguard! She hated to have anyone hover over her when she was working. Especially an overzealous, Kevin Costner wanna-be!

She leaned against the cool glass and watched the traffic below. *Well, as long as he stays out of my way, we won't have a problem.*

CHAPTER THREE

Scott Weller aced his serve and was set to try again when his opponent, Alex Rivera, dropped to the floor in exaggerated exhaustion.

"Whoa, man, give me a break. I worked graveyard last night."

Scott tossed a look over his shoulder. Alex's solid six-foot frame was sprawled out on the hardwood floor. "Cut the shit. You worked the three-to-eleven shift." He flicked the wet hair from his forehead and turned back to the wall.

"Yeah, but I worked my ass off," Alex said.

Scott shook his head and gave up his stance. Dropping the blue racquetball and racquet onto the hardwood floor, he moved to the corner of the square room and pulled two towels and two water bottles from a cubby in the wall.

"Sorry, I've got a lot on my mind." He tossed Alex a towel and one of the bottles and leaned against the wall to catch his breath. He had hoped their weekly racquetball game would help shake off his tension from work, but even after nearly an hour of playing, he still couldn't get his mind to unwind from his current situation. He tugged at his police academy t-shirt, adjusting the sweat-drenched fabric away from his body.

"Must be pretty bad," Alex said, his voice a thick Texas drawl mixed in with a Spanish accent. He sat up and wiped the sweat from his face before he took a gulp from his bottle. "But at least it's helping your game. You're usually not much competition." He didn't have a chance to duck

Scott's towel before it connected with the side of his face. Alex laughed and draped the towel over his shoulder. "So, what's up? You're usually not the type to let something get stuck in your craw."

"The captain put me on desk duty for the next few weeks. Internal Affairs started their witch hunt, and he doesn't want to give them anything else to investigate. Like I'm some sort of hot head or something," Scott growled under his breath.

Alex looked at him with a crooked smile. "Nope, not at all."

Scott tossed the water bottle back into the cubby and resumed his position at the serving line. He looked back at his friend and cocked a brow. "You going to play or sleep?"

With a heavy sigh, Alex stood and recapped his water. He tossed it into the cubby with the towels and stood behind the blue line, ready to receive.

"So this I.A. thing is just routine, isn't it?" Alex asked, grunting as he returned the hard serve.

"Nothing is ever routine with I.A.," Scott ground out. He connected on the ball with such force it ricocheted off the wall like a bullet and shot toward the ceiling. Alex charged the ball and took the serve.

"It's not like they've never tried to bust your balls before. Why is it getting to you now?" Alex dropped the ball and in one fluid motion, slammed it against the wall with a thundering pop. He pivoted and moved back as Scott came in for the return. They volleyed back and forth until Scott won the serve.

Scott exhaled a deep breath, bouncing the ball on the court. "It's not so much the I.A. investigation as it is the desk duty. Since I can't get on the streets, the captain's assigning me grunt work."

Serve, volley, point.

"There's some big shot coming in who's requested police protection. They even went through the mayor to get it. Like anyone needs a bodyguard in Rosehill!" Scott dropped the ball and slammed it against the wall, acing his serve again.

Alex raised his hands up, huffing out a breath. "That's it. That's game. You're killing me, man."

They grabbed their towels and left the court. It was immediately occupied by two men who had been sitting outside, watching the competition.

Scott peeled off his shirt as soon as he entered the locker room and used it to wipe the sweat from his body. He tossed the shirt into his gym bag, glancing at the small mirror installed on the inside door of his locker. The six-inch scar that ran jagged down the center of his chest was a reminder of his brush with death, yet he rarely thought about that night five years earlier when he had been face down in the street bleeding to death. His attitude was, and always would be, that it was just part of the job, just as his father and his father's father had said before they each took a fatal bullet.

Scott had long ago accepted that it was his destiny to die on the job. But since that fateful day when he'd been used for target practice, he made sure he wore a bulletproof vest when he went out on a call. After all, destiny didn't need his help.

"So, who's this big-shot you have to babysit?" Alex asked. He sat on the bench and removed his shoes.

"I don't know. I'm supposed to meet him—" Scott looked at the watch in his locker and swore under his breath. "Ten minutes ago. So much for a quick shower." He grabbed his clothes from the hook in the stall and quickly put them on.

"Well, not a very good first impression. Here." Alex tossed him a can of deodorant and laughed. "I think you're gonna need this."

Scott used the spray then tossed it back. "Thanks. And sorry about the game."

"Like I said, I worked my ass off last night," Alex said. "You had me at a disadvantage." He wrapped a towel around his naked waist and started toward the showers. "Oh, by the way, if you're not too busy tonight, Jenn wanted me to invite you over for dinner."

Scott's fingers stopped on the buttons of his shirt and he sent Alex a cautious look. "This isn't another one of her attempts to fix me up, is it?" Like most married women seemed to feel the need to do to their single friends, Jennifer was always trying to find a suitable mate for Scott. It wasn't that the women she chose weren't lookers, they just weren't the type he would want a permanent relationship with—if he ever decided to go that route, which wasn't likely. Marriage wasn't exactly on his list of long-term goals. Not that he hadn't considered it once. Of course he was only seventeen at the time and in the middle of mind-numbing sex with

Carole Moreno in the backseat of his mother's Lincoln.

Maybe his mother was right, and he just hadn't found the right girl. No, marriage to a cop was hard enough. Being the widow of one was even worse. He wasn't about to risk putting someone through that. He adored Jennifer though, so he didn't make a fuss when she tried to fix him up. He'd just grin and bear it and most of the time, enjoy it.

"No, nothing like that," Alex said. "We're just having a few people over. My baby sister's coming into town for a visit, and Jenn wanted to welcome her back with a few friends. Besides, she's not your type. She's educated."

Scott laughed at Alex's playful smirk, not the least bit offended. He had certain rules he liked to follow when it came to dating. One was never date your best friend's sister, and he considered Alex too good a friend to even consider the thought.

"So, is six o'clock okay for you?" Alex asked.

Scott thought about the short, balding man he would be sitting with that night, which is how he pictured C. J. Martinez—a short, middle-aged bald man who popped antacids like candy. He'd never met Alex's little sister, but he guessed she would be more appealing company. He could probably get someone from the station to cover him for a few hours.

"Sure, six sounds great. Do you want me to bring anything?"

"Nah, just your appetite. Oh, but you can bring Denise, if you want," Alex said, referring to Scott's latest girlfriend. When Scott grimaced, Alex laughed and added, "Or not."

Scott grinned and grabbed his gym bag. "I'll see you at six."

Scott turned up the volume on his radio and tapped his fingers to the gritty rock of Nickleback as he maneuvered his Jeep onto the street. The breeze swept thick strands of hair across his brow, which he didn't bother to push aside. What was the point of having a jeep if you didn't ride without the top on? He'd removed the Jeep's canvas top earlier that morning, hoping the weatherman's prediction for sunshine all day would ring true. So far, he seemed to be right on the money.

The drive from the gym to the precinct only took twenty minutes. Since traffic was light at the moment, Scott didn't bother to speed. He was already late. What were a few more minutes? Besides, he was in no hurry to take this assignment. He was a cop, not a fucking babysitter. Although, if Alan Broussard and the rest of those slimy assholes from Internal Affairs had their way, he'd be lucky to get even that assignment.

They didn't have anything on him, anyway. After all, it wasn't his fault his last arrest resulted in a broken leg and dislocated collarbone for the suspect. The dumb shit shouldn't have tried to play Superman and jump a five-foot ditch. Okay, so maybe the tackle Scott gave him helped with the injuries a little and, yeah, he did hit him once to garner control. But what was he supposed to do? Let the son-of-a-bitch get away?

Scott tightened his fingers around the steering wheel as he thought about the suspect. A twice-charged pedophile who'd kidnapped and raped a twelve-year-old girl and left her for dead in a ravine. The girl survived long enough to identify her attacker, and the DNA tests confirmed her account. When they went to arrest the man, he ran out the back door and fled through an open oilfield near his house. It took Scott twenty minutes to catch the guy. Now the bastard was screaming police brutality, and because it was nearing an election year, the chief assigned Internal Affairs to look into the incident. Scott had no doubt he would be cleared of all the charges, but the fact that his supervisors were even considering that asshole's side made his blood boil.

He slammed on his brakes, skidding to a stop in front of the police station. The tires protested with a squeal and the odor of burning rubber. He sat a moment and took a deep breath, opening then clenching his fists to calm his anger. It wouldn't do any good to go into this meeting with a scowl. His captain would do enough of that for the both of them.

He stopped by his desk and grabbed a pack of gum. The stick of Doublemint he put in his mouth as he entered the office kept him from cringing at the large man who glared at him from behind the desk.

"You're late, Weller!" Captain Franklin Knowles growled. He was a large man, nearing fifty years of age, with thinning salt and pepper hair and a pushed in face that made him look like a bulldog. Rumor had it his nickname had been Bulldog in his rookie years, but since becoming captain, he decided it was best to drop the label. He snatched a file from the bottom of his inbox and gripped it in his hand while he waited for Scott to close the door.

Scott dropped into a chair across from the desk. Most days he found his captain's annoyance amusing, picturing the man with a half-chewed cigar in his mouth and looking much like the bulldog Spike from the old "Looney Toons" cartoons. However, at the moment, neither of them was in a humorous mood.

"Look, Captain, there's got to be someone else you can put on this," he said. "Get one of the boots to handle it, and let me get back to doing real police work."

"This is coming from directly from Chief Braddock, and he asked specifically for you. I would think you'd want to be away from the desk for a while."

"Give me a break. You know he only asked for me because of the Gutierrez case. It's his way of letting us know who's in charge," Scott said, biting off the words as if they left a bad taste in his mouth.

"He is in charge, and those are your orders." Captain Knowles slapped the file on the desk and slid it across the veneer top. "I'm not any happier about this than you are, but as long as he's signing the checks, we'll do as he says."

Scott stared at the file a moment then grabbed it off the desk. He sat back in his chair, cursing under his breath as he flipped through the meager pages inside. "C.J. Martinez. Christ! At least let him be a dignitary or something," he murmured. "Really? A writer? So what, is the mob after him because he wrote about all their dirty little secrets?" *At least that would make the job more interesting.* A spark of excitement shot through him as he scanned the pages. He straightened in his chair with a slight grin. "A stalker, huh? Possibly dangerous?"

"Wipe that look off your face, Weller. This one belongs to the Feds."

"Right, and we all know how much they like to share," he said dryly. He'd had the misfortune of working with the elite bureau eight years earlier after the disappearance of a young Mexican national. The agents had charged in like Custer and swept his case out from under him. Though they eventually allowed him access, the case ran for eighteen months before they closed it unsolved. He still hadn't gotten over the outrage of that.

He removed the stapled pages then looked up. "Well? Where's the rest of it?"

"Right now, what's there is all we get as far as the Feds are concerned.

Forget it, Weller," he said before Scott could protest. "The only stake you have in this is to stay by Martinez's side and act as an assistant. You're to be as discreet as possible." He grabbed another file and slapped it on his blotter. "The address where she's staying is right there," he said waving at the file Scott held. "She flew in from JFK this morning and was supposed to check in when she got to town, but hasn't yet."

"*She?* Wonderful," Scott said with a scowl. It was bad enough when it was a man. Now he was stuck babysitting Miss Daisy.

"You're to go to her home, introduce yourself, and get to work," Knowles finished. "Now get out! And for Christ's sake, clean yourself up!"

Scott pushed himself out of the chair and barely resisted the urge to stalk out of the office. Damn the Feds if they thought they could lock him away as a babysitter to keep him off their case. It was his neck going on the line for their witness. He had every right to know what they were working on.

He stopped at his desk and grabbed a small address book from the top drawer. He paused, tapping the black binder against his palm.

"Screw it," he said, shoving the book in his back pocket. "It's not like they can stick me on desk duty."

CHAPTER FOUR

It was almost noon when Casey arrived in Rosehill. With a brooding sigh she dropped her suitcases on the queen-size bed. The leather bags bounced once before settling on the mattress.

She hadn't left New York right away. She'd made excuses, stalling as long as she could, until Jo called her travel agent and booked the flight for the trip herself. Jo had even contacted Alex to let him know Casey would be in town for an undetermined amount of time. Once that call was made, she had no choice but to follow through.

She flexed her fingers, which were still sore from the death grip she'd given the armrests once the plane descended into Houston's Airport. She'd been booked on a connecting flight to the county airport in Rosehill, but at the last minute decided to bypass the airbus and rent a car for the remaining two-hour trip to the coast. She'd hoped the drive would help calm her nerves and give her more time to get used to the idea of being back in Texas. She hadn't counted on the traffic or endless construction detours which added a stressful hour to her trip. As she neared Rosehill, the pungent odor of sulfur from the refineries lining the narrow two-lane highway was another reminder of why she didn't miss the town.

She took a resigned breath and did a cursory study of the bedroom. At least she'd been able to talk Jo into renting her a house on the beach thirty miles away from town. She might need to find closure from the pain of her past, but she would do so at a distance.

33

The room was a decent size with various seascape watercolors decorating the ivory colored paneling. A wide fishing net with several multicolored seashells sewn into the webbing hung above the bed. The adjoining bathroom was spacious and came with a shower stall as well as a claw foot tub. The tub had actually been a selling point for her, since she liked to unwind from time to time with a long hot bubble bath and a glass of wine.

A gust of wind fluttered and snapped the thin drapes on the open bay window. The smell of sea and wet sand filtered into the room. Casey stepped to the window and leaned out, allowing the warm breeze to sweep across her face.

She'd agreed to a two-week rental on the house with an option to extend if she decided to stay in Texas and write her next book. She gazed out at the shrimp boats anchored deep in the waters of the Gulf of Mexico. She wasn't sure if she would take that offer. Jo was right about one thing— it wasn't easy being back.

The high-pitched ring of the telephone nearly made her jump out of her skin. She pressed her hand to her heart and gave herself a moment to calm down before moving to the bedside table.

"Hello?"

Silence answered her.

"Hello?" she said more forcefully. She gripped the phone, straining to hear someone on the other end. Nothing. She slammed the phone down and took a step back. "It was just a wrong number. No reason to panic," she said.

The phone rang again. A startled cry escaped her throat. She hesitated then snatched the phone.

"Who is this!"

"Ms. Martinez, it's Agent Simms. I'm sorry I'm calling from my cell and lost the signal. I didn't mean to scare you."

Casey eased the breath from her lungs and sagged onto the bed. "What can I do for you, Agent Simms?"

"I wanted to make sure you settled in okay."

"Yes, everything's fine. Nice and quiet."

"Good," he replied, passing over her sarcasm. "Have you contacted the local police department yet?"

"No, not yet."

"Well, make sure you do. They're expecting you. I'll be in touch," he said.

Casey stared at the phone when the connection ended. She pushed off the bed and dropped the phone back on its base. The commanding tone in the agent's voice irritated her enough to forget that he'd scared the hell out of her.

"Screw your orders," she muttered. She did what she was told and left town, but that didn't mean she had to agree to the bodyguard. She could take care of herself. She lived in New York, for crying out loud.

The sound of laughter lured her back to the window. A couple strolled across the sand with a small child sitting tall on the man's shoulders. The woman handed something to the child, clapping when the little girl tossed the object into the air to be caught by one of the hovering seagulls. The loneliness that had followed Casey throughout childhood closed around her like a shroud. She turned away and moved back to the bed.

She pulled her clothes out of the suitcase and transferred them to the mahogany dresser against the far wall. She looked at her reflection in the full-sized oval mirror. A pathetic child in a worn, secondhand dress stared back at her.

She pushed her fingers though her hair with a frustrated breath. She was not that girl anymore. She would not let this town or its people make her feel that way again.

"It's just for two weeks," she said, stepping back to the window. "I can do two weeks." She rested her shoulder against the frame and stared at the beach. The young couple were each holding the child's hands and lifting her to jump over the waves rolling onshore. Their muffled shrieks of laughter floated through the air.

A stab of jealousy pierced through the pain in Casey's heart. There had never been any carefree moments like those for her family. Her father had made sure of it the night he killed her mother.

After the funeral she and her brother were sent to Rosehill to live with their maternal grandmother. Herlinda Martinez had been a hard woman who'd never approved of her daughter's husband. And she had no qualms about letting Casey and Alex know exactly what they came from. Casey thought she would find refuge in school until she realized the teachers had no expectations of her either. The school, as well as the town, became a constant reminder that she would never be more than the poverty stricken, welfare orphan she was. She hated when the holidays rolled around, knowing the food drives set up by the local churches in their need-to-feel-charitable-to-those-less-fortunate creed would result in a care package of food left on her grandmother's doorstep for the whole neighborhood to see. The humiliation of it burned in her, even now.

Casey rolled her shoulders to ease the tension and push away the memory. She'd spent too many years working to overcome her insecurities, only to have them resurface the moment she stepped into town.

She moved back to the bed and grabbed another suitcase, dumping the contents out. A framed photo dropped onto the mattress. She smiled at the picture of her brother and placed it on the bedside table.

She never understood why Alex chose to stay in Rosehill with all its bad memories. He certainly couldn't *like* living here. Maybe staying was his way to be close to their mother since she was buried in the pauper's cemetery on the edge of town. But, whatever his reasons were, they hadn't been the same for her. She'd wanted out and would have run away when she was fifteen if not for Alex. But as much as she loved her brother, she just couldn't stay in Rosehill.

The drapes fluttered in again, a soft dance of fabric in air. Casey rubbed her hands over her face and pushed out a heavy breath. As much as she hated coming back, she had no choice but to be here. She might as well try to make the best of it.

She rummaged through the clothes on the bed and picked out a navy-colored sports bra and running pants. A quick run would help her relax and clear her mind. She still had a few hours before the dinner party Alex planned, and she didn't want to show up brooding.

She stripped off her shirt and headed toward the bathroom. At the last minute she remembered the note propped against the welcome bowl of fruit on the counter. The guest bathroom was out of order and the plumber was coming in to fix it.

"I really need a run."

᪥

He watched her unpack in the bedroom where she would sleep, the one with the bay window overlooking the beach. His breath caught as she removed her blouse, the fabric sliding off her skin like a caress. Excitement kindled his blood. He wanted desperately to give in to his desire and climb the deck to the open entrance. But he had to hold back. She wasn't ready for him. Not yet. He needed to be more patient. He couldn't spoil it now. He needed to wait just like he'd promised.

She stepped onto the upper deck, using the rail to stretch out her muscles. Her leg came up to rest on the thin board. Her arms reached up and she lowered to the rail like a ballerina at the barre. Long, lean limbs stretched taut.

His pulse quickened.

God she was beautiful. Just as he remembered. He wanted so much to take her in his arms, touch her smooth skin. Feel the weight of her breasts in his hands. They would fit so perfectly. Taste so sweet.

He clenched his hands and pressed them into his thighs until he felt the bruises forming. He wanted her so much it hurt. She'd made him wait so long. Just one taste. That's all he needed was just one taste.

He pounded a fist against his leg. *No! Not now, not yet.*

But soon.

Yes, it would be soon. Only a little while longer, and she'd be in his arms and in his bed.

He picked up the book lying on the seat beside him and gently stroked the picture on the back of the cover. His book. She'd written it for him. He'd known it the minute he saw it on the shelves. The minute he read the first page.

He opened the book, smiling at the first sentence. *Some things are meant to be.*

He looked up as she jogged down the stairs and took the path to the beach. The running clothes she wore hugged every curve. His arousal grew. He gripped the book to ease the pain. He could wait. He would wait. She wasn't going anywhere. Not again. He would make sure of that. She would never leave him again. They were destined to be together.

And this time, only death would separate them.

CHAPTER FIVE

Agent Simms stood in front of the evidence board, studying the crime scene photos with a small magnifying glass. His wall looked like a menagerie of death. Rows of photos taken of the various murders discovered since he'd been assigned the case covered the white backboard. Each had been marked with a date and the name of the city where the murder occurred.

He'd been handed the case three years earlier, after the body of Michelle Castillo, the daughter of a high-profile attorney in Manhattan, had been found in a motel outside White Plains. She'd been raped and mutilated, her body sprinkled with shredded strips of paper they later determined were ripped from a book. The press had quickly jumped on the story, dubbing it the *Paperback Murder*. Within a week he'd received calls from several major cities around the United States about an unsolved case involving the rape and mutilation of young Hispanic women, each covered with the shredded pages of a book.

He picked up a photo of Casey given to him by her agent and held it up to the other pictures tacked to the board. From day one he'd always believed there was a link between the women, one sole reason why they had been killed. The murders hadn't been random acts by a madman. These women had been chosen. Not because of where they lived or worked, but because of whom they looked like.

"NYPD never followed up on the Bibles and notes Ms. Martinez gave them, but they kept them locked up in their evidence room. We were able to get some decent prints off them." Hawthorne entered the room carrying two cups of coffee. "They're being run now, but I'm not holding out hope for a match anytime soon."

Simms took the cup Hawthorne offered and set it on the desk. "It's the closest we've come to a break in three years. I think I can be a little patient with the prints." He nodded a greeting to their profiler Alexandra Bronson as she stepped into the office. "You have anything new for us?"

"Yeah, more or less." She moved into the room and handed him a folder, stealing a wistful look at his coffee. "I reworked the profile, adding in Ms. Martinez's connection. Given the age of the victims, I'd say our UNSUB is somewhere in his late twenties, early thirties. It's possible he has a job that requires he travel so we shouldn't rule out truck driver or pilot. His cuts on the vics are precise, so he knows how to handle a knife. I don't think he's a doctor, though, but he might have some medical training." She stepped to the backboard and tapped on one of the photos from the Catherine Flores crime scene. "He seems to know enough about crime scenes. He uses the blanket for his initial strike so it catches the blood and keeps it from splattering, leaving us with no usable trace evidence."

"You think he could be law enforcement?" Hawthorne asked.

She turned to look at him and shrugged. "It's something to consider. Of course, it's possible he's just been studying the forensics side of a crime. Nowadays you can learn almost anything from T.V., the Internet or even a book."

"Terrific," Simms said. "Thanks to the entertainment industry we're training every psycho in the country to get away with murder."

"Gotta love progress," Agent Bronson said. She glanced at his coffee again. "You going to drink that?" Simms picked it up and handed it to her. "Thanks. Anyway, like I was saying, he's smart enough to know what he needs to do to get away with these murders. And he's not going to give himself away until he's ready."

"So, he's trying to see how long he can outsmart us?" Agent Hawthorne asked.

Agent Bronson picked up the photo of Casey and turned back to the board. "No, I don't think that's his game. He's not choosing his victims at random. He's choosing them because they look like Ms. Martinez. It's as if he believes she's wronged him somehow. Whatever he thinks she did, it's fueling his anger. And the longer he has to think about it, the angrier he's going to get," she said. "And he's going to take that anger out on his next victim."

"I don't think he can get any angrier," Simms said stepping beside her.

"Yeah, well, he will," she said grimly. "You see this first murder in L.A.? Or what we assume is the first murder." She pointed to the picture of a young Hispanic woman lying face up across a full-sized bed. Strips of paper littered the body, sticking to the blood. "This was practice for him. He chose a woman no one would miss. A hooker. He probably figured the police wouldn't look too hard to find this woman's killer.

"The victim was killed instantly, stabbed straight through the heart. The second victim was another indigent in New Orleans." She pointed to the second row of pictures. The woman sat propped against a metal Dumpster, her once white bra stained dark with blood. Torn pieces of paper had been strewn in her hair like confetti. "And that one was a little more violent. The guy raped her, stabbed her in the chest and left her near a rat-infested dumpster.

"Our killer is becoming angrier with each kill. This latest victim? Look at her face. It's practically destroyed. The SOB beat her before, and I'm sure, after death."

"Jesus, could this get any worse?" Simms growled.

"Oh yes, it can. He's losing it. He made it clear with this last murder that Ms. Martinez is his intended victim. Which means he's going to start getting more anxious." She turned to look at him. "Have we put her into a safe house yet?"

"Not exactly, but she agreed to leave town and get twenty-four-hour protection."

Agent Bronson nodded and looked back at the photos. "Well, whoever she has better be on his toes. Because this guy wants her dead, and nothing's going to stop him from making sure that happens."

"Terrific. If it isn't the phone, it's the door." Casey stepped out of the shower and reached behind the door, her nails scraping against wood. "Damn it, where'd I leave my robe?" She grabbed a beach towel and wrapped it around her, tucking it in at her breast to keep it in place.

"Just a minute," she called as she stepped out of the bedroom. She used her fingers to brush the wet curls from her face. The knocking turned into pounding. "For crying out loud, what happened to being laid back in Texas?"

She stole a peek through the blinds on the window and saw a handsome man standing on the narrow deck. Feet planted. Arms locked across his chest. Thick black hair fluttering in the breeze. He wore a dark cotton shirt tucked into a pair of faded Levis. His scuffed brown cowboy boots added an inch to his slender six-foot height. *The plumber.* She swung the door open, peering around the frame to stay hidden. The heat in his blue eyes sent a pleasant ripple of warmth to her insides which she quickly banked.

His hand went to his back pocket. "Ms. Martinez, I'm—"

"Yes, I know." She offered him a friendly smile and opened the door wider. "I'm sorry, I was in the shower. I wasn't expecting you for another hour. Come on in. The room's over there." She waved her hand at the closed door on the other side of the room. "I'll be out in a minute. Could you close the front door, please?"

Scott stepped inside and watched the woman disappear through the door of the bedroom, a flash of long legs and dark chocolate hair. The slap of lust he'd received from her wet and well-tanned body settled nicely in his gut. His lips curved with a pleased smile. Maybe he wouldn't have to be an assistant to the old broad after all, but it sure will be nice getting to know the one she has.

He closed the door and studied the large living room, making mental notes of the area as he walked through. The house wasn't as small as it appeared from the outside, but it was definitely larger than his one bedroom closer to town. He hooked his thumbs in his pockets and continued his perusal of the room. It was fully furnished and though the furniture didn't look new, it had been well cared for. An overstuffed sofa and love seat in a print of red and blue flowers sat in the center of the room.

A dark wood console rested behind the sofa with a vase of long-stemmed roses placed on top. The floors were hardwood and covered in places by multicolored throw rugs which made it easier to clean the sand carried in from the beach. Various seascape watercolors hung on dark paneled walls.

A large kitchen and dining area opened to the left. The aroma of coffee drifted in from a pot on the L-shaped counter which separated the two rooms. Along the far wall stood a wide armoire that he suspected concealed a big screen television or maybe an expensive stereo system. Next to the armoire was a built-in bar flanked by two high-back bar stools.

It surprised him that the place C. J. Martinez chose to rent out during her two-week stay was a beach house. He expected something more pretentious, like the penthouse floor of the nearest Hilton.

He reached behind the bar and grabbed a bottle of cola, then sat on one of the stools and made himself comfortable. On the edge of the bar was a stack of mail and a worn Bible with several of the pages folded in at the corners. He picked up the book and turned to a dog-eared page in Proverbs. He read over the highlighted passages, then tossed the book back on the counter.

The woman stepped from the bedroom wearing a pair of navy slacks and an expensive-looking pale blouse. Her hair was still wet, but she'd managed to tame it. She took guarded steps into the room and sent him a look that would chill an Eskimo.

"Excuse me, but if you're charging by the hour I'd appreciate it if you would go into the bedroom and get to work," she said.

Scott looked her over, his lips spreading into a wide grin. The woman's voice was rich and satiny, with the slight hint of a Spanish accent. The warmth of his lust kicked up a notch.

"Well now, sweetheart, exactly what kind of work do you want me to do?"

"The toilet?" She lifted her chin with an indignant frown. "You're not the plumber, are you?"

"Damn, I sure wish I was. Sounds like it could be fun." He stood and plucked out his wallet. "I'm Detective Scott Weller, Rosehill P.D. I was told to meet with Ms. C. J. Martinez at this address. Has she arrived yet?"

She glanced at the badge then raked her gaze over him, unruffled by her error. "It's *Casey*, and I'm her." She didn't bother to hide her annoyance.

"Well now, you don't look anything like Miss Daisy," he answered with a slow, approving nod.

She ignored his remark and stepped behind the counter. "Look, I'm sorry to have inconvenienced you, but I won't be in need of your services. So, you can go now." She snatched the Bible off the bar and tossed it into a small wastebasket before grabbing a bottle of water.

Scott rubbed the stubble on his chin and sent her a crooked smile. "Well now, *Casey,* my orders are to watch over you while you're here," he said. "And I always follow orders."

She swept her gaze over him again as he returned to the stool and stretched out his legs. Her expression told him she found that statement hard to believe.

"Listen, Detective. I don't know what you were told, but I am not in any danger here, so I don't need a bodyguard. And I am within my right to refuse protection, am I not?"

Scott crossed his arms at his chest and nodded. "Yes, you are. However, this is coming from the mayor, and he has friends higher up the food chain. So why don't you just let me do my job so everyone's happy?" *Except me.*

She sent him a tight-lipped smile. "Look. I'm sure you have better things to do with your time than hang around here and irritate me. Like maybe arresting the town drunk or those pesky little jaywalkers."

"Why shucks, ma'am, we don't rightly mind 'tall splitting our time between you and Otis," Scott quipped, grabbing his drink to hide his smile. He'd never met a woman who wore pretentious as well as this one. It was actually a turn-on.

Unamused, Casey stepped from behind the counter and took his drink, setting it on the bar. "I'll tell you what…" She cupped his arm at the elbow and ushered him to the door. "I will call whomever I need to call and tell them not to worry, and I assert my right to be left alone. Thank you. Goodbye."

Scott grinned and rubbed his palm over his chest when she closed the door smartly in his face. Well now, he couldn't say he didn't try. If Miss High and Mighty didn't want him around, he sure as hell wasn't going to fight her on it.

Damn, if this didn't make his day.

❦

"Hey bro, glad you made it," Alex said as Scott stepped through the front door.

"Are you kidding? I wouldn't have missed it." Scott shook Alex's hand then turned to the young woman standing beside him. "Hi beautiful," he said, planting a kiss on Jennifer's cheek. She stood four inches shorter than him, with long auburn hair and light brown eyes. She was the definition of quiet beauty, with a sultry accent that made him think of Scarlett O'Hara. "Tell me, darlin', when are you gonna leave this loser and come away with me?"

Jennifer laughed and slid her arm around Alex's waist. "Well, if he keeps spending more time at that hospital and less at home, I just might take you up on it."

"The ICU's been packed lately," Alex said, with a shrug. "But it's starting to let up."

"It better," Jennifer said. "Come on back, Scott. Most everyone's here already."

They stepped onto an extended patio furnished with a wooden picnic table and various lawn chairs. A group of men and women milled around the stone-paved deck, drinking beer and talking. Several called out their hellos to Scott and continued their conversations. Near the edge of the lawn, smoke drifted out of a large, barrel-shaped barbeque pit. The air carried the spicy aroma of grilling meat.

"So, where's this sister of yours? I do hope she isn't as ugly as you are," Scott said with a playful smirk.

"Cassandra? She's running a little late. She should be here soon, though." Alex handed Scott a beer from the ice chest next to the back door. "Hey, what about that guy you were supposed to babysit for? Was he as bad as you expected?"

"He was actually a *she*. A real cold fish, with the bite of a rattlesnake. She waived her right to protection. Unfortunately, it isn't going to fly with the mayor, so I'm still stuck with her. I was able to get one of the boots to cover for me tonight, though."

They stepped to the barbeque pit, and Alex turned the meat inside. "What? The great Scott Weller actually found a woman immune to his charm? I didn't think there was a woman left in the world who wouldn't jump you at the wink of an eye."

Scott hunched his shoulder with an exaggerated shudder. "Please, I don't think there's enough antivenin in the world for this one. She is quite a looker, though." He pressed a hand to his heart and sent Alex a wicked grin. "But don't give up on me, yet. By the end of the week, we could be tearing up the sheets."

"Thank God. For a minute there I thought you'd lost your touch. You know I live vicariously through your conquests," Alex said with a laugh. From inside the house the doorbell chimed.

"I'll get it. You take care of that meat before you burn it," Scott said. He handed his beer to Alex and went back into the house with a familiar ease. There were few places that made him feel right at home and part of a family. He and Alex had become fast friends during his recovery in the hospital. Of course, it was hard not to feel a connection to someone whose hands had been in your chest. Alex was the brother Scott never had, and he valued every moment of their friendship.

The bell chimed a second time as he swung the door open.

The bright smile on Casey's face disappeared when she saw him. Her brown eyes darkened. "What the hell are you doing here?"

"Took the words right out of my mouth." Scott leaned against the doorframe, his lips curving into a wide grin. He managed to keep his surprise in check. Seeing her again was a pleasant shock to his system.

So, this is little sister Cassandra. Lord, you sure do like irony.

He thought he saw something familiar about her at the beach house and wondered why he didn't make the connection until now. If he'd looked closer, he would have noticed the golden brown Hispanic features were very similar to Alex's. Although, too bad for her, Alex got all the personality.

He was caught off guard when her hand gripped his shirt and she yanked him from the doorway. His arms circled around her and pulled her firmly against him to steady them both as they stumbled down the stoop. She smelled lightly of jasmine and the scent shot a glorious blaze of heat to the pit of his stomach.

He glanced down at the bottle she held between them and sent her a crooked grin. "Now, isn't this the part where you say, *that a bottle of wine or am I just happy to see you?*"

Casey's panicked gaze darted at the house then back to Scott. "What are you doing here? Why are you following me?"

"Relax. I was invited."

"What? I didn't invite you." She glared at him, her voice a pitch above a whisper. "I told you I didn't want or need your help. How am I supposed to explain this to my brother?"

It slowly occurred to Casey that his arms were still around her, and her body was pressed firmly against him. Her pulse quickened to a staccato beat, and her blood warmed to what she was sure was an unhealthy degree. She wanted to push him away but the command wouldn't go from brain to hand. Her body seemed to be telling her she'd been away from a man's embrace for much too long.

The amusement she saw glitter in his eyes was enough to make her forget her libido. "What is so damn funny?"

Before he could answer, the front door swung open, and Jennifer rushed out of the house. "Cassandra!"

Casey sprung back so fast she nearly dropped the bottle of wine. Heat fused her cheeks.

Jennifer hurried down the steps and flung her arms around Casey. "Oh, it's so great to see you." She pushed back to arm's length. "Look at you! Oh my gosh, you're gorgeous. Isn't she gorgeous, Scott?" Her excitement emanated in waves, adding to Casey's discomfort. Jennifer didn't wait for Scott to answer and pulled Casey toward the house. "Come on, come in. Alex has been climbing the walls waiting for you."

Casey shot a searing look at Scott as she followed Jennifer into the house.

"This is Scott Weller, one of our dearest friends. Scott, this is Alex's sister, Cassandra."

Scott continued to smile, the humor dancing in his eyes as he extended his hand. "Cassandra. That's a beautiful name. It's a pleasure to meet you." He lifted her hand to his lips and brushed a kiss over her fingers.

She jerked her hand back. "Mr. Weller."

"Cassandra!" Alex rushed in with a whoop. He grabbed Casey in a hug, lifting her off the floor.

"Alex! Put me down, you big ogre," she said with a laugh. He set her down, and she held him back at arm's length to study him. At thirty-three, he was five years older than she, with the same coal-black hair as their mother and trimmed short around an angular face. He was much broader in the shoulders and his skin darker than she remembered. "Look how grown up you are," she said with a laugh. She wrapped her arms around him with a fierce hug and kissed him on the cheek. "I've missed you so much."

"Not as much as I missed you," he said. He draped his arm over her shoulder and turned to Scott with a wide grin. "Scott, I'd like to introduce you to my baby sister, Cassandra."

The pride in Alex's voice made Scott smile. "We've met." His blood still hummed from their unintentional embrace. Of course now that he knew who she was, he would need to be more careful with his thoughts.

"She's a big-time writer now. She's got some great stuff," Alex said.

Casey gave him a playful push. "Right, like you read my work."

"Sure he does. Just not the sex scenes," Jennifer said with a laugh.

Scott cast a sly look at Casey. "Sex scenes? Sounds like my kind of book."

She ignored him and draped her arm over Jennifer's shoulder. "So, guys, when are you going to start having babies so I can spoil them all rotten?"

Jennifer sent her a casual shrug. "Well, if you give us another six months…."

Casey stopped and stared at Jennifer with wide eyes. "What?"

Jennifer laughed, tears forming in her eyes. "We're going to have a baby!"

"No shit? Way to go, buddy." Scott grinned, slapping Alex on the back.

"Thanks. I had a little help."

"Why didn't you say something before?" Casey placed her hand on Jennifer's flat stomach with a look of astonished wonder.

"We wanted to wait until after the first trimester. Just in case."

"There's no just in case. You're going to have a beautiful, healthy baby. I can feel it," Casey said before pulling her into a hug.

Scott leaned in to kiss Jennifer's cheek and gave her a quick hug. "Well now, this calls for more than just beer."

Casey lifted the bottle of wine. "Then it's a good thing I brought this. And we'll find juice for the momma-to-be. You can figure this out right?" She slapped the bottle against Scott's chest and walked with Jennifer and Alex into the kitchen.

Scott shook his head and ripped the seal from the neck of the bottle. "New Yorkers."

❧

Casey stretched out on a wooden lounge chair with a contented sigh. The party had ended an hour earlier, but she wasn't quite ready to return to the empty beach house.

Her brother handed her a wine glass before taking a seat on a lawn chair across from her. "There's still one glass left of that fancy wine you brought," he said.

"Thanks. I was shocked I even found it in town. I didn't think the stores here carried anything but Miller Lite," she said. "In fact, I was surprised to see how much the town has changed in the past ten years. They're close to becoming a real city. I think I even saw what could pass for a mall."

"Yes, ma'am," Scott said with a slow drawl. "We even have us a real movie the-a-ter. Shows them talking pictures and everything."

Casey spared him a glance. He sat next to her in an Adirondack chair, his legs stretched out and crossed in what she suspected was a habitual position for him.

"Ignore him. He has no class," Alex said with a laugh.

"Nope. But I do have a job which demands I get to first thing in the morning." Scott unfolded himself from the chair and stepped in front of Casey. "Cassandra, it was indeed an honor to meet you."

Casey sent him a short nod. "And you, Mr. Weller." His lips spread into a wide grin when she hesitated to take his offered hand. As if knowing it would annoy her, he pressed a kiss across her fingers. The warmth of his touch shot a spark up to her elbow. She bit the inside of her lip to keep the reaction from showing on her face, but the gleam in his eyes told her she hadn't succeeded.

Scott turned to Jennifer and pulled her into a hug. "Congratulations again, Jenn. You're going to be a terrific mom."

"Come on, I'll walk you out," Alex said, moving beside him.

Casey frowned as they disappeared into the house. She shook the tingle from her hand, annoyed by her purely female reaction to the kiss. "What's his deal?"

"Scott? Don't worry, he's harmless," Jennifer said.

"Really?" Casey said dryly. She thought about how it felt to have his arms around her earlier and the way her body had reacted. Whatever Scott Weller was, it was not harmless.

She had watched him throughout the night, a little envious of his easy manner with all the people who came out to the party. He seemed to know every female in the room, and they had no problem entertaining him as well. So what? He was hardly her type.

Jennifer laughed. "I guess it would depend on who you ask. Scott is Rosehill's most eligible bachelor, and he's very much determined to stay that way. But that doesn't seem to stop the women from throwing themselves at him."

Casey stole a look through the open doorway of the house. Her eyes met Scott's as he turned the corner toward the front door. His smile was quick and sexy and sent a hot current through her veins that settled in the pit of her stomach like a fiery stone. *Definitely not harmless.*

"I don't think I've ever heard you mention him before. How did he and Alex become friends? Did Scott give him a parking ticket or something?"

"No. Actually, Alex was putting in some overtime in the ER the night Scott was brought in with a gunshot wound to the chest." Jennifer stood and moved around the deck, gathering the empty bottles left by their guests. "He'd gone out on a domestic disturbance call and the guy came out shooting. Alex assisted with his surgery and was his nurse when they brought him up to the ICU. They just hit it off and have been best friends ever since. It's been about five years now, I think."

"Wow. And he's still on the job?" Casey looked back at the empty house. She wondered what it must have been like for Scott to be at death's door, and why he would continue to put himself in that position. She didn't know whether to respect him or consider him a fool.

"Oh yeah, he'd never quit. Scott's third generation police officer. It's in his genes. And boy howdy, does he wear those jeans well," Jennifer said with a wink.

"Shame on you, Jen. I thought you only had eyes for my brother."

"Of course I do, but I'm not dead. I can still look."

Casey had looked, too, and though it was a very nice package, he was not her style. She rose from the lounge chair and helped pick up the empty dishes.

Jennifer slid a mischievous glance at Casey as they entered the kitchen. "You know, I saw y'all on the sidewalk earlier. If you're interested, I could fix you up."

Casey stopped and shook her head. "No, no. That's quite all right. I like a little less redneck in my men." *When I find the time for them...*

"Scott is not a redneck. He and Alex are best friends..."

Casey held up her hand. "I know you like to play little Miss Matchmaker, but I didn't come here to find a date."

"Well, don't take this the wrong way, but why *are* you here?" Jennifer asked.

Casey hopped onto the counter to sit, avoiding her sister-in-law's watchful stare. "I'm on vacation?"

"Here? In Rosehill?" Jennifer shook her head. "I don't buy it. You've been back only once in ten years and even then you couldn't leave fast enough. Something's wrong."

"Nothing's wrong. I just needed to get out of the city, and I missed you guys."

"This is about that guy, isn't it?" Jennifer asked.

Casey went still, her fingers tightening on the wine glass. Damn it, she hadn't expected them to hear about the murders in New York. She'd asked Agent Simms to keep her involvement out of the investigation so Alex wouldn't find out. The son-of-a-bitch lied to her. "Guy?"

"The one in Chicago? What was his name? Allen?"

"Aaron," she said, relief washing over her like a cool wave. "No, I haven't heard from him since I moved back to New York."

"Well, something's going on. I can feel it."

"So, what? Being pregnant makes you psychic?" Casey said, reaching for the wine bottle to refill her glass.

"Casey, I've known you since you were twelve years old. I know when something's bothering you." Jennifer reached out to touch Casey's arm.

"You can talk to us. You know that, right?"

"Of course. And don't worry, there's nothing wrong." She took a drink from the glass, the wine bitter against her lie. She pasted on a smile and tried for jovial. "So, this was a nice party," she said. "You guys sure have a lot of friends."

Jennifer accepted the change in subject with a sigh and turned to finish loading the dishwasher. "They're mostly from the hospital. Your brother is quite popular over there."

"Well, that's not surprising. He's always been good at making friends." *Unlike me.* Until she'd met Jo, she'd never had a real friend. Male or Female. She mentally shook off the dismal feeling. "So, uh, I didn't see Tony here. Are he and Alex still friends?"

"Yeah, they are. Alex called him but he couldn't make it. His girlfriend was here for a little while, but I think she left before you got here."

"Girlfriend?"

"Her name's Alicia. They've been dating off and on for about five or six years, I think," Jennifer said, pushing buttons on the dishwasher. The machine hissed as the first rinse cycle started. She turned to look at Casey. "That doesn't bother you, does it? That Tony moved on?"

"What? No, of course not. I'm...happy for him." An image of a young man flashed in her mind. Tall with a wiry body and shoulder-length hair the color of sand. He was the first man she'd ever dated. The first man to tell her he loved her. On her eighteenth birthday he'd surprised her with an engagement ring and, though she knew she didn't love him, she'd accepted his proposal. She thought, with enough time, she would develop those feelings. But as the days passed and her high school graduation neared, the guilt at leading him on became an unbearable weight.

Jennifer stepped closer, her eyes narrowed. "You're not still blaming yourself for what happened, are you? What Tony did wasn't your fault. You shouldn't feel guilty."

"He tried to kill himself after I called off our engagement. How is that not my fault?" Casey said, fighting down the rush of guilt. When she'd told Tony she couldn't marry him and planned to leave Rosehill, he'd broken down into tears and threatened to kill himself if she left. Although she didn't take his threats seriously, in order to appease him she'd lied. She convinced him she wanted to take some time for herself and travel the country before she came back to settle down. Tony told her he would wait for her to come home.

When she'd returned for Alex's wedding two years later, Tony expected them to pick up where they left off, but she'd avoided him and left town again as soon as the ceremony was over. A few days after she returned to New York, Alex called and told her Tony had swallowed a bottle of pills.

Casey drank half the wine in her glass, hoping the alcohol would burn away her guilt. "I didn't think Alex would ever forgive me," she said, staring into the half empty glass.

"What? Oh, sweetie, there was nothing to forgive. Alex was never angry with you. Hurt, maybe, because you didn't talk to him first, but he understood why you moved away." Jennifer took Casey's hand, tugging to make her look up. "What Tony did was stupid and wrong and he should never have made you feel guilty about it. It wasn't your fault and Alex knows that. He loves you more than anything and only wants to see you happy." Jennifer gave her hand a reassuring squeeze. "It was a long time ago, sweetie. Tony is fine now. He's moved on. You need to let go and move on, too."

Casey nodded. She did move on and that's what shamed her. Once her decision to leave had been made, she'd buried every part of her past. She dismissed the town and Tony and everything she'd ever been. She even changed her name to Casey Martinez so she wouldn't remember what she came from when she saw her name in print. But now that she was home, she would have to face the unwanted memories and the guilt that always came with them.

She placed her glass down beside her and hopped off the counter. "It's getting late. I'd better go. Thank you for the party. I had a good time."

"You don't have to go back to the beach. You know you're welcome to stay here with us," Jennifer said as they walked toward the front of the house.

"I know. But I miss the beach, and it'll help me relax so I can get some work done. But don't worry. I'll come back." She placed a hand on Jennifer's stomach and smiled. "We have a baby to get ready for, remember?"

"Oh yeah, my morning sickness won't let me forget," Jennifer said with a laugh.

Scott was pulling out of the driveway when they stepped outside. He sent her a crooked grin and waved. Casey followed his subtle nod toward the dark sedan parked on the corner. She swallowed an oath and sent Alex a bright smile as he stepped onto the stoop.

"I'm going to be a little busy for the next few days so don't worry if you can't reach me. I'll swing by when I can," she said, giving him a hug.

"Is that your way of saying, don't call me, I'll call you?"

Casey gave him a nervous laugh, stealing another look at the sedan.

Alex placed his hand on her cheek, his eyes soft. "Don't worry, sis. I know you need some time. But I'm here, okay?" He leaned in to kiss her cheek, lingering by her ear. "Welcome home."

CHAPTER SIX

Casey poured herself a cup of coffee as someone knocked on her front door. She carried the cup with her, frowning when she found Scott on her deck. *Great, he's back.*

Like the day before, he wore a pair of faded Levis, a dark cotton shirt and scuffed brown cowboy boots. A nine-millimeter handgun was strapped into a leather holster at his side, along with a clip-on police badge. He flashed a smile, his eyes dancing with a humor Casey didn't understand. *At least he shaved.*

She exhaled a tired breath. "What are you doing here?"

"Now is that any way to greet your bodyguard?"

"You are not my—"

"I brought breakfast," he said, holding up a square box that smelled sinfully of chocolate. "You know how we cops feel about our doughnuts."

Casey eyed the carton. It wouldn't hurt to share a doughnut with him. She was hungry, and maybe they could discuss this situation like rational adults. She'd spoken to the chief of police after she kicked Scott out the day before, and like it or not, she was stuck with the man for the remainder of her stay.

She stepped back and waved him in with very little enthusiasm. "I see you even brought flowers. Trying to butter me up?" she asked, referring to the vase of daisies he picked up before he walked in.

"Actually, they were sitting on the deck." He handed her the vase, then sent her a crooked grin. "But if that's all it takes."

She sent him a bland look and set the daisies alongside the roses on the console as he continued into the kitchenette.

"Where do you keep the plates?"

"Hmm? Oh, cabinets above the sink." She took a small tag from one of the stems. "'Absence sharpens love, presence strengthens it. It's good to have you home.' Hmmm."

"Who are they from?"

Casey shrugged. "They didn't sign the card, but they're probably from Alex. He's the only one who knows I love daisies."

"Alex quoting Thomas Fuller? Can't picture it," Scott said, grabbing a mug from the cupboard.

Casey sent him a dubious look. "You know who Thomas Fuller is?"

"I think I may have seen that on a bumper sticker," Scott answered with a grin. "Give me the name of the florist. I'll check them out."

"They're just flowers, Detective. I haven't been in town long enough for anyone to want to poison me with pollen." She tucked the note in the vase then wandered into the kitchen and waited while Scott filled his mug with coffee. He bypassed the cream and sugar she'd left out and drank as if desperate for the caffeine boost.

"So, uh, listen, I wanted to…well…thank you for not mentioning anything about this problem to Jenn and Alex last night."

Scott grinned at her discomfort. "Glad to see you didn't choke on that. My Heimlich isn't very good." He held up his hand when she glared. "You're welcome. It's really up to you to tell them you're being stalked. But the fewer people who know about it, the better."

"I am *not* being stalked! Regardless of what the Feds think, whatever was happening in New York was not about me. And besides, even if it were, it isn't likely the psycho is going to follow me to some insignificant hick town two thousand miles away." She grabbed a chocolate doughnut from the box, ripped off a piece and shoved it in her mouth.

"That may be true. But right now my orders are to keep you safe. So, you'll be under twenty-four-hour watch until I'm told otherwise. Which means, you don't go anywhere, see anyone or do anything unless I know about it first." He tore a piece from her doughnut and popped it in his mouth.

"I never agreed to this! You can't follow me around without my consent. That's harassment," she said, irritated that she was very close to pouting.

"Look, for whatever the reason, the chief of police ordered this on behalf of the FBI, the mayor, and the governor of our fine state. You have a problem with it, write your congressman." He finished his coffee and placed the cup in the sink. "By the way, while I'm thinking about it, give me your cell phone number."

"I don't have a cell phone."

Scott looked at her as if she had three heads. "You do know this is the twenty-first century, right? Everyone has a cell phone."

She glared at him. "Well, I don't. It's just one more annoyance I don't want to have to put up with."

He shook his head and turned toward the front door. "I'm going to take a look around the grounds, check all the locks on the doors and windows. When I get back, we'll go over whatever plans you have for the day." He strode from the room and out the door before Casey could argue.

❧

Scott stepped onto the narrow deck, a warm gust of wind sweeping his hair across his brow. Two weeks. That's all he'd committed to. With any luck the Feds would catch her stalker before then, and he wouldn't have to deal with the pompous princess any longer.

He followed the deck around to the back of the white cottage-style home where it opened up to a large patio facing the beach. Two heavy plastic lounge chairs and a round patio table with matching seats were in the center of the area. A sliding glass door made a second entry into the house by way of the living room. The doors were closed at the moment and a long pole that looked like a broomstick, had been set into the grooves.

On each side of the house were two large picture windows framed by soft blue wood-slat shutters. He shook his head when he noticed the window to Casey's bedroom was open. He would have to warn her about that, and he hated giving lectures almost as much as he hated receiving them.

He stepped to the next set of windows. At least they were locked. He checked the tension on the large clasp, then peered inside. The room was furnished with a full-sized bed and a wide armoire. Since it was closest to the front door, he decided to take it as his room.

A narrow set of stairs was the only entrance that led to the top deck. He took them down to a carport and another patio with a wooden bench swing hanging from the rafters. He looked at the silver Mercedes parked under the awning in the narrow driveway and shook his head. *Pretentious.* He continued around the car and circled to the back of the house.

Like most of the surrounding beach houses, this one was built far enough from the shore to avoid the tide at its highest—provided there was no hurricane forming in the warm waters of the Gulf. The house stood on eight-foot pylons with a narrow trench grooved around the base and leading to the beach. The yard was at least an acre and made up of mostly weeds and small burrs that grabbed onto your clothing like barnacles on a ship's hull.

Scott wiped away the sweat beading his forehead and scanned the beach. Saltmarsh cordgrass and bulrush sprouting from small sand dunes bordering the area, swayed with the steady breeze. The air was thick and humid with the sharp smell of salt and sea. From his position near the edge of the deck he counted five lounge chairs, shaded with over-sized umbrellas, on the sand. Two small children splashed in the foaming waves under the watchful eye of their mother. In the distance three people stood knee-deep in the water trying their luck at fishing and probably had their lines tangled in a wiry mess.

There were several more beach houses farther down the road. Some of them were still under construction, the original foundations destroyed by Hurricane Ike a few years earlier. He'd already checked with the realtor to see who rented the homes and found out the other completed houses weren't currently occupied. Of course, once school ended more families would converge along the shore, renting the houses for weeks at a time. By Memorial Day weekend, the place would be a zoo.

He turned around when he heard Casey come down the stairs and would have choked on his gum if he were chewing any. She'd changed into black running shorts and a grey tank top that emphasized the mouth-watering curves of her body. She'd twisted her hair into a braid that draped over her shoulder and rested on the curve of her left breast.

A knot coiled in his stomach. His blood warmed a degree with each step she took. It was a purely male reaction and not the least bit unpleasant.

She locked her arms tight across her chest with a defiant look that told him if it was his job to stay by her side, then she was going to make him work. "I'm going for a run, Warden. Is that okay with you?"

Scott looked down at his jeans and brown leather Ropers. It wouldn't be the first time he'd had to run in them, though usually it was to collar a criminal.

With a heavy sigh, he took off his boots and socks and tossed them next to the steps. He cuffed up the hem of his jeans, checked his gun to make sure it was secured on his belt then tucked his badge into his front pocket.

He gestured to the beach with a barely contained scowl. "Let's go."

Casey bit back a grin and started on a slow jog down the sandy trail leading to the beach. The tide was in, so she ran along the edge for better traction. To her annoyance, Scott ran alongside her, keeping a steady pace as he scanned the beach. Before they hit the first mile she'd mentally marked off, he pulled off his shirt and tucked it into the waistband of his jeans. She had to admit he had a magnificent body. His arms were sculpted solid and well tanned. An eagle-in-flight tattoo colored his left bicep.

She tried not to let the tight, gleaming muscles along his back distract her, but she was female after all. When she nearly stumbled in the sand after a quick glance at his butt, she glared at him and he took the hint that he should ease back.

They ran two and a half miles before she turned around. Scott continued to stay several paces behind her and didn't lose the gap even when she increased her speed. With a half mile to go she slowed to a trot, tossing a look over her shoulder to gauge his distance. She guessed him to be at least ten feet behind. With a mischievous smile she bolted.

When she reached the spot in front of the beach house she stopped and kicked off her shoes. Wading into the water, she leaned over and closed her eyes as she slowed her breathing. The waves rolled over her feet, and she lost herself to the sensation of being pulled into the water as it receded.

Before she could straighten, her feet slipped out from under her. She'd barely let out a scream before she was carried into the water and dropped into a large, salty wave.

"You looked like you could use a cool down," Scott said between breaths as water slapped against his calves.

A wave splashed against Casey's back, leaving a thick branch of seaweed in her lap and sand in her mouth. She spit out the rancid taste and pushed her wet hair from her face. She pinched the brown, gnarled stem with her thumb and forefinger and lifted it off her lap with an exaggerated polite smile.

"I guess I deserved that. You're in better shape than I gave you credit for." She held out her hand for him to help her up.

"Uh-uh. My momma didn't raise no dummy. Get yourself out." He stepped back and didn't try to hide his amusement as Casey struggled to stand against the force of the waves.

&

Casey took a drink from her water bottle, swishing it in her mouth to wash out the remaining taste of the Gulf. She had showered as soon as they returned from their run, but the mouthwash she'd rinsed with wasn't enough to override the foul taste of the seawater. *They should probably put that on the label. Kills 99% of germs, but not the taste of seawater.*

She grinned as she thought about how foolish she must have looked fighting the waves and seaweed. It may have been a dirty trick, but she liked a man with a sense of humor. Not that she had any intentions of liking Scott Weller, but she could still give him points for his wit.

She turned on the laptop she'd left on the breakfast table and brought up the file she'd started earlier that day. She couldn't quite mask her smile when Scott came out of the bedroom smelling like her floral scented body wash.

"I'm going to have to remember to get some manly soap when we go out," he said.

"I don't know, I think you smell kind of pretty."

"Thanks. That's exactly what every man wants to hear." He rubbed his hands through his wet hair and brushed it back with his fingers.

Casey looked at him and smiled. He'd left his shirt unbuttoned, giving her a mouth-watering glimpse of his broad chest and well-honed abs. An image of her hands roaming over that hard, smooth skin flashed in her mind. She could almost feel the tingle in her fingers as she explored his sculpted muscles, trailing a path down to his narrow waist and the dusting of hair around his navel. Would those large hands of his be gentle as they stroked and worked to pleasure her body? With that lazy smile and laid-back nature, she didn't doubt he was a patient and attentive lover.

She swallowed the lump forming in her throat and turned her attention back to the computer. *Where the hell did that come from?*

Scott moved alongside the table as he finished rolling up the sleeves of his shirt and strapped on his watch, oblivious to her carnal assessment. He picked up the paperback book she had taken out of her satchel.

"So you really write about sex, huh?"

Casey kept her eyes on the screen and tried not to inhale his scent. How was it her soap smelled sinful on him?

"I don't write about sex. My stories include a romance and sex just happens to be a part of that."

"I'll bet the research is a lot of fun," he said, the humor evident in his voice.

She looked at him from the corner of her eye. "I have a very active imagination, Detective. Research isn't necessary."

"Yeah? How active?" He thumbed through the book and stopped at a page to read. He whistled out a slow breath. "That's quite an imagination. Can people really do that?"

Casey grabbed the book and tossed it back on the table. "Do you mind?"

Scott flashed a smile and picked up the book again. "So, why the pseudonym?"

Casey hesitated then cast a sidelong look at him. "I thought it might be easier to sell if the publishers thought I was a man." *It's not a complete lie.*

She tapped the keys and tried not to notice the flush in her body when he moved closer. It'd been three years since her last physical relationship. It was only natural to feel the twinge of desire for this man. That didn't mean she would act on it.

"A man writing romances?" Scott thumbed through the pages and stopped to read another passage.

"You'd be surprised at how many men write romances. And they're *paranormal* romances."

A low appreciative whistle sounded from him. "This is better than *Playboy*."

Casey glared at him and snatched the book from his hands, shoving it back into the satchel. "I'm trying to work here. Don't you have a pickup to tune or something?"

"Actually, I drive a jeep," he answered with a wide smile. "So, what're you fixing for lunch? That run worked up an appetite."

"I may have to put up with your company, but I don't have to feed you. Get your own food." She closed the computer and carried it with her to the bedroom.

Scott bit back a laugh when the door snapped shut.

"Okay, then. I'll just sit over here and do some work of my own." He buttoned up his shirt as he moved to the sofa. He didn't know what it was about her that made his blood hum, but he was enjoying every electrifying jolt.

He picked up the duffle bag he'd brought with him and pulled out his cell phone. Dropping onto the sofa, he propped his legs on the coffee table and tapped in some numbers.

"Hey there, darlin'," he said when the familiar voice answered. "How's my favorite records clerk?"

CHAPTER SEVEN

Casey sat on the queen-sized bed with her legs crisscrossed under her. The laptop rested on a bed tray in front of her. Her fingers lay unmoving on the keys.

She had been at the computer for the past three hours trying to work on the outline for her next novel, but she couldn't seem to keep her mind from wandering. She looked out the window at the foam-covered waves in the distance. The sky was a canvas of brilliant blue and clear as glass.

She blew out a frustrated breath and slid her hands away from the computer. Why had she let Jo to talk her into coming here? She'd never be able to get any work done. Not as long as she continued to remember. But remember is what Jo wanted her to do. Remember, accept and get closure. *Closure. Yeah, right.* How was she supposed to get that when she would never learn to accept?

A gusty sea breeze swept into the room, sending the drapes floating above the floor before they settled against the windowsill. Outside a seagull swooped at the water, arcing back up as it missed its prey. A distant memory played in her head. Five years old, sitting on the edge of the beach, building a sandcastle with her mother. Their shrieks of laughter filled the air as one wave after another moved inshore and threatened to swallow their creation. Her mother took her hand and led her into the water.

"Don't be afraid, Mami. I have you," her mother said, gently tugging

Casey into the water. They held hands and splashed as they jumped over the rolling waves surging toward the banks of the shore.

Casey closed her eyes and rested her head against the headboard as the memory faded. It was the last day they shared together before her mother's violent death.

Although the events of that day were clear, Casey always had trouble picturing her mother's face. As the years passed, she'd become only a shadow of memories.

She sat up and closed the file she'd been working on and opened up another one. A photo of a young woman in a wedding dress appeared on the screen. Casey traced her finger over the face. It was the only picture she had of her mother. The only one she dared to take from her grandmother's attic. She'd had it reconditioned and scanned onto her computer so she wouldn't forget.

"B*esos de mariposa* …butterfly kisses," she whispered. They were the last words her mother said to her before she died.

Over the years Casey had tried to forget that horrible night, tried to push away the bad memories and remember only the good. But, as it seemed with most memories, only the bad ones remained. Even now she could hear the hinges on her door creak as her father crept into her room. Hear the heavy shuffle of his footsteps as he neared the bed. Smell the pungent odor of stale alcohol that seemed to permeate every pore on his body. His wide hands were hard and rough when they settled on her small thigh.

She fisted her hand in her lap and shuddered out a breath. Her father came into her bedroom that night and had it not been for her mother—she didn't want to think about what would have happened if her mother hadn't come into the room. Her mother saved her life that night. But Casey did nothing to save her.

She squeezed her eyes closed as the memory flooded her mind.

Casey clutched the blanket against her, watching in horror and awe as her mother charged into the room. Her dark brown eyes were glazed with fury as she grabbed her husband by the collar of his work shirt. She shoved him out of the bedroom and out of the house with a strength Casey always knew her mother carried.

She rushed back to Casey and pulled her tiny, trembling body to her chest.

"Oh my baby, I'm so sorry. Are you okay, hijita? *Did he hurt you?" She cupped Casey's face and searched her eyes for confirmation.*

Casey shook her head and wrapped her arms tighter around her warmth. She laid her head against her mother's chest, pressing against the jack-hammer pounding of her heart.

"He'll never do that again. You hear?" She held Casey tighter. "I promise, I will never let him hurt you like that again."

She held on to Casey, planting kisses on her head and stroking the thick ringlets of her hair. She rocked back and forth, cooing softly in Spanish. When Casey yawned, her mother gently laid her back onto the pillow and pulled the blanket up to her neck.

"You don't need to be afraid ever again, hija. *You're going to be safe." She leaned over and kissed Casey's forehead. "Te* quiero, *my brave little girl."*

"I love you too, Mommy."

Her mother smiled and brushed her hand over Casey's soft curls. "Besos de mariposa." *She leaned over and swept her long lashes against Casey's cheek.*

Casey returned the kiss with a giggle, then rolled over and snuggled into her pillow. She didn't wake again until she heard the scream.

Casey pressed her hands to her face and pushed away the tears burning her eyes. Her mother was barely thirty years old when she died at the hands of Alejandro Rivera.

During the funeral Casey sat quietly with her brother and grandmother, fighting the tears that wanted to pour out of her. Everyone thought she was in shock or just didn't understand what had happened. But she did understand; more than they knew.

She closed the computer with a snap and climbed off the bed to stand at the window. She jammed her fisted hands in the pockets of her slacks, then pulled them out and locked her arms across her chest. With a frustrated growl, she whirled away from the window and paced the room. She needed to get out, get some air, take a walk, *something* before she made herself crazy.

She turned to the closed door with a scowl. *Not that I'm allowed to do anything with Sheriff Taylor lurking about.*

Flexing her fingers open and closed, she stepped out of the bedroom. She drew in a deep, calming breath before she moved any farther into the room. The spicy aroma of food and the sizzling sound of frying meat slammed into her. It made her mouth water and her temper flare. *Well, he just makes himself at home, doesn't he?*

She'd heard him moving around outside her door while she worked and at one time heard him speak to someone. Because she planned to ignore him, she didn't venture out to see who it was. Apparently he'd asked someone to bring him food since the kitchen hadn't been stocked yet.

Trying her best to ignore him again, she squared her shoulders and marched to the sliding door to the deck.

"Going somewhere?" Scott asked from his position at the stove.

"I want to go for a walk and get some air. Is that okay?" she snapped.

"Hold on. I'll come with you." He turned off the burner under the skillet sizzling on the stove.

She scowled at him. "Never mind!"

Scott shrugged and turned the fire back on, then flipped the meat frying in the pan.

Casey stalked to the kitchen table and grabbed the pack of cigarettes she'd left there. She tapped one out and lit it up, taking a deep drag and blowing it out in a huff.

"Those things will kill you, you know," Scott said, glancing at her.

"Yeah, well, so do gunshots," Casey retorted. Shame burned her cheeks when she realized what she said. Scott continued to cook and showed no indication it had bothered him. She took another draw from the cigarette before tamping it out in the crystal ashtray on the kitchen counter. She stole a peek over his shoulder to look at the food sizzling on the stove.

"That isn't possum or something disgusting like that, is it?" she said, in a feeble attempt at an apology.

"You know what they say. 'Tastes just like chicken.'" He laughed at her appalled look. "Don't worry. It is chicken."

Casey moved into the kitchen and pulled a bottle of wine out from the refrigerator. "Where did you learn to cook?" she asked, reaching into the cabinet for two glasses. She didn't quite pull off the casual tone.

"My grandmother," he answered with a proud grin. "She made the best southern fried chicken in the state. She could even give the Colonel a run for his money."

Casey felt the pang of regret. The only thing her grandmother taught her was how weak and simple her mother had been, and how she was destined to become just like her. It was something she fought against on a regular basis. She poured wine into the two glasses and offered him one.

He shook his head and held up a bottle. "Water's fine for me."

Casey shrugged and poured his drink into her own glass and took a long drink.

Scott lifted the golden brown pieces from the skillet and blotted them on a plate of paper towels. He turned to look at her, studying her over the lip of his water bottle as he lifted it to take a drink. She was leaning on the counter, her shoulders relaxed and not as squared as they had been when she'd stepped from the bedroom.

"I meant to ask. How'd you come up with the name Casey Martinez?" he asked. "I mean, Casey is a given, short for Cassandra. But where does the Martinez come from?"

She hesitated and, for a moment, he thought she was going to ignore him. Then she shrugged and said, "It was my mother's maiden name. Pretty much the only thing I had left of her when she died."

"I'm sorry." Scott knew the story of her mother's death and her father's incarceration. He'd heard the story from Alex several years earlier. Growing up without a parent was a common link in their friendship.

"My father killed her." She said it simply, as if it were something that happened in every family. "Condensed version? My mother kicked him out because he was a drunk and an addict and he liked young girls. But, see, he was superior. The king of his castle. He wasn't going to allow any woman to treat him like that. So to teach her a lesson, he beat her, raped her, then stabbed her to death while Alex and I slept in the next room." She stopped, her fingers white on the stem of her glass. "Then he had the nerve to blame it all on the drugs."

Although she murmured the last part under her breath, he heard her voice break. Her shoulders sagged as if weighted down by her grief. With a trembling hand she swallowed down the rest of her wine, then grabbed the bottle and refilled her glass. It unsettled him that a part of him wanted to take her in his arms and help her forget the nightmare of her childhood.

Casey held on to the bottle a moment, her eyes fixed on the wine in her glass as if it held solace for her. "I don't know why I told you that," she said in a clipped voice.

"Believe it or not, people actually find me easy to talk to," he said. "I'm very sorry for your loss. Where's your father now?"

"As far as I'm concerned, he's dead."

"But you don't know for sure?"

"I don't care. As soon as I was old enough, I left that life and everything about it." She took another swallow from her glass and set it on the counter with a snap.

Scott turned back to the chicken, removing the remaining pieces and placing them onto the plate. He understood the venom in her words and didn't blame her for how she felt. Changing her name had probably been more about distancing herself from her father. He wrestled with the urge to ask her more questions but decided against it. He wasn't going to push—not yet anyway. He knew as well as anyone some things just needed more time to heal.

She pulled in a breath as if to settle herself, then said, "So, are you going to share that?"

He turned and offered her a smile. "Of course. Help yourself."

He grabbed the plate of chicken and handed it to her. She carried it to the table while Scott gathered the salad and a dish of wild rice. He sat at the table, biting back a laugh when Casey chose to sit at the far end.

She served herself before she sat down, then sent him a cautious look. "You aren't going to say Grace, are you?" she asked.

"Only if you want to," Scott said, setting his plate in front of him. He wasn't a religious man, but that didn't mean he couldn't pray.

"No. I don't."

"Then let's eat," he said with a smile. His grin spread when Casey picked up a knife and fork to cut a slice from the chicken. "Sweetheart, there are just some things that are meant to be eaten by hand." He grabbed a chicken leg and bit into it.

Casey looked at him a moment then set her knife and fork on the table. She picked up the chicken and took a large bite. Her eyes closed as she savored the taste, a soft smile playing the corners of her mouth. "This is really good. Your grandmother would be proud."

"Thank you," Scott said, barely masking his surprise. Color flushed her cheeks. He wondered if she always had trouble giving compliments or if it was just him. He decided it was the latter when she turned her attention back to her plate and ate as if she were alone in the room.

"So, Cassandra…" Scott said to break the silence that had plagued them throughout the meal.

Her eyes turned hard. "It's Casey. My name is Casey."

"Casey, then," he corrected. "Tell me about New York."

She picked up her wine glass, her expression going blank. "Well, it's the largest city in the United States, affectionately known as the Big Apple. There are five boroughs …"

"Cute. Tell me what happened to send you packing."

She lifted her chin and twirled the wine in her glass. "Nothing happened, and nothing sent me packing."

Scott raised his brow and waited for her to continue. His source at the FBI office in Houston wouldn't be able to get back with him for a few days so he figured he'd pull what he could from Casey. It was likely she knew more than he did anyway.

"Fine," she said. She set her glass back on the table and turned it absently. "Some psycho is running around killing women, and the FBI seems to think it has something to do with me. I personally think they're being paranoid, but they insisted I leave town anyway. And hire you."

Scott ignored the bite of the last statement and sat back in his chair, crossing his legs at the ankles. "Do they have any leads?"

"None they've bothered to share with me."

"Hmm. Well, it's obviously someone you know."

Casey narrowed her eyes at him. "Excuse me?"

He laughed at her indignant response. "In general. Usually in cases like this it turns out to be someone you know. Have you given them a list of possibilities? Ex-boyfriends, roommates, all-around enemies?"

"Yes, Detective. I did. It was a very short list," she said.

He grinned at her. "Well now, would that be called arrogance or confidence?"

"I don't socialize much, Detective, and unlike you I'm choosy about who I spend my time with."

"Sounds like you lead a dull life, Ms. Martinez."

"No, just a careful one." She lifted her chin and picked up her wine glass. "Why are you asking me these questions anyway? Didn't you get a report or something about the investigation?"

"It was a bit vague. Apparently the feebs haven't learned to share yet." In his experience the FBI didn't share information about their investigations unless they found it essential to their case. And evidently they didn't think including a small town police department would make a difference.

"Ohhh, too bad. Feeling out of the loop, are we?"

He shrugged off her patronizing tone. "I've been bounced off the streets for a while. I guess I'm just anxious to get back to real police work instead of getting stuck as a glorified babysitter." He silently kicked himself when Casey bristled, her back going ramrod straight.

"You can leave anytime, Detective." Her look cooled along with her voice. "It was not my idea to have you here, and I certainly do not need a keeper."

"What, and miss all this engaging conversation?" He gave her his most charming smile, but it didn't thaw her expression. "Look, I'm sorry. That just came out wrong. Regardless of how either of us feels about these arrangements, I have a job to do, and I'll do it. So you have nothing to worry about."

"I'm not worried. As I said before, I believe the FBI is overly paranoid. However, I will placate them since I really have no choice in the matter and you can continue to do your *job*." She picked up her plate and took it to the kitchen. "Thank you for dinner, Detective. Now, if you'll excuse me, I have a job to do as well."

Scott rubbed the back of his neck as she returned to her bedroom. It amazed him how she could make the word *detective* sound so derogatory.

CHAPTER EIGHT

Agent Simms pinned an index card into the evidence board and stepped back to view the montage. Nine states, twelve murders, five years. The only real consistency was that each happened during the months of April or June.

He stepped to his desk and picked up the book found at Catherine Flores' apartment and thumbed through the pages. It was a new copy, since the original was still with forensics.

"Recreational reading?" Agent Hawthorne said as he entered the office.

"Not exactly my cup of tea." He closed the book and tossed it back on the desk.

"Mine either, but I have to admit, they *were* entertaining."

Agent Simms gestured to the file he held. "You find something?"

"The prints came back on the Bible." Agent Hawthorne flipped through a manila folder. "They belong to an Alejandro Rivera, ex-con who did time in Texas for murdering his wife."

"Ms. Martinez said cons were some of her biggest fans."

"Yeah, but what she didn't say was this particular con is her father."

"What?" Agent Simms snatched the folder and pulled out the page. "Why didn't this come up on our background check?"

"The files were sealed during the trial to keep Ms. Martinez and her brother protected. Afterward they were stored, and no one bothered to reopen them. When the prints came in I contacted the prison where he was incarcerated and had them fax the information," he said. "According to the files Rivera was sentenced to twenty-five years for manslaughter. Ms. Rivera—uh, Martinez—was only five at the time but she was a key witness at his trial. He served nineteen years and was given early parole about three years ago. According to his jacket, he's currently living in Houston. I don't know how close that is to where Ms. Martinez is staying, but I have the Houston office on alert. Do you want them to pick him up?"

"No, just have them watch him. It's probably better if he doesn't know Ms. Martinez is in the same state. He might have been the one sending the Bibles, but I don't think he's our killer."

Hawthorne nodded and took the folder back. "I've been trying to figure out what it is about the books that ties into the murders," he said, moving to the map. "And look at this. Out of the twelve murders so far, six of them happened in the same state where one of her books was set."

"Yeah, I noticed that, too," Simms said, sitting against his desk to study the map.

"Our guy must have assumed that because the books were set in these states, Ms. Martinez lived there." He picked up the book and flipped it open to the back page. "Her bio says she's from New York and likes to travel, but doesn't list where she lives now. Maybe our guy thought she lived in the towns she wrote about, but when he arrived he realized they were just made up. He gets angry because she made a fool out of him, and he takes his anger out on the first person he sees who resembles Ms. Martinez."

"It's plausible," Simms said. "So, why only April and June?"

"Well, we already know her birthday is in April, so that could be one reason. The only other thing I can think of for June is Father's Day."

"So our killer wants her to think of her father?" He considered the notion then shook his head. "I don't know. Something tells me Ms. Martinez doesn't waste much thought on the man. The day would be like any other for her." He picked up his phone on the first ring. "Simms. Thanks, I'm on my way." He hung up the phone and stepped around his desk. "Coroner is finished with the autopsy. Keep going over the files and see what else you can come up with. If this bastard stays on his regular pattern, we have less than a month before he kills again."

❧

"What did you find?" Agent Simms asked as he pushed through the swinging doors of the morgue. Catherine Flores's nude body lay on a steel table, a white sheet pulled down to her waist. The blood had already been washed from her skin, the lacerations from her attack stitched closed. A Y incision trailed from her shoulders to her chest extending down to her lower extremities.

The coroner looked up with a nod as she finished the sutures. "Be with you in a minute. Make yourself at home," she said with a thin smile.

Agent Simms squared his shoulders and stepped back. Sometimes ME's were as bad as the local police departments when it came to jurisdiction on a case.

The doctor pulled the sheet up to cover the body then stripped off her latex gloves. She pushed her protective glasses up to rest on top of her head and picked up the metal file at the foot of the table.

"The toxicology report just came back," she said, stepping beside him. "Her alcohol level was point zero one. I also found traces of Benzodiazepine in her system. It's a sedative most commonly found in Rohypnol. I don't think it was enough to kill her, just enough to leave her unconscious for about twelve hours. She was raped repeatedly. There's a lot of bruising and tearing of the vaginal wall. He likely used a condom. I found traces of latex and some spermicide." She moved to the wall where the X-rays hung and flipped on the bright fluorescent light.

"She'd been badly beaten across the face. Her cheekbones are crushed, her nose is broken, her jaw is dislocated. It looks like he used his fist, but again, he used the blanket as a buffer. There's no foreign blood or skin and nothing under her nails. It looks like he trimmed them. Did a pretty damn good job of it, too.

"She had twenty-five stab wounds in the upper and lower extremities and another twenty-five slashes on her face." She pointed to the marks, speaking with a professional detachment. "My best guess for his weapon of choice would be a hunting knife with a blade about eight to twelve inches long. The wounds are deep in some places, shallow in others so it's inconclusive." She paused and sent a pitying look at the body. "It's almost like he tortured her with the knife. She pretty much bled to death. The poor soul was so drugged up I doubt she felt any of it."

"God, I hope not," he murmured. He took the chart she handed him and scanned the pages. Anger burned through him, settling tight in his chest. The only link they had to the murders, other than the book by Casey Martinez, was the fact that the women had been given the date-rape drug, Rohypnol. At last count he'd had twelve bodies and no suspects. Now, he had just been given victim number thirteen. "That's it?" he asked.

"As much as I enjoy your company, that's not why I called you." She tapped the page he'd just flipped to.

"You found a hair." Simms looked up, forming a smile.

"Yep. The SOB didn't clean up as well as he thought. I've already sent it to the bureau for a DNA analysis. If he's in the system, you should have him."

CHAPTER NINE

Curled up on a lounge chair, Casey stared at the beach as the waves rolled and foamed onshore. The sun sat just above the horizon, a kaleidoscope of soft colors among the whisper of white clouds. A group of seagulls ventured out to the offshore shrimp boats in a search for breakfast, their siren cries fading as they moved farther away from land.

The dream Casey thought she'd left behind with her childhood woke her an hour before sunrise. She'd shot awake, short of breath, her heart pounding so hard she thought it would explode. Tears burned her eyes until she could no longer hold them back. They fell like a waterfall down her cheeks and into her pillow, leaving her feeling drained and defeated.

Casey hugged her knees to her chest and closed her eyes. Images flashed in her head like a cruel slideshow. She was back in the small clapboard-shuttered house. Muted light seeping in through dirty windows. Yellowed paint chipping off the walls. Silence stilled the air, the quiet almost deafening.

She crept down a long narrow hallway toward her mother's bedroom. The thin cotton nightgown she wore whispered against her legs as her bare feet scraped across the hardwood floor. A dim bulb flickered on the ceiling, casting ghostly shadows in front of her. The floorboards creaked under her weight, and she realized she was no longer five years old, but a grown woman.

Reaching the end of the hall, she closed her hand around the crystal doorknob. A chill skittered across her skin like icy fingers. The faint copper smell of blood seeped under the door.

She flattened her hand against the cold wood and gently pushed it open. Fear froze her to her spot and seized her with an unrelenting grip. On the bed her father crouched over the butchered body of her mother. His head came up when he heard her frightened gasp. His mouth curled into a cruel smile. The glassy, dead stare of his black eyes burned into her.

"There's blood on your hands, Cassandra."

She spun around and ran, the dark, husky threat of his voice ringing in her ears.

Casey pressed her fingers to her eyes and wiped furiously at the tears. He was right. If she hadn't run away, if she'd been the brave little girl her mother thought she was, she could have saved her. It didn't matter that she was only five years old when the nightmare happened. She still could have done something, anything to help her. But instead she'd cowered in her closet and saved herself.

"Good morning."

Scott's voice jolted her from her thoughts. He handed her a cup of coffee before continuing to the railing to stare at the beach.

Casey rubbed her eyes and glared at his back. "Can't I even get a few minutes of privacy without you lurking about?"

Scott kept his back to her and continued to scan the empty beach.

"I gave you thirty minutes. And you looked like you could use some coffee." He wanted to give her a moment to compose herself. He'd heard her in the living room an hour earlier and saw her step out onto the deck through the open doorway of his bedroom. Since she still wore the t-shirt she'd slept in, he knew she wouldn't venture any farther than the deck.

He'd planned to give her a few hours alone until he saw her shoulders drop as if a heavy hand had fallen on them. The way she wiped at her face told him she'd been crying. He debated the thought of offering her comfort and decided she would probably bite his head off if he tried.

He turned around to face her. The misery was gone from her eyes and replaced with the bright light of annoyance. Yep, she not only would have bitten off his head, she'd have spit it in the garbage disposal.

"So, what exciting things do you have planned for today? Going to stick your nose into your computer again?" he asked, leaning against the railing and crossing his legs at the ankles. He sipped his coffee to hide his amused grin. Damn, if she didn't look sexy when she was irritated.

Casey wrapped her fingers around the mug and turned her attention to the beach. "I'm going into town this morning. I have some things I need to pick up at the store, and I want to do a little shopping." She sipped the coffee and paused but didn't comment that he'd fixed it the way she liked.

"Okay. Whenever you're ready. And no, you aren't going alone. But don't worry. I'll keep a safe distance."

Her shoulders squared, and he knew she was going to start another pointless argument. He didn't know why she even bothered since he could out-stubborn anyone, but it was cute the way she tried.

"I'm not going to walk around town with you tailing me like a lovesick puppy," she said. "I don't want your company. I don't like your company. I'm perfectly capable of going shopping alone, and I can take care of myself."

"I don't doubt it. And hopefully in a couple of weeks, if there's a God, you'll be able to do just that. Until then, darlin', I'm your shadow." He pushed off the rail and strolled back into the house before she could respond, but he didn't miss her murmured, "*Pendejo.*"

෴

They left the beach house after breakfast and took separate cars, which Scott had expected and didn't mind. It was their first venture into town since her arrival three days earlier, and he wanted to make sure no one was tailing her.

Their first stop was at the post office. He followed her inside and bought a book of stamps at the machine in the lobby while Casey stepped to the counter to mail a package. After a short drive through several neighborhoods (he wondered if she was either lost or trying to shake him) she parked her car along the curb in downtown Rosehill and got out to walk.

Scott did as promised and kept a discreet distance between them. He shook his head with a short laugh when Casey ducked into one store after another as if she were still trying to lose him. She could Houdini all day but it wouldn't matter. He'd walked these streets often in his early years on the force and knew every entrance and exit to each of the stores. She couldn't escape him even if he were blindfolded.

After two hours of window shopping he followed her into a boutique. He stepped behind her and had to stop himself from imaging her in the black lace teddy she held. "Very nice, though I pictured you to be more of a negligee type," he said, leaning close to her ear.

Casey bristled and tried to ignore how the warmth of his breath made her pulse jump. "I suspected you were a closet drag queen." She placed the teddy back on the rack and picked up another one.

"Nah, I prefer to take them off, not put them on," he answered with a sly grin.

"Scott Weller." A young saleswoman stepped to them with a bright smile. She leaned forward and pressed a kiss to Scott's cheek. "I haven't seen you in ages. To what do I owe the pleasure?"

"Hey darlin'. I just stopped in as a favor to my mother. She was here a few weeks ago and asked you to order something for her. I was checking to see if it was in," he said.

"I'll go look. Ma'am, is there anything I can help you with?" the woman said to Casey.

"No, thank you. I'm just looking. You have some lovely things here."

"Thank you," she answered with a proud grin. "I'll be right back, Scott."

Casey tossed a dry look over her shoulder. "Your mother?"

Scott shrugged and gave her a dazzling smile. She bit down on the jolt to her system.

He raised his brow with interest and nodded at the teddy. "So are you going to buy that thing?"

Casey didn't miss the humor in his voice. She picked up a sheer white chemise that left nothing to the imagination and stroked her hand along the inside so he could see just how sheer it was. "I find most clothing to be too confining when I sleep. But there's something about the touch of silk against my skin." She caressed the fabric over his bare arm and leaned next to his ear, dropping her voice to a low, sultry tone. "It's just so…erotic. Don't you think?" She eased back and smiled at him. He looked as if he'd just swallowed his tongue.

The saleslady returned, flipping through pages on a clipboard. "It came in a couple of days ago, Scott. We shipped it out already."

Scott looked at the young clerk and blinked as if trying to bring her into focus. "What? Oh …yeah…thanks."

Casey returned the chemise to the rack and nodded to the girl. "Thank you. I enjoyed your shop," she said before sauntering out of the store. She stepped onto the sidewalk and heard the clerk tell Scott to call her and his absent-minded, "Uh huh, sure."

Slipping her hands into the pockets of her jacket, she continued along the sidewalk, taking in the other stores lining the street. They hadn't changed much in the ten years she'd been gone. As a child she had loved to look at the colorful displays in the windows, fantasizing that she was one of the models posing in the window. On the days she was with her grandmother they would push along an old shopping cart Alex had found in a drainage ditch. They used the cart to carry their packages home since her grandmother couldn't drive a car. Until Alex got his license, their ventures out were either on foot or by bus. It had never occurred to her to be ashamed of public transportation until she overheard one of her classmates sneer, "Only trash ride on the bus." After that, she swore she would never step foot on a bus again, a promise she'd kept for nearly fifteen years.

She pushed the memories away and looked up at the clock on the City Bank's marquee. One thirty. Her stomach growled. Time for lunch.

She spotted the diner on the corner, surprised it was still open after all these years. When she was a teenager, the small mom-and-pop diner was considered the place to hang out. Juniors and seniors would gather on Friday and Saturday nights after football or whatever school sport had been played and turn the parking lot into a giant party. But she'd never been invited to join them.

She hesitated, then with a mental kick, squared her shoulders. She wasn't in high school anymore.

She settled into a red vinyl booth with a Formica table and scanned the laminated menu the waitress handed her.

"Mind if I join you?" Scott asked, stepping to the table.

Casey kept her eyes trained on the menu. "Yes, I do," she answered.

He laughed and slid into the booth across from her. "I was beginning to wonder if you were ever going to stop for lunch. I've heard of women who could shop till they drop. Never thought I'd ever meet one."

The waitress, a young woman with thick black hair pinned back into a bun, stepped to the table and set two small glasses of water in front of them. "Well, hey there, Scott. We haven't seen you around here much. How you been doing?" she asked, with a toothy grin.

Casey clenched her jaw and resisted the urge to cringe. The woman's thick Texas drawl scraped her nerves like fingernails on a chalkboard.

Scott gave her a curious look before turning to smile at the young girl. "Not too bad, Heather. How's everything at home?"

"Everyone's doing great. Jimmy and his wife are about to have the baby soon, so we got a baby shower coming up. I tell ya, I didn't know having a baby could be so crazy and fun all at the same time."

"You're going to be a terrific aunt. Give them my best, will you?" Scott said.

"I sure will. So, are y'all about ready to order or do you need some more time?" Heather asked.

"Let me have my usual, darlin," Scott said with a wink.

"Okay." The young girl turned to Casey. "And you, ma'am?"

Scott tapped the menu when Casey continued to stare at it. "There's only one side to the menu, darlin' and not much to choose from."

She sent him a scowl before turning to the waitress with a polite smile. "The grilled chicken sandwich, please. Do you have bottled water?"

"No, sorry. Just straight out the tap," Heather said with a lift of her shoulder.

"An iced tea, please."

"I'm sorry, but you sure do look familiar. Do I know you?" Heather asked. She studied Casey's face as she picked up the menu.

Casey held her breath, making an effort to relax the muscles that had bunched along her back. It was inevitable as well as unavoidable that she would run into someone from her high school. She'd even tried to prepare herself for their usual disdainful remarks. It was pointless, of course, she would always be thought of as the trash from the other side of town.

She stole a glance at Heather's polyester waitress uniform. At least she could take comfort in knowing one of her classmates didn't get very far in life.

"This is Cassandra Rivera. Alex's sister." Scott stared at Casey, his brow cocked as if he thought she were from another planet.

"Oh, of course. You look just like him. Oh, I just adore Alex. He is such a sweetheart," Heather gushed. "He took care of my daddy last year when he had his heart attack. He made us feel so secure during that horrible time. I tell you, he's the best nurse they got at that hospital."

Casey turned to get a better look at the girl. She was barely out of high school. Shame washed over her like a cold wave. Had she become what she hated most about the town?

"My family and me just love him to death. He's just terrific," Heather continued.

"Yes, he is terrific," Casey said. "Thank you."

"You give him my best, you hear? And his wife, too. She's a great lady, too. Well, I'll go put your order in."

Casey watched Heather hurry off. She wanted to apologize for being rude, although the girl didn't seem to notice. She felt Scott's eyes on her and looked up, keeping her expression cool. "What?"

"I don't think I've ever seen anyone go from tense to arrogantly superior in the blink of an eye before." He leaned back in the booth laying his arm across the back of his seat, an amused grin on his face. "You're a tough one to figure out, you know?"

"Then don't bother." She turned her attention to the handful of cars stopped at the intersection. A rusted pickup truck coasted to the stoplight then picked up speed as it passed the diner.

"You're a walking contradiction, you know that?" Scott continued. "All flash without the fire. Oh, I've seen your type before. The high and mighty who seem to think they're better than everyone around them."

Casey ground her teeth and focused on a store display across the street.

"See, you try to come across as this pompous, New-York-tough, self-important bitch." His grin widened when she glared at him. "But, I don't think you're really like that. I think you're just a regular person like the rest of us, only you're more afraid to be yourself because you think you have something to prove to everyone here. Like, maybe if they stop seeing you as who you were and see you as who you are, you'll be able to overcome some inferiority complex you had as a child. I'll bet you're just waiting for the day when you can stand on the steps of Rosehill City Hall and holler, 'Look at me! I *am* better than you!'."

"Spare me your pseudo-cowboy analysis," Casey said, resisting the urge to squirm at his near accurate assessment. "You don't know me or anything about me. You're the hired help right now, Detective. Don't forget that." She shifted in her seat and pulled out her pack of cigarettes. "Now, if you don't mind, I'd rather eat alone."

Scott grinned and slid out of the booth, keeping his eyes pinned on her as he spoke.

"Hey, Heather, wrap that up for me, will ya, darlin?" he said. "You have a nice lunch now, Ms. Martinez, and just let me know when you're ready to continue your strut downtown." He winked at her then headed to the counter to pay for his meal.

Casey pulled out a cigarette and lit it up. She blew the smoke out on a tight breath and watched him leave. She'd heard the playful tone in his voice but still had to resist the impulse to sulk. He didn't know what he was talking about. She was not pompous and had never been self-important. She was just careful, that's all. Just because she tried to make something of herself and didn't want to be reminded of where she came from didn't mean she was stuck-up.

She glanced around at the handful of people in the diner. Her gaze stopped on an elderly Mexican man at the counter, dressed in worn jeans and a dirty T-shirt. She took a drink of water to wash away the disdain and turned away.

Okay, so maybe she *had* developed a bit of an elitist attitude where this town was concerned, but that didn't make her a bad person, did it?

The man turned and looked at her with a thin smile before he left.

Casey felt the shudder down to the bone.

Chapter Ten

Scott waited in his jeep as Casey made her way back to her car parked on the corner. She looked tense—her back straight, her steps rigid. He wondered if he'd hurt her feelings with his playful jibe during lunch. She didn't seem like the type that let anything bother her, but he could be wrong.

He parked along the curb as Casey pulled her car into the HEB parking lot. Sliding from the seat, he waited for the traffic to clear and followed her inside the grocery store. He had an unsettling need to know if he'd hurt her feelings.

He found her in the frozen foods section, debating on which box of Hotpockets she wanted to buy. Cold air blew across his arm from the open freezer as he stepped beside her. She had already placed several frozen pizzas and burritos, as well as a couple of cans of ravioli at the bottom of her cart.

"That looks nutritious," he said, shaking his head.

She scowled at him and grabbed another box. "Who are you, my dietician?"

Scott held open the freezer door while she made her decision. "Look, I'm sorry about lunch. I didn't mean to hurt your feelings with what I said."

She looked at him, her eyes cool. "You didn't, since that would require me to care about anything you have to say. And I don't." She tossed the two boxes of Hotpockets into her cart and moved to the next isle.

"Ouch," Scott said with a laugh. He stepped behind her again when she turned into the hygiene isle, casting a look at the colorful display of shampoos.

"You know—" He placed his hand on the cart to stop her before she could leave. "Since we're going to be living together for the next couple of weeks, why don't we pool our groceries? I mean, since we both have to eat, it'll make more sense to follow one grocery list instead of getting double of everything. And we can just split the costs."

Casey stopped and looked at him. In the small basket he carried were fresh vegetables and several packs of chicken, pork and beef steak. So far they weren't doubling up on anything, she thought dryly. And, as much as she hated to admit it, he was right. It would be more practical to follow one grocery list instead of two, and she liked to think she was a practical person.

"Okay, Detective. We can pool our groceries," she said. "Here, you can buy these, too." She pulled a box of tampons from the shelf and tossed them in his basket.

He barely resisted the wince. "Funny. Personal items are separate." He picked up the packet and set it back on the shelf as Casey continued to the next isle.

She arched her brow and looked at him when he stepped beside her. "May I get cookies or will you chastise me for that as well?"

"As long as they're Oreos," he said, setting his basket in her cart.

"Double stuffed. What else is there?" She grabbed a bag from the shelf and set it in the cart.

Satisfied they had enough to last the next two weeks, they headed to the checkout. Casey pulled the groceries out of the basket and separated them on the belt to give them each an even amount to pay.

"Make sure that all comes out even now," Scott said with an amused grin.

"I just want to make sure we each pay our fair share."

Scott laughed and turned to the cashier. "Just ring it all up together, darlin'." He looked at Casey and smiled. "We can divvy it up when we get home."

"It isn't home," Casey said before she could stop herself. "Fine. Are you sure you can count that high?"

"That's why God invented calculators," he said with a wink.

❧

"So, are we finished or is there somewhere else you need to go?" Scott asked once they loaded the bags into Casey's rental.

"We're done for now. I'll see you back at the beach house." She climbed into the car as he crossed the street to his jeep. "Eventually."

She pulled out of the parking lot before Scott could get into his driver's seat. She'd conceded to trying to lose him downtown—the man was like a bloodhound, so it became pointless. But she was in a car now, and it was definitely faster than being on foot.

She gunned the engine and zipped past the stoplight seconds before it turned red. She checked the rearview mirror and spotted Scott caught behind two cars at the light.

"See if you can keep up now, Detective," she said, increasing her speed.

She turned right at the next intersection and slowed her speed so she could take in the old neighborhood. It surprised her how much of the town had changed since she'd moved. Not that she really cared, but so much of what she remembered was different now. Even the salespeople in the boutiques and stores downtown didn't seem as haughty as they once had.

She turned down a narrow two-lane street, scanning the once-familiar block. The large vacant lot near the high school was now a strip mall with a McDonald's on the corner. The drive-in theater, where she saw her first Disney movie with Mama and Alex, had been torn down, the lot now an empty field of overgrown weeds. It saddened her to know it was gone since it was one of the few good memories she could pull up of her childhood.

She continued over a rusted railroad track, stopping at the red light. Traffic trickled through the intersection, the occasional blare of a horn followed by a friendly wave. Definitely unlike the gridlock that was such a satisfying annoyance in New York.

She studied the neighborhood as she waited for the never-ending light to change, taking in the old, unkempt houses which were still paneled with asbestos siding. An old woman sat hunched on a wooden rocker, watching the traffic as if she were at a parade. In the neighboring yard, two small children, barefoot and in need of a bath, chased a small ratty dog.

Casey turned away and swallowed the bitter taste of shame at the back of her throat. It's funny how the things you try the hardest to forget are the ones that stay with you, she thought soberly.

She strummed her fingers on the steering wheel and surveyed the rest of the neighborhood. Her hand froze as her gaze landed on a metal sign posted on a large stone wall. It took a moment for the words to register. Green Lawn Cemetery. The place where her mother and grandmother were buried, side by side.

She waited for the traffic to clear then did a quick U-turn and pulled into the entrance. The road curved and opened to the spacious grounds. After a moment of coasting along the narrow road she stopped along the edge of the grass and searched the area, looking for anything familiar.

She turned off the engine and climbed out of the car. Nothing about the place was as she remembered. The grounds were neat and well manicured. Several of the graves had fresh flowers laid across them, while lighted eternity candles in brass holders stood on the markers of some others. The stone mausoleum, placed off to the side, was new. Through the glass doors she could see brass sconces attached to the walls, each filled with flowers.

Tears tightened her throat as she looked at the grounds. It all looked so different. So foreign. It was no longer the pauper's cemetery she had once been ashamed to visit. Someone had finally cared enough to give even the less fortunate a beautiful resting place.

She heard Scott's jeep stop behind the Mercedes. He didn't climb out right away, and instead watched her from behind the steering wheel. She couldn't tell if he was angry at her for taking the side roads in an attempt to lose him. But he seemed to want to give her some privacy.

As if sensing she was lost, he climbed out of the jeep and stepped quietly beside her. She glanced at him then turned her attention to a large stone memorial with a picture of the Virgin Mary.

"I don't know where to go," she said hopelessly. "Isn't that the most horrible thing you've ever heard? My mother is buried here, and I don't even know where she is."

"It's been a while since you've been here. I'm sure the place has changed a lot in that time," he said, turning to look at her.

"Yeah. I guess." She crossed her arms, her fingers gripped tight around the flesh.

"We can ask the caretaker if you want. His office is up toward the front," Scott offered gently.

"No. Forget it. It's okay." Casey turned back to her car. It disturbed her that she almost turned to him for support. She didn't need a man to lean on. She could handle her problems on her own just as she always had.

Scott laid his hand on her arm and stopped her. "Casey, you don't have to feel guilty about this. I'm sure your mother knows you're here." He dropped his hand when she looked up and blinked at him.

"I'll see you at the beach house." She stepped to the car and climbed inside.

Her fingers tightened around the keys as she fought down the ache in her chest. The guilt over her mother's death would always consume her and there was nothing anyone could do to change it.

It was her fault her mother was here. She was going to have to continue to live with it.

The phone rang as they stepped into the beach house. Scott set the groceries on the floor and held up his hand to stop Casey from picking up the handset.

"Grab the cordless in the kitchen but don't answer until I tell you to."

He moved into the bedroom and stood by the bedside table. Casey grabbed the phone and waited in the doorway, tapping her foot.

Scott nodded. "Okay, now."

She pushed the call button at the same time Scott carefully lifted the phone from its cradle.

"Hello?"

"Hi, Casey."

"Jennifer. Hi." Casey smiled at the sound of her sister-in-law's voice.

"How's everything at the beach house?" she asked.

"*Todo esta bien, menos la rata que esta en la recámara de huésped*," she said. "Hold on a sec." She covered the mouth piece with her palm and glared at Scott. "Do you mind?"

Scott shrugged and carefully set the phone down. Casey closed the door behind him when he left and settled on the bed.

"What did *that* mean?" Jennifer said with a laugh.

"Nothing. Sorry." Casey leaned against the headboard and stretched her legs out. "So, how are you feeling?"

"Well the good news is the morning sickness finally passed. But now I'm starting to crave fried peanut butter and banana sandwiches."

"That's really gross, Jenn."

"I know, and Alex is threatening to name him Elvis, even if it's a girl. But the baby wants what the baby wants," she said with a laugh. "So, listen, I know you're busy so I won't keep you. I just have a favor to ask. How open would you be to doing a book signing? That's what it's called right?"

"Yeah—"

"See, it's for a fundraiser we're doing Thursday for the hospital to help rebuild the children's wing. It was hit pretty hard during Hurricane Ike, and the money the hospital got for damages went to the other units. Some of the businesses in town have offered to donate twenty-five percent of their sales and the manager of the mall said he would donate a percentage of a full day's sales to the hospital, too. So I thought, maybe if you helped us out by doing a signing at the bookstore in the mall we could raise even more money."

"That sounds great, but—"

"I already spoke to the manager at the bookstore, and when I mentioned that you're my sister-in-law and you're in town for a while, he said he'd love to host your signing. All you have to do is give a little talk or something then sign your books. It'll only be a few hours, and all the proceeds go to the hospital. Did I say that already? The manager even said he'd donate fifty percent of the whole day's sales. Isn't that great?"

Casey bit her lip. Would the FBI even let her do a book signing? She was supposed to be in hiding. Of course, it wasn't as if whoever the Feds were looking for was going to find out about an impromptu appearance fifteen hundred miles away. If she kept it off her website and made sure it was only publicized locally, it shouldn't be a problem.

"Oh, I'm sorry. I didn't mean to put you on the spot," Jennifer said. "If you're not allowed to do it, that's okay. I don't want to get you in trouble."

"No, Jenn, I'd love to do it. I was just thinking, maybe I could call my editor and ask if she'd be willing to donate some of the books. That way we can get more money for the hospital."

"Oh, that would be wonderful. Thank you," Jennifer said. "I'll call the store and let them know you said yes. I'll call you later with the details."

Casey lay back against the headboard and blew out a resigned breath when the call ended. She hoped she wasn't making a mistake.

She returned to the kitchen and found Scott leaning on the counter, eating the Oreos. He'd already put the other groceries away.

"Everything okay?" he asked.

"Yes. Jenn wanted to know if I'd help with a fundraiser for the hospital." She placed the phone back on the wall and turned to grab a cookie. "I told her I would."

Scott nodded and moved to the cabinet to grab a glass. "I didn't know you spoke Spanish."

"Of course I do. I choose not to."

"Why?" he asked, pulling the milk out of the refrigerator.

"I have my reasons."

Scott handed her a glass of milk. "So, what did you say? To Jennifer, when she asked about the house."

"I said it's fine." Casey bit her lip and shrugged. "Except for the rat in the guest bedroom."

He laughed and bit into another cookie. "You know, that's just one of those things that sounds better in Spanish."

CHAPTER ELEVEN

Scott paced the living room of the beach house while he waited for Casey to come out of the bedroom. She'd been closed off in the room for the past thirty-six hours, only emerging long enough to cook herself a frozen dinner.

He'd understood her need to be alone after the trip to the cemetery and didn't try to coax her out of the room for company. Shortly before midnight last night, she'd crept out to let him know Jennifer had called back to tell her the book signing had been set up for this morning.

He glanced at his watch and swore under his breath. It irritated him that she'd waited until the last minute to tell him about the plans and he told her, or rather argued with her, that their morning run would put them behind schedule. But, as usual, she wouldn't listen. The signing was scheduled for ten and it was already nine o'clock. The drive to the mall took forty-five minutes—not that they would have much traffic to deal with, but he hated to be late for anything. Plus, he wasn't happy that Casey would now openly expose herself to whoever was after her. Okay, so far there hadn't been any problems with a stalker and maybe she was right with thinking the FBI were being paranoid. But that was beside the point.

He stepped to the window, pushing the drapes aside to look out. *For someone who's being stalked, she sure has a careless attitude.* He dropped the curtain and went to the terrace doors to make sure the pole was still in place.

At least he wouldn't have to stand by and act as her assistant, he thought with relief. He'd been assured that the store manager and his employees would handle the entire setup and signing arrangements. All he had to do was take care of security which, lucky for him, hadn't been a big problem.

Scott checked his watch again as Casey stepped out of the bedroom. She wore a short navy-colored skirt with a matching blazer over a soft pink blouse. Her hair fell loose across her shoulders. Her makeup was soft and subtle. His pulse jumped.

Definitely worth the wait.

"Are you ready?" he asked.

"Yes, I'm ready," she said. "Is there any coffee left?"

"No, and you don't have time. Let's go."

She started to speak then shook her head. "Fine." She did a cursory check of her small handbag then looked up at him. "Are you going like that?"

Scott looked at his clothes. He wore a pair of faded jeans and his cowboy boots as usual, but his shirt was fresh and fairly new.

He pulled his sunglasses from his shirt pocket and slipped them on with a wry grin. "Sorry, I left the tux at the cleaners."

"I didn't mean…never mind. Let's just go."

☙

They reached the mall with ten minutes to spare. It was still too early for the stores to open, so there weren't many people. A handful of senior citizens were taking advantage of the air-conditioned building to do their daily walk, marking the distance with the bronze mile markers imbedded into the brick walls.

A tall man with wide-palmed hands and long, spindly arms met Casey and Scott at the entrance to the bookstore. "Ms. Martinez, it's such an honor to have you here," he said, shaking Casey's hand with too much enthusiasm. "We don't get many authors signing their books in our store, so this is a wonderful experience for us. And it's even better knowing one of our own hometown girls has made it big."

Casey fixed a polite smile on her face. She would never be a 'hometown girl.'

She slid a quick look at his name tag. "Thank you, Mr. Edmunds. It's a pleasure to be here."

He led them to the back of the store where a six-foot table had been set up. Arranged on top of the table was a stack of the books Casey's editor had shipped overnight. A padded chair had been placed behind the table for Casey to sit on. A carafe of what she assumed was cold water sat on the opposite side of the books along with a tray of pens.

"We still have about ten minutes 'til we open. Would you like anything before then?" the manager asked, his expression pleased with her reaction to his setup.

"A very large cup of coffee would be great right now. I haven't had any yet," Casey said with an irritated glance at Scott.

"I want to take a look at any other entrances you might have besides the main one," Scott said.

"Of course. There's only one. Our delivery door. It leads out into a service foyer."

Mr. Edmunds led Casey to the small break room and showed Scott the rear exit.

Scott checked the door then asked the manager to make sure the lock was secure. It would be easier to stick with one entrance and exit. He had posted two uniformed officers inside the mall with orders to be on the lookout for anyone who appeared to be watching Casey with intense interest. He checked the handheld radio clipped to his belt and turned the volume just above a whisper. The familiar crackle sounded before he heard a voice say all was clear on the west end.

Scott found Alex and Jennifer standing with Casey when he returned to the front of the store.

"Hi Scott. What are you doing here?" Jennifer greeted him with a quick hug.

"Working security." He shook Alex's hand.

"Ah, crowd control, huh?" Alex said with a grin.

"Yeah. I hear these romance fans can get pretty wild," he said dryly.

"You just might be surprised." Casey nodded toward the front entrance.

Scott turned to find a large group of people pressed against the gate. There had to be at least fifty giddy females waiting to come in. On a normal occasion he'd be delighted, but at the moment, he was nearly terrified.

"I suggest standing away from the door when it opens," Casey said with a smug smile.

Scott took her advice and chose a spot near the rear of the store so he could watch the people enter as well as keep an eye on Casey. He moved around the store as best he could while he tried to keep her in his line of sight. The manager and his employees managed to regain some control over the eager crowd, pushing them back two feet from Casey on the other side of a roped-off barrier.

Scott watched her take charge of the crowd, entertaining them with stories about her travels and her writing. She read an excerpt from her latest book then took questions from the group. He had to admit, she was in her element. She hadn't been the least bit intimidated by the mad rush of people and when the signing itself started, she'd made an effort to talk to each person as if she actually knew them. So far, everyone who stepped to the table appeared friendly and not the least bit threatening or suspicious.

"This is so exciting. I've never been to a book signing before." Jennifer moved beside him in the Science Fiction section. "Just look at Casey. She's so calm. Doesn't she look wonderful?"

Scott slid a look at her. The tone of her voice told him she was in matchmaking mode again. He wondered how Casey would react if she knew what her sister-in-law was scheming?

"She looks like she knows what she's doing," he answered cautiously.

"Yeah, she does. She's amazing. And the people just love her," Jennifer continued. She cast a sidelong glance at him. "You know we've been trying to talk her into moving back home. Maybe find a really great guy and settle down. She'd make a great catch for someone."

Uh huh, Scott thought.

"She's definitely a looker," he said. He cocked his head and studied Casey. "You think she's ready for a serious relationship?"

Jennifer's eyes lit up. "Oh yeah. And Casey is one of the most loving people you'll ever meet."

"I'll bet she is. You know, I think I might have the perfect guy for her. My friend Dwayne has been looking for a good woman. He lives up in Beaumont." He pulled out his cell phone. "Dwayne runs his own sewage cleaning business, there. Good money in that, you know?" He paused, his finger over the number pad. "Hey, you don't think your sister-in-law would mind a little sewage smell, do you?"

Jennifer frowned and punched him on the arm. "You aren't the least bit funny, you know."

Scott laughed and leaned over to kiss her cheek. "Yeah, I am. I gotta get back to work. But you keep working on the matchmaking thing if it makes you happy."

❦

It was almost noon when Scott glanced at his watch again. Casey told him the book signing would only take two hours but from the look of the crowd still waiting it would be at least another hour. He started to walk toward the manager to have him end the signing when he spotted the sales clerk in the suspense section. She was gathering books off the floor and cursing under her breath. He stepped behind her as she bent to pick up several books and barely missed a clip to the chin when she straightened.

She yelped and pressed her hand to her chest. "Good heavens, you scared me," she said.

"Sorry. What happened?" he asked nodding at the books she held. It looked like someone had swept the whole shelf onto the carpet.

"Oh, nothing. It's just kids. They do this all the time. Grab books and start reading like we're a library or something. Usually it's in the children's section, though." She placed them back on the shelf while Scott bent to pick up the books still lying on the floor.

"This one looks damaged." He flipped it over and found Casey's photo on the back. *Oh yeah, she's a looker.*

The clerk peered at the book and shook her head. The cover was ripped and several of the pages were crinkled and torn. "Yeah, it happens. Wes isn't going to be happy but he's used to it. Every once in a while some teenage girls will come in and try to find something their parents won't let them read. They always end up tearing a few of the books while they look for the good stuff. It's usually Ms. Martinez's books we have to write off. You know, because of all the…*sex* she writes about." She said the word in a hushed voice.

Scott bit back a grin and nodded.

"You know…" The clerk shifted her gaze along the isle to make sure they were empty and lowered her voice. "I'm really surprised we had such a large turnout for her."

"Why's that? Because of all the *sex* she writes about?" Scott said with a

95

conspiratorial whisper.

The girl grinned, dismissing his words with a wave of her hand. "No, that's probably what brought them all in. It's just... in her first book Ms. Martinez didn't paint a very kind picture of Rosehill. In fact, she was downright hateful about us. Calling us mindless hicks and making us look like shameless heathens," she said with a touch of indignation. She turned and placed another book on the shelf. Her drawl thickened as she spoke. "And let me tell you, people were just livid about that. I thought for sure they were going to burn all her books. They talked about her on TV, on the radio. Everywhere you turned someone was griping." She turned to look at Scott, a light of humor in her eyes. "But, you know, as mad as people were, they gobbled up them books. We couldn't get them on the shelves fast enough."

"So what do you think happened to change everyone's mind?"

"Tourism," she said simply. "People started coming to town wanting to know what The Boudain Hut is and where they could find Pleasure Island."

Scott laughed and handed her the books. "I'll bet they were disappointed to find out it really is only an island."

"Yeah, but once they learned about the fishing, they got over it pretty quick. Of course there are still a few out there who can't seem to move on. We even got a few phone calls from some of those holier-than-thou groups when it was announced Ms. Martinez would be here."

"Really? What did they say?"

"Oh, the usual. We shouldn't promote such filth, and they were going to picket our store. We even had one guy call and say he was going to come set fire to the place if we didn't get rid of her books. Some people are just plain crazy." She shook her head, tucking the ruined books against her chest. "But, I guess it's a good thing you're here, right?"

"So they tell me," he murmured. "Listen, do you think I could take those?"

She looked at the ruined books and sent him a curious look. "Sure, but you'd have to pay for them. At a discount of course."

"Not a problem. And if you have any of her older books toss them in there, too."

He pulled out his wallet and handed her a credit card then carefully took the books from her. If Casey made it a habit to put parts of herself into her stories then maybe he could find out more about her and the real reason why someone was stalking her.

A scream shrieked from the front of the store. He spun around in time to see a short round woman throw herself at Casey and grab her in a hug.

"It really is you!" the woman shrilled.

The table wobbled, sending the stack of books crashing onto the floor. Casey's eyes widened, her hand striking out to grab hold of the table before she toppled over, too.

Scott rounded the bookshelves to help her, but the crackle on his radio stopped him. He pulled it off his hip and brought it to his ear. At the table, the woman's face was flushed with excitement as she shoved her book across the table for Casey to sign.

"Scott, looks like there's some trouble over in the food court. I'm going to check it out."

"Let me know what you find." Scott turned the volume lower on the radio and looked at Casey. She'd taken control of the situation and was saying something to the woman that made her screech with laughter. She passed her the book she'd signed and thanked her for stopping by. It was a very smooth dismissal, and Scott wondered if the woman even noticed.

Casey turned to look at him and smiled. The warmth of it sent of ripple of pleasure straight to his gut. He attempted a smile back, grateful when his radio crackled and saved him from looking like an idiot. "Talk to me," he said, turning away to answer the radio.

"It was nothing. Someone set off a cherry bomb in the boys' room. Stinks to high heaven out here. Except for that prank, it's been a pretty quiet day."

"Yeah, copy that. I'm going to see about ending this thing. You guys make another sweep and call it a day."

"You got it."

He clipped the radio back to his hip and went to search out the manager.

☙

"Well, that was certainly interesting," Scott said when he and Casey finally left the bookstore. "I don't think I'll ever look at a bookstore the same way again. I don't know how you do it."

"You get used it," she said, handing him her shopping bag. She couldn't resist buying a couple of books for herself, especially when the manager gave her such a large discount. "When did Alex and Jennifer leave?"

Scott adjusted the bags to one hand. "A couple of hours ago. I told Alex you'd call them later. So, how about lunch? I'm starving."

Casey looked at him and shook her head. "It's a wonder you aren't as big as a house. All you seem to think about is food."

"Darlin', there are only two things in this world I think about on a regular basis. One of them just happens to be food," he said with a slow grin. "Come on, there's a great, authentic Mexican restaurant on the other side of the mall. Unless, of course, you find that too trite."

Casey sent him a sour look and adjusted her jacket. "I find you too trite." She shook her head with a bemused sigh when he laughed. There was no insulting the man. Why did she like that about him?

"Fine," she said. "Let's eat. I'll even treat since you were such a good sport about today."

Scott raised his brow with mocked surprise and grinned. "Better watch out, Ms. Martinez. I might start to think you actually like me."

She sauntered past him, tossing a wry smile over her shoulder. "Don't press your luck."

Alejandro Rivera tucked himself back into the shadows of the wall as Casey and Scott left the store. He'd been watching the book signing for the past hour, debating whether or not he should go inside. Would his daughter even know who he was? He snarled, curling his hand into a fist. He'd spent twenty years rotting away in a cell because of her. She'd better damn well know him. And if she didn't? His lips curled into a smile. Then he was going to have to show her. Just like he had her mother.

He pulled a small packet from his pocket and carefully unfolded it. He put it up to his nose, pressed one nostril closed with his finger, and breathed in the powder. He rubbed the remaining powder on his gums and watched Casey continue across the mall, her hips swaying seductively. She tossed a sassy look over her shoulder to the man walking beside her. Alejandro's stomach flipped.

Exactly like her mother.

CHAPTER TWELVE

Scott settled on the sofa with the books he'd bought at the mall while Casey took advantage of the remaining daylight to lounge on the deck and get some work done. He stole a glance outside through the sliding patio doors to make sure she was still in her lounge chair. She'd changed into a pair of khaki shorts and a peach-colored shirt that hugged her curves. Thin straps crisscrossed her back, leaving her slender shoulders bare. A pair of dark lens Ray-Ban sunglasses rested on her nose, and a Cubs baseball cap sat on her head, her hair tucked haphazardly underneath. A laptop lay on her thighs, and her fingers danced over the keys with the grace of a concert pianist at Carnegie Hall. On the patio table was the bouquet of handpicked flowers they'd found at the bottom of the steps when they returned from the mall. There'd been a note attached with a badly written poem about eternal love. Since the note wasn't the least bit threatening (unless he counted what it did to his lunch) they passed them off as a gift from one of the young boys Casey often spoke to on the beach during their morning run. Not that the barely adolescent teenagers had a chance with her, but he couldn't blame them for the infatuation and almost felt sorry for them.

He propped his feet on the coffee table and picked up one of the books. It was her recent title and the fourth one he'd looked at. He hadn't bothered to read the full stories, but what he read was enough to get a glimpse into Casey. So much of her was in the characters she wrote about —the stubbornness, the determination, the sassy attitude—not to mention they were each sexy as hell—and, although he didn't think she actually practiced black magic, he wondered how much of her life was also included in the stories.

His cell phone chirped as he flipped to the back page of the book and the grainy black and white photo of Casey. "Weller."

"Hey, Scott, it's Jolene." His favorite Fed. "I managed to get hold of those files you were asking about."

Scott smiled and tossed the book on the coffee table. Finally, answers. "What'd you find?"

"Are you familiar with the Paperback Murders?"

"Yeah." He'd heard about the murders three years ago when a high profile case landed in New York. The body of Michelle Castillo had been found murdered in her home with strips of what appeared to be a paperback book by her side. Within weeks of the murder the FBI sent out a wire about a possible serial killer, listing the body count as five, although in the preceding years the count had risen to twelve. The press had jumped all over the story, dubbing it the Paperback Murders.

Scott sat up, his pulse spiked. "Are you saying Casey Martinez is involved with the case?"

"Right now, she's their only lead but they haven't been able to figure out how, exactly, she fits. The murders happen twice a year, one in April and another in June, but she's not connected to any of the victims. The only thing they're certain about right now is that the books left with the bodies were written by Ms. Martinez. According to the agent in charge, a recent murder in New York pointed at the possibility that Ms. Martinez is going to be the next target."

"Fuck me," Scott murmured, getting up to pace. She didn't have just a psycho stalker, she had a fucking serial killer after her. "Have they come up with any suspects yet?"

"A few persons of interest, but nothing's panned out. They have a decoy in her apartment in New York to try to draw the guy out."

"If they think he's still in New York, why the detail in Texas?"

"Just covering all the bases. They aren't going to take chances with a witness, especially since several murders occurred in cities where she lived," Jolene said. "I'm sending you the file. You should have it in a couple of days.

It's still missing some details, but you'll get the gist of it."

"Thanks, Jolie. I owe you one."

"Yeah. You do."

❦

Dusk settled in quietly with the whisper of soft grey clouds in the distance. A steady breeze blew in from deep off the warm Gulf waters where several shrimp boats had anchored for the night. On the beach, a group of teenagers were taking advantage of the empty shoreline and building a small bonfire. The bright red embers wafted across the sand, and a country western tune filtered out from the speakers of a nearby pickup truck.

Casey was so engrossed in the scene she was writing that she didn't notice when Scott stepped beside her until he pulled off her sunglasses. He carried a plate of food and two old-fashioned bottles of Coke.

"Do you always get this absorbed in your work?" he asked.

"Doesn't everyone?" She took the hat off and shook her head to let her hair tumble free before taking her glasses from him to tuck into the V of her shirt. She looked up at the lights of the shrimp boats in the distance. The sun had vanished below the horizon. The darkened sky was now a burst of glimmering pinpoints of light.

"What time is it?" she asked.

"Almost nine o'clock. Here, I thought you might be hungry." He handed her the plate of food and one of the bottles of Coke.

Casey peered at the plate to inspect the food. Fried pork chops, mashed potatoes and baby peas. "It looks delicious. Thank you." She closed the computer and moved it to the table before she took the plate. "You really didn't have to cook for me. I'd have fixed myself something eventually."

Scott shrugged and sat in the patio chair on the other side of her. "It was no problem. I like to cook and thought you could use something more nutritious than Hotpockets or frozen pizza."

Casey bypassed the knife and fork and picked up the meat with her fingers. She bit into the pork chop, closing her eyes to savor the taste. A satisfied hum rose from her throat.

Scott followed the path of her tongue as she licked the taste from her lips. The careless movement punched his chest with a burning fist of desire.

He drank half the bottle of Coke to extinguish it.

"This is really good. You should consider quitting your day job," she said, digging into the food.

"Cooking is a hobby. I like my day job," he answered. Although he liked to cook, he'd never really prepared a meal for a woman before. It was, without a doubt, too intimate and indicative of a long-term relationship, and he wasn't in the market for one of those. But it gave him a wondrous sense of pride to know she enjoyed the meal.

He gave her several minutes to eat before he spoke again. "So, how long have you lived in New York?" he asked.

"Off and on, about ten years." She ripped off a piece of meat and shoved it in her mouth.

"Off and on?" He turned his attention to the beach when she licked her fingers. Damn it, if he'd known how erotic she'd look eating a pork chop, he'd have fed her a bowl of cereal.

"I moved to New York right after I graduated high school. I lived there for a few years, working for Jo. When I started writing, I set the story in Washington, D.C.," she said, oblivious to his reaction as she slid the fork between her lips. "Since I'd never been there before, I decided to relocate for a while to get a feel for it. I stayed for two years, went back to New York for a while, then moved to St. Louis. I stayed there for about a year before I moved again."

"You must really like to travel."

"Not really. I just haven't found anywhere I want to call home," she said with a shrug before biting into a fork full of potatoes.

"Why did you leave Chicago?"

She cocked her head to look at him, her brow arched. "Been reading my file, Detective?"

Scott grinned and lifted his shoulder with a noncommittal shrug. "You won't let me read your work, and I had to have something to put me to sleep," he said. To his surprise she laughed. Maybe she was starting to like him after all. "So, what happened in Chicago?"

She went silent and picked up her drink, taking a slow sip. He wondered if she was going to answer him. He thought about the books sitting in his bedroom. The story she'd set in Chicago dealt with betrayal. He'd assumed she'd based the character's suffering on her own father's actions, but maybe she'd been the one betrayed by another man.

Casey set her drink down and shrugged. "It became a bit too windy for me."

Scott nodded thoughtfully and took a casual drink from his bottle. She returned her attention to the food and he let the silence linger a moment before he asked, "How long ago did you live in L.A.?"

She stopped eating and narrowed her eyes at him. "You know, Detective, I've worked around enough law enforcement to know when I'm being interrogated. Would you like to stop hedging and tell me what the point of this conversation is?"

Scott shrugged. "I'm just curious about this case of yours. No big deal."

"There is no case," she said through clenched teeth. "Whoever the FBI is looking for has nothing to do with me. Yet, they kick me out of my home and stick me in this stupid hick town where the only annoyance I've had to deal with it you!" Her fingers whitened around the neck of the bottle and she closed her eyes as if giving herself a moment to calm before speaking again. "You've obviously been looking into the case. If you know something, I'd appreciate it if you tell me."

Scott tapped his fingers on the neck of his bottle, turning his gaze to the snapping logs on the bonfire. He wasn't sure how much he should tell her. The information he'd gotten had been vague at best, and he wouldn't know anything more until he got the file in a couple of days. Regardless, she needed to know what she was up against, even if she didn't want to believe it.

He shifted in his seat to look at her. "In the last five years there have been thirteen murders of young Mexican women."

"Tell me what I don't know."

He sent her a knowing look. "L.A., Chicago, Washington, New York. Sound familiar?"

She set her plate on the ground and stood, moving to the edge of the deck. A loud whistle cut through the air, followed by a bright burst of colorful lights. The group of teenagers on the beach planned to give them a light show.

"You've just named four cities with very high crime rates, Detective. I fail to see that it's more than a simple coincidence." She watched the burst of red and blue lights with little interest. The delayed crack of the fireworks exploded like a gunshot. She jolted then went still, huffing out a breath as if chastising herself for the needless panic.

"Your birthday is in April, right?"

Her terse silence was broken by the pop of a bottle-rocket. "Yes," she answered.

"Six of the murders happened in April. That's hardly a coincidence. It's more like a pattern."

"That's only six murders. I still don't see the connection."

Scott rose from his seat and moved beside her. It wasn't stubbornness that furrowed her brow. It was denial. "What's important about June?"

She turned to stare at him. "What?"

"Is there anything important to you about the month of June?"

"No," she said, grinding her teeth and turning back to the look at the beach.

He waited as she pulled the pack of cigarettes from her pocket and tapped one out. She lit it up with a deep inhale of breath. After a moment her expression hardened and she said, "My father was born June twentieth. On Father's Day. How's that for irony?" She started to take another pull from the cigarette but stopped. She turned to look at him, her eyes round and alert. "Wait. Are you telling me the other women were killed in June? That this…son of a bitch could be coming after me because it's almost June?"

Scott placed his hands on her shoulder and gently squeezed against the tension in her muscles. "Look, you have nothing to worry about. You're a thousand miles away from New York and you're safe here. The Feds are going to find this guy before he can kill anyone else."

She nodded but it wasn't convincing.

A strand of hair swept across her cheek and he tucked it back behind her ear. "I won't let anything happen to you. I promise."

Something unreadable flickered in her eyes. She swallowed and took a step back. "It's getting late. I think I'll go to bed." She moved to the table and crushed out her cigarette.

Stopping in the doorway, she turned and offered him a strained smile. "Thank you for dinner."

Casey glanced at the clock next to her bed and sighed. Sleep was a luxury she didn't pack for this trip. Tossing the blankets aside, she crawled out of bed and grabbed her cigarettes from the end table. She had left the window open so she could listen to the sounds of the night and the crash of waves, hoping they would lull her to sleep. But three hours later, she was still wide awake.

After lighting a cigarette, she climbed out of the window and stood on the deck. A gusty breeze blew in from the beach, carrying the lingering odor of burning wood from the bonfire. She waited a moment, straining to listen for Scott. She'd heard him go into his bedroom an hour after she did, but that didn't mean he wouldn't hear her. The man had built-in radar where she was concerned. She didn't know whether to be impressed or annoyed.

Satisfied he wasn't nearby, she crept down the stairs to the deck below, feeling much like a thief on the prowl. The trill of crickets and cicadas broke through the silence of the night. The waves rolled in the distance like a subtle applause. She moved to the edge of the patio to watch them curl inshore. The full moon glistened an endless trail on the water. Lights from the oil-rigs glowed in the distance like a cityscape.

The conversation she'd had with Scott earlier played back in her head. In two weeks it would be June. If his theory was right, in two weeks she could be dead. She resisted the urge to shudder and filled her lungs with the cigarette. It wasn't possible. He had to be wrong. Just like the federal agents. No one wanted to kill her. The fact that her books had been left with the victims was just an unfortunate coincidence. There was no proof that the killer would come after her, at least no proof that she had been made aware of.

L.A., Chicago, Washington, New York. Sound familiar?

No! It's a coincidence, that's all.

Agent Hawthorne's voice echoed in her mind. *If you've been getting unwanted mail then you may have a stalker, and he could be anyone.*

She pulled on the cigarette, pushing the smoke out with a huff. She refused to believe their killer was after her. Scott and the FBI could assume and theorize all they wanted, but she was not going to cower in fear or believe she was the target of a madman!

The breeze kicked up and snapped the American flag mounted on the deck next door, the noise resounding like a gunshot. Casey jumped and pressed a hand over the pounding in her chest. *Dammit!* Irritated with herself, she turned around in search of an ashtray. And froze.

Sitting on the swing was a package the size of a small shoe box. An icy chill rolled over her. Swallowing hard, she took a slow step toward the swing. The wind gusted through the tunnel of the patio, lifting the flap on the package.

She bit into her bottom lip, her fingers shaking as she reached for the Bible. A page had been folded in half. She opened it and read the highlighted passage.

For the life of flesh is in the blood and I have given it to you upon the altar to make atonement for your souls.

A noise rustled from the dried marsh behind her. She dropped the book and spun around as a small dark figure raced across the beach and dove into the thick grass. Two bright eyes glittered behind the blades. The rush of panic washed over her like the crash of the waves. She wheeled around and slammed into a solid form. Panic seized her and lodged a scream in her throat.

"What are you doing out here?" Scott said, one arm hooking around her waist to keep her from falling back.

Casey gulped in a breath, her heart hammering against her ribcage. "Jesus Christ! You scared the hell out of me!" she said, pressing her hand against her breast. "Don't you know it's dangerous to sneak up on someone?"

He grinned and tightened his hold. "I'm the one with the big gun, remember?"

She glared at him and pushed away. "Don't flatter yourself." She took another breath, this time to settle the heat his touch sent through her. She really needed to stop getting so close to him or she was going to spontaneously combust.

"What are you doing down here so late?" he asked.

"I wasn't trying to get away if that's what you thought," she said, lifting her chin and trying not to look chastised. "I couldn't sleep and I wanted some air. Why the hell are you lurking around? I thought you went to bed hours ago."

"Guess we're both suffering from insomnia."

Scott glanced down at the pale camisole she wore. The low-cut bodice gave him an eyeful of her golden skin. Every muscle clenched, and his jeans suddenly became a size too small. *Looks like I'm going to lose even more sleep.*

He cleared his throat, praying he wouldn't stutter. "I came down to check the grounds and heard you sneaking around. I was just about to say something before you barreled into me."

"I didn't barrel. I turned and you were there." She pushed her hands down her sides as if looking for pockets. Her eyes widened and her cheeks turned a bright shade of red when she realized she didn't have any. She took another step back, though the dark shadows of the patio didn't quite conceal her. "I was just about to go in. Excuse me."

He nodded toward the beach when she started to step around him. "It was a tomcat," he said.

Casey stopped and sent him a cautious look. "What?"

"The thing that scared you. It was a tomcat."

She glanced at the marsh then turned back to him. "I wasn't scared. Now, if you'll excuse me, I'm going back to bed." She hurried around him and made it to the foot of the stairs before he spoke again.

"You forgot your Bible." He picked up the book and brought it to her.

She hesitated, looking at the book as if it were a snake about to bite her, then snatched it from his hand.

"So what's this aversion you have for the good book?" he asked before she could leave. "That's the second time you threw it in the garbage."

"*You* put it on the swing?" Though she tried to sound annoyed, he heard the underlying relief in her voice.

"I saw it in the trash bin." He leaned against the handrail, trying to keep his eyes from lowering below her neckline. Although, if he were going to lose sleep, he might as well make it worthwhile. "So, what? Are you a devout atheist or something?" he asked.

Casey clutched the book against her chest, the pressure enhancing the fullness of her breasts, and he couldn't stop his eyes from taking a quick look at her smooth flesh. "No. I thought someone may have left it..." She paused, then shrugged and said, "I've been getting these Bibles for a while, but I never paid any attention to them because I considered them harmless. But now..." She pressed her lips together and looked out at the beach.

"But now with the Feds chasing a serial killer, you're a little more worried?"

She turned to him with a firm look in her eyes. "I told you before, I'm not worried."

"You know, you don't always have to be so tough. It's okay to be scared. You'd be a fool not to be." He gestured to the Bible before she could react. "So that's the book from the bar that first day? Was it here when you arrived?"

Casey glanced down at the book, her fingers white on the binding. "No. It was in the mail I brought with me," she answered. "They're just highlighted proverbs from some religious nut. They aren't death threats."

"Maybe not, but we should probably send it up to the crime lab in Austin. See if they can get some prints off it." His fingers brushed against the silk of her skin when he reached for the book. The heat vibrated to his toes. He thought he saw something flicker in her eyes before it was quickly pushed aside. She thrust the book into his hand and took a step back.

"You do that," she said. "In fact, why don't you go with it and wait on the results. I'm going to bed."

Scott whistled out a breath and rubbed a palm against his chest as she hurried up the stairs and snapped the door shut behind her. He could still feel the warmth of her skin on his fingertips.

"Keep your hands to yourself, Weller," he murmured. "A tumble in the sheets isn't worth your job." Although a part of him was willing to take the risk.

❧

A dark figure crouched behind the thick blades of marsh, watching as Casey disappeared into the beach house. The plan had been easy. Wait for her to go to sleep and climb into the open bedroom window. Finish what should have been done five years ago. There wasn't supposed to be a bodyguard. Not that it was a problem. He could be dealt with.

The figure clutched a knife, turning it to catch the glint of moonlight on the steel blade. There was still time. Casey Martinez won't have a bodyguard forever. When the time is right, she'll wish she'd never come back to Rosehill.

CHAPTER THIRTEEN

Agent Simms tapped the paperback against his palm and stared at the colored pushpins jutting from the map covering half his wall. Each pin was flagged with a number and date marking a murder. He'd been staring at the wall for hours on end. They were missing something. He just couldn't figure out what.

He turned and studied the stack of file boxes lining his wall. Cases he'd collected over the past three years. All the same M.O. All connected to Casey Martinez through her books. But *why?* Why had he made her his target? "There has to be a something we're missing."

"We've gone over every one of these cases at least ten times. If there's another connection, I'll be damned if I know what it is," Agent Hawthorne said, pulling a folder from one of the file boxes.

Agent Simms moved to the map. "We know several of the murders happened either in states where Ms. Martinez set her book, or states she happened to live in at the time." He tapped the map with his pen as he spoke. "Victims one and four were found in California, two years apart. But Ms. Martinez didn't set a story there until her third book, so what was it about the first victim that got her killed?"

"Practice? Maybe he wanted to make sure he could get away with it before he went after his real target."

"If that's true then it means he planned to target Ms. Martinez from the beginning."

"Maybe he did. From the looks of it, he seems to be tracking her through her books." He pointed to the pins marking each state. "Victim eight was killed in Chicago. Victim six was found in St. Louis and victim number ten in D.C. She not only set books in these places but she also lived there."

Agent Simms shook his head and tapped the map. "Right, but victim number two was found in New Orleans two months *after* victim one. Ms. Martinez didn't live there or use the city as a setting for a book."

"Then those victims were probably because he *thought* they were Ms. Martinez," Agent Hawthorne said, the frustration tight in his voice. He dropped the file back in the box. "Fuck, I don't know."

Agent Simms looked at the book still clutched in his hand. "The answer's buried here somewhere. We just have to keep digging until we find it."

Hawthorne exhaled a heavy breath. "Even starting at the beginning, we have shit."

Simms glanced up, his expression grim. "Except now we know his next target."

⌘

Scott was used to the long hours on the street or in the station, and he didn't mind at all. Being a cop was his life, and he knew what to expect from it. But the last couple of days sitting with Casey were beginning to wear thin. The friendly relationship he thought they'd generated after the book signing quickly chilled when he accompanied her on a trip to the mall in the next town. She accused him of rushing her through the overcrowded department stores each time she stopped to browse. (Could he help it if he hated to shop?) They argued over the amount of time she spent signing stock copies when they stopped into yet another bookstore.

He enjoyed a good fight every now and then, and it seemed Casey did too, since for the last two days every time she spoke to him, it ended in a battle of words. However, the brief arguments and his purely male reaction to the sexy heat in her eyes were causing him to lose even more sleep. It was all he could do to keep from locking her in the bedroom and cuffing her to the bed.

The image filled his mind. Her arms raised above her head, her naked body writhing under him, moving with a steady rhythm, moonlight glistening off her golden skin. His hands roaming over her, teasing her most sensitive spots, her back arching begging him for more.

"Christ!" he growled, shaking the images from his mind. Even when he wasn't asleep, he was dreaming about her.

He grabbed a file from the corner of his desk, tossing the flap open. Thank God he'd managed to talk his captain into adding a unit to cover the night shift so he could cut out by midnight. Although, if his captain knew he was using the extra time off to do his own investigating into Casey's stalker, he'd have his ass in a sling. But he was willing to risk it. The sooner the bastard was caught, the sooner he could kiss this assignment good-bye and get back to his normal routine of pushing papers.

It had been eight days since Casey arrived to make his life miserable and, aside from a few flowers left on the stairs, she'd had no unwelcome visitors. No one watched her while they were on their morning runs or when they made the occasional trip into town. No one tried to contact her through the mail or by phone. Maybe Casey was right and the Feds were wrong about who her stalker was. It wouldn't be the first time they'd mishandled a case.

Inside the file he found a more detailed report on the Paperback Murders. His contact in the bureau had been able to get him access to more of the files once they learned he was the officer assigned to protect Casey. So, maybe the Feds weren't so selfish after all.

The profiler's report was standard. White male from a lower to middle class background, in his mid twenties to late thirties. May have been physically or emotionally abused by his parents.

Couldn't get any clearer than that, Scott thought sourly.

The hair on the back of his neck prickled. He didn't need to look up to know Alan Broussard from Internal Affairs had stepped to his desk. *Great.*

"Detective Weller. You're working late."

Scott looked up from the reports not bothering to hide his disdain for the man. "Broussard. What happened? The rats kick you out of the sewer for stinking up the place?"

The man's thin lips curled into an un-amused smile. "I thought you'd like to know we've finished our investigation on you." He paused as if waiting for Scott to answer. He didn't. "I was just doing my job, Detective. Just like you were."

"Your job is nothing like mine," Scott countered. "And since I don't spend my days wallowing around knee-deep in bullshit with my integrity shoved up my ass, don't ever compare your job to mine."

Broussard went rigid, color rising up his neck. "You may have been cleared this time, Detective, but keep in mind, you screw up again, and I'm going to show you just how far up your ass my integrity will go."

Scott sat back in his chair as Broussard stalked from the room. *Just doing his job.* It was the excuse they used when they tried to ruin the name of a good cop. Like they'd done to his father.

He'd been ten years old when the white sedan had pulled up to his house. He'd sat at his mother's side, holding her hand, waiting, knowing what his father's partner had come to tell them.

His father had been shot trying to save a life. The fact that he'd also taken out the suspect before he went down didn't seem to matter to I.A. While the doctors tried to restart his father's heart in the operating room, Internal Affairs opened an investigation into unnecessary use of force. It had taken nearly a year to clear his father's name, but the damage had already been done.

Scott absently rubbed his chest, then grabbed the report and shoved it into his briefcase. So much for getting any work done.

CHAPTER FOURTEEN

"**I**'m meeting Jennifer for lunch in a possibly crowded restaurant. Unless the cook plans to poison my food, I'm going to be perfectly safe." Casey put the finishing touches of her make-up on and looked at Scott's reflection in the mirror. He was watching her from his position on the large rattan chair in her bedroom.

"Fine, I like restaurants. And I don't even mind sharing a table with you," he said.

"I've been here over a week and nothing has happened, like I knew it wouldn't," she said. Okay, so maybe she didn't mention the other notes she'd received with the flowers. They were silly poems and not the least bit threatening, so she didn't see the point. "I've done everything you've asked of me, short of wearing a tracking device. I think you should at least grant me this one thing."

She turned to face him, resisting the urge to squirm at his watchful gaze. For the past three nights she'd seen that face in her dreams. Those blue eyes hungry with desire, watching her with a burning intensity. His mouth hot on her breasts, his hands roaming with quiet knowledge over her body. She would awake on the edge of an orgasm and furious at him for invading her mind. She was more than relieved when he moved back to his apartment two nights earlier. She'd become tired of fighting all the time, since it was better to fight with him than to let him know how he affected her.

"Look, Detective," she continued, trying to keep her voice patient, "you told me yourself it was best if no one outside of us knows about the Fed's case. If you show up to the restaurant with me, Jen is going to ask questions. She's already wondering why I haven't been to see her all week."

"You could always tell her we've fallen madly in love and you can't get enough of me," he said with a wink.

"Yeah, right. Like that would ever happen." Her mind jumped back to her dream, sending the familiar warmth to her stomach. She turned back to the mirror and bit her nails into her palm, irritated with herself for allowing that image to come back into her head.

Scott laughed. "I'll tell you what. I will give you two hours for lunch and two for shopping. I need to check in at the station and take care of some paperwork, anyway." He'd already planned to let her go, but it was so much fun irritating her.

Casey raised her brow at him. "Two hours for shopping? Have you met my sister-in-law?"

"Fine. Three hours."

"Thank you," she said, turning to him with a warm smile.

He fought to extinguish the heat she shot through him with that mere look. God, she was going to be his undoing.

"Just make sure you're back by five. Stick to the more crowded, public places. And keep your eyes open for anything out of the ordinary." He sighed at the wearisome look she gave him and pushed himself out of the chair. "Let's go. I'll follow you into town."

❧

Casey and Jennifer rummaged through a rack of clothes, removing some at random and laying them across their arms.

"This should be enough for now. Let's go try them on. I think the rooms are back this way." Jennifer draped the clothes over her shoulder and gestured to Casey to follow.

They found the dressing rooms and took one next to each other in the far corner away from the entrance. The cubicles were the size of a walk-in closet and furnished with a small wooden bench and floor length mirror.

Separating them were thin paneled partitions which started at the floor and ended six inches from the ceiling. Casey hung her clothes on the metal hook on the wall and began to get undressed.

"So, you and Scott seem to be spending a lot of time together," Jennifer called over the wall between them.

Casey's hands froze on the buttons of her blouse. "What do you mean?"

"Well, he was at the book signing, and I saw him at the beach house the other day."

"You were at the beach house?"

"Well, I swung by. But then I saw his jeep parked in front, and I didn't want to intrude."

Casey closed her eyes and swore under her breath. "No, you wouldn't have been intruding on anything." She continued to strip off her clothes and folded them neatly, placing them on the bench. "Scott and I aren't friends or anything remotely close to it. He must have happened to stop by that day. He was probably checking up on me or something." She picked up the vibrant red evening dress, holding it up to inspect before stepping into it.

"Oh. I'm sorry. It's probably Alex's fault that Scott's out there. I think he may have talked him into checking up on you from time to time. He's been a little worried about you being at the beach all by yourself. With the Memorial Day coming up, that place can be quite the zoo. Don't be mad."

"No, I'm not mad." Casey raised her eyes to the ceiling and mouthed the words *thank you*. "But please tell my brother that I am not in need of protecting. I can take care of myself just fine."

Jennifer laughed. "Yeah, like he'll listen. But, don't worry. I'll yell at him for you."

"Thank you. Okay, I'm ready. Let's see what you've got." She stepped into a pair of red stilettos before leaving the room.

Jennifer came out of her cubicle wearing a maternity peasant top. She stopped to examine the tight red dress on Casey and wiggled her brows. "Oh my. Sinful," she said. "Too bad you're not seeing Scott. That would really knock his socks off."

"I'm not planning to buy it. I just wanted to try it on."

"Why not? You look hot. Scott would be stepping all over his tongue if he saw you in that." She twirled around before Casey could respond. "So…what do you think? Do I pull off pregnant yet?"

"It's a little on the large side, isn't it?"

"I'll grow into it." Jennifer turned to look in the mirror, putting her hands under the blouse and pushing it out.

"You're flat as a pancake. I don't think you're going to get very big."

"Don't say that. I want to get fat. I can't wait until my clothes start getting tight. Oh, you'll probably never hear that come out of a woman's mouth again," she said with a laugh. She adjusted the blouse then sighed. "Okay, maybe you're right. I'm going to go see if I can find a smaller size. Don't try anything else on till I get back. I won't be long."

Casey returned to her room as Jennifer disappeared around the corner. She stepped out of the shoes as she considered the pair of Wranglers on the plastic hanger. She hadn't worn blue jeans since she moved to New York because it was one more thing she associated with Texas. Though she'd argued against it, Jennifer suggested she try them on since jeans were considered an international fashion and everyone looked good in jeans. As Casey studied the dark fabric she had to admit they weren't so bad.

She reached her hands around her back to unzip the dress. The lights shut off, plunging the room into total darkness. She went still, a rush of panic skittering down her back.

"Hey. There's someone in here." She waited, listening for footsteps. "Not funny, Jenn," she said. "I think you've been with Alex too long. His lack of humor is rubbing off on you."

She strained to adjust her eyes to the dark and put her hands out to use the wall as her guide. She made her way back to the bench, sweeping her hands across the wood until she felt the soft leather of her purse. Reaching inside she pulled out her cigarette lighter and flicked on the flame. Her shadow danced along the floor as she turned around.

Footsteps shuffled outside her room.

"Jennifer? Is that you?"

The knob twisted. The door rattled. Casey staggered back, falling against the wood bench and dropped the lighter. She swallowed hard, biting her nails into her palms to ease her panic. The door shook with more force.

"Who's there? What do you want?" Casey said with as much courage as she could muster.

"Bitch!" a voice growled.

Casey swept her hand along the floor, looking for the lighter. The sound of breaking wood sent her heart to her throat. Her fingers touched on one of the shoes. She grabbed onto it and held it up. She was not going to let the son-of-a-bitch scare her. Not now. Not ever.

She squeezed the shoe tighter, relying on the false sense of courage it gave her and stood. Taking a cautious step, she reached out until she felt the doorknob.

I'm coming for you, Cassandra.

She forced her father's voice from her mind and drew in a deep breath. Pulling hard on the door, she charged forward.

The lights flashed on. The scream jerked Casey to a stop. Jennifer stumbled back and fell against the wall.

"Casey, what are you doing?"

"Oh my God, Jenn. I'm sorry, are you okay?" Casey helped her stand as she took a quick scan of the room. It was empty.

"Shit, you scared the hell out of me!" Jennifer said her hand splayed across her chest. "Another few months and I'd have been in labor. What the hell happened? Why were the lights turned off?"

A young saleswoman rushed into the room. "I heard a scream. Are you ladies okay?"

"Yes, fine. I just got a little spooked when the power went out," Casey said. She relaxed her hand on the shoe she still held and placed it behind her back.

"The power?" The woman shifted her gaze between them.

"It was probably just a kid playing a prank or something," Casey said with a shrug. "I guess whoever it was took off."

"I didn't see anyone when I came in," Jennifer said. Her gaze shifted to the dressing room. Her eyes widened. "What happened to the door?"

Casey turned to see a large split in the center of the wood slats, as if someone had tried to break through them. She swallowed the rise of panic, keeping her gaze even when she looked at the sales clerk.

"I'm sorry. The door was stuck. I did that when I was trying get it open. I'll pay for the damages," she said. "If you could get me an address, I'll take care of it right away."

The woman nodded, her expression wary. "Okay. I'll go get the manager."

Casey bit her lip and tried not to think about how the break had really been made in the door.

Jennifer touched Casey's arm. "You're white as a ghost. Are you sure you're okay?"

"Yes. I'm fine." She fisted her hands to keep them from trembling and forced a smile. "I guess I just don't know my own strength. Do you mind if we don't mention this to anyone? I feel foolish enough."

"Sure, no problem. I'm not exactly anxious to let anyone know you knocked me on my butt," Jennifer said with a laugh. "Come on, let's forget about shopping for now and go have some ice cream. I think I'm having a craving."

❧

It was nearly seven o'clock when Casey returned to the beach house. Scott pounced the minute she walked in.

"Goddamn it, Casey! Where the hell have you been?"

She lifted her chin with a chilled look and tossed her packages on the sofa. "Don't yell at me. I'm not a child."

"Then don't act like a damn child! You were supposed to be back here two hours ago. It would have been my ass if something had happened to you. I trusted you, dammit!" He slammed the door shut, rattling the windows.

"And don't curse at me, either." She stalked to the bar and pulled out a water bottle from the mini refrigerator, her voice clipped. "I'm sorry. I lost track of time. It won't happen again."

"You're damn right it won't," Scott fumed, marching to the bar. "Because from now on, no more favors! You so much as walk across the fucking street, you'd better damn well let me know about it first!" He grabbed the water from her and slammed it on the bar. The bottle cracked, spilling water over the veneer counter top. He'd been told his temper was legendary. He didn't like to lose it, and he was usually good at keeping it under control. But the damn woman brought out the worst in him.

"Fine!" Casey stormed to the sofa and grabbed a package from the cushion. "Here! I don't know why I bothered getting this for you, anyway. It's not like I actually like you or anything. I must have been delusional!" She threw a box at him and didn't try to hide her disappointment when he caught it at his chest.

Scott eyed the package cautiously then looked at her. "What's this?"

"Running shoes. If we're going to run every morning, you should at least have a decent pair of running shoes." She continued to grab the shopping bags, jerking them off the sofa as she spoke. "I had to guess at the size. But with any luck, they'll give you blisters."

Scott looked at the box as the heat of his anger cooled to guilt. He was used to getting gifts from women, but for some reason this one touched him more. He set the box on the bar and took a calming breath before he stepped to her. "Thank you. They're perfect. Look, Casey…"

"Forget it," she snapped. She turned on her heel and went into her bedroom.

Scott pushed his hand through his hair, wincing when she slammed the door behind her. Were women born with a talent for making men feel like idiots? Okay, he could admit he wasn't being fair. It wasn't her fault they were stuck with each other. The situation was stressful for the both of them, yet she still did everything he'd asked of her with no complaints…okay, very little complaining. Plus she was right earlier when she said they hadn't had a single ounce of trouble since she'd arrived in town. And even though she was late coming in from her shopping trip with Jennifer, she'd come back in one piece.

Maybe the least he could do was lighten up.

With a resigned sigh he stepped to the door and tapped softly against the wood.

"Go away!"

He blew out a sigh of relief. Anger was better than tears. He was a sucker for a woman's tears. He opened the door a crack and waited. She hadn't thrown anything at him yet, but it didn't mean she wouldn't if he gave her a big enough target.

Casey stopped clicking at the keys on her laptop and glanced up, fury lighting her eyes. "What part of *go away* do you not understand?"

She sat rigidly on the bed, the shopping bags scattered, untouched, on the floor. The flush of anger glowed on her skin and made his blood stir.

He swallowed the pressure in his throat before he spoke. "Listen, I'm sorry…"

"I'm not interested in your apologies."

Scott tensed and ground his teeth. *He* had the right to be angry, not her. "Okay, fine. No apology then. How would you like to get out for a little while?"

"I was just out, remember?" She spared him a glance and fixed her eyes back on her screen.

"I mean go out and have some real fun, not like shopping. Though, I still don't understand where the fun in that is." Satisfied she wouldn't throw anything at him, he pushed the door open wider. "There's a Heritage Festival going on in the next town."

"Redneck is a heritage now?" she said curtly.

Scott tightened his fingers on the doorknob, the muscles along his back going taut. So much for holding his temper. "You really are a bitch, aren't you? I thought maybe it was just an act to show everyone how New York tough you are." Had he really tried to be nice to her? "Never mind. I thought you might want to get out of here for a few hours. But you can just stay there and pout."

Casey's head came up, regret clouding her eyes. "I don't pout, I stew," she murmured. "I'm sorry," she said before he could leave the room. "That was very rude of me and uncalled for. It's been a long day and being back in this town seems to bring out the worst in me."

Scott didn't expect the apology, and his own regret was instant. "I'm sorry I called you a bitch."

"Don't be. I am," she said with a small smile.

Scott grinned and stepped toward the bed. "Come on, I think we could both use a night out."

She considered him a moment, then pressed the keys to save her work. "Okay." She took the hand he held out and skirted from the bed.

Scott planted his feet and pulled her up to stand toe to toe with him. "We can call Alex and Jennifer to join us if you're afraid of being alone with me," he said with a slow grin. He had intended to lighten her mood some more, but found himself drawing his eyes to her mouth. The sudden need to sample those full, red lips built to a surprising ache inside him.

She sent him a feline smile and hooked a finger in the V of his shirt, tugging him closer. "You think I'm afraid?" she said with a cooing voice.

Scott slid his hands down her arms, locking his eyes on hers. The flutter of anticipation settled like giant bat wings in his stomach. She was close enough to taste and dangerous enough to burn. And definitely not his type.

She moistened her lips with a quick sweep of her tongue and pinned him with her dark eyes. His heartbeat quickened, making his blood hum as if tiny electrical currents coursed through his veins. Her hand flattened against his chest, the touch burning straight through his shirt. His breath caught, his body vibrating with tension as she leaned in. Images of her cuffed to the bed, arching against him in a welcome invitation, filled his mind. *Screw his type.*

Casey pushed hard against his chest jolting him from the erotic fantasy.

"I'm not afraid of anything," she said. "Least of all you."

Scott shook the fog of lust from his head as she sauntered into the bathroom. He rubbed a hand over the spot where she'd touched his chest and laughed.

Yeah, women were real good at making men feel like idiots.

CHAPTER FIFTEEN

The annual Nederland Heritage Festival was set up in the older downtown area of the neighboring town. The first four blocks of the main street had been blocked off to all automobile traffic to allow more room for the various food and game vendors. Though the festival had originally been created to celebrate the seventy-fifth birthday of the small town, it had been such a big success it became an annual event.

Casey stepped over a thick black cable snaked across the pavement to avoid stepping in a puddle of water. *Probably wasn't a good idea to wear Anne Klein to a street fair.*

The aroma of smoked meats and fresh, buttered popcorn scented the air. The rush of a small roller coaster rustled overhead amid screams of delight from the passengers. From somewhere down the street a band played country-western music.

She couldn't remember the last time she'd been to a Heritage Festival, or any festival for that matter. She'd spent the last seven years perched in front of her computer, writing down the stories that swarmed in her head and had never given any thought to enjoying the day-to-day carefree moments. When had her life become so dull?

Scott waited patiently, his lips curved with an amused grin as she sidestepped the food and garbage on the ground as if she were walking through a minefield. She sent him a careless shrug in return.

Their night out wasn't nearly as bad as she'd thought it would be. She had planned to ignore him and focus on having fun, but found herself enjoying his company along with the festival. He had an easygoing, playful way about him she found hard to ignore. And, she could admit now, she didn't want to.

"It's too bad Jennifer was too tired to join us," Scott said when she'd made it safely to his side. He tore off a piece of the funnel cake Casey had bought and popped it into his mouth.

"Yeah, I guess all that shopping wore her out. Plus, with Alex working, I don't think she'd have enjoyed herself as much. But we found some great stuff at the mall," she said. The incident in the dressing room flashed through her mind. A chill shivered over her.

Scott tore another piece off the funnel cake, sending her a boyish grin she couldn't help but find endearing. She knew she should tell him about what happened at the mall, but he was in too good a mood and she didn't want to spoil it. Besides, it wasn't as if she'd been hurt.

"Something wrong?" he asked.

She shook her head. "No. Everything's fine." *It can wait until morning.*

She took the last piece of funnel cake Scott offered, careful to shake off the excess powdered sugar. She ignored his grin and turned to look at the prizes hanging from a game booth. "Oh, look! Jenn would love that purple elephant for the baby. Win it for me." She passed over his groan and tugged him to the booth. "Oh, come on. This should be easy for you. All you have to do is shoot out the little star."

"These things are rigged, you know." Scott pulled out his wallet and handed the gangly man behind the counter his money. He had to admit he was actually enjoying his night out with Casey. She seemed more relaxed and high-spirited then usual and much less reserved than when he first met her. He wondered if she noticed her facade was starting to crumble.

He rolled his shoulders before lifting the BB gun chained to the booth's counter. He brought it up, resting it against his shoulder, then tossed Casey a serious look. "Step back now, ma'am. This takes some serious concentration."

Casey gave him an obedient smile and quietly moved in beside him while he adjusted the butt against his shoulder. He set up his aim and was about to shoot when she leaned forward and blew a soft breath in his ear.

His hand jerked, sending a round of rubber BB's bouncing off the toys. Heat shot straight down to his toes.

"You want this thing, right?" he said with a laugh.

Casey stepped back with a self-satisfied smile.

Scott re-aimed the rifle and pulled the trigger. The small bb's pelted out in a steady staccato, tearing a hole in the thin sheet of paper tacked to the wall.

"We have a winner!" the barker announced to no one in particular.

Casey squealed, throwing her arms around his neck. "Oh, I knew you could do it!"

Scott circled an arm around her waist and pulled her closer. "If I'd known this would be my reward, I'd have played more of the games."

Casey sprang back, her face flushed crimson. "I'm sorry. I didn't—"

"Don't be. I'm not complaining," he said. His body was still kindling from her breath in his ear. It was a wonder he didn't just go up in flames.

"Well, well, well, look at what the cat done dragged back to town," a male voice drawled from behind Casey. "Now, I'd heard a little rumor about you being here, but I just couldn't believe you'd swing into town and not come see me."

Casey turned around and found herself face to face with a set of bright chestnut eyes and a broad smile. It only took her a moment to recognize him. "Tony." She smiled back and managed to keep it in place when his long arms wrapped around her, pulling her tightly against him. She rose to her toes and awkwardly returned his hug. Drawing away, she took a step back to look at him.

He was much larger than she remembered, broader in the chest. His once thin arms were thick with muscles; the angles of his face were more refined. He wore dark jeans and a navy blue T-shirt with the Rosehill Police Department insignia on the left pocket. A wide, black Stetson covered most of his head and wisps of brown hair peeked out below the rim.

"It's good to see you," she said, sliding her hands in her pockets. "You look good."

"And you're still as beautiful as ever, Cassandra," he said with a wistful smile. He glanced at Scott. A brief look of disapproval passed through his eyes before he extended his hand. "How's it going there,

Scott?"

"Not too bad," he answered, returning Tony's laconic greeting. "How was fishing? Catch anything?"

"Just the reds, brother. Just the reds," he said with a laugh.

"The reds? You told me you didn't catch anything." A young woman stepped beside him, locking her hands around his arm. She stood an inch taller than Casey, her long black hair falling in thick curls around a lovely olive-colored complexion. Her dark eyes skimmed over Scott and Casey, not altogether friendly.

"That would be the red-ass, sugar. She hates cursing," Tony said with a mischievous smile.

"I'm not too crazy about it myself," Casey said with a glance at Scott.

He gave her a careless shrug and shoved his hands in his pockets. "You two been out here long?" he asked Tony. He'd kept his voice light but Casey heard his annoyance.

Tony furrowed his brow at Scott's question then turned to the woman next to him as if he'd forgotten she was there. "Forgive my manners. This is Alicia Morales. Alicia, this here is Cassandra Rivera. The first woman to ever steal my heart," he said with a wink.

Casey smiled to hide her discomfort, though Alicia didn't seem to notice. "It's nice to meet you." She extended her hand but Alicia ignored it and turned to Tony.

"Tony, you promised me a drink. The line is starting to get long," she said.

"You bet, sugar. Cassandra, it's great to have you home." He pulled her into a hug and pressed a kiss to her cheek. "I'll see you soon, and we can catch up on old times," he said, gently squeezing her hand.

"Yes, of course," Casey answered. She eased out a breath as Tony lead Alicia toward a trailer advertising long tall slushes. "Well, that was awkward," she murmured.

"I didn't realize you two knew each other that well," Scott said. He took her arm and led her in the opposite direction.

"Tony? Of course. He and Alex have been friends since high school. And, we were sort of engaged once," she added absently. She wrapped her arms around the purple elephant Scott won for her and tried to shake off the discomfort from the meeting.

"Engaged?" Scott stopped at another trailer and ordered two bottles of water. "What happened?"

"Some things just aren't meant to be," she said. She accepted the water he offered and twisted off the cap.

"Must have been hard for the two of you. Breaking up, I mean." He took a drink from his bottle, watching her over the rim.

"It was amicable, and he's happier now, so that's all that matters." She shrugged, hoping he'd take it as a hint that she would not be interrogated. She glanced back and caught Alicia's eye. She attempted a smile. The woman glared back at her.

Shouldn't she feel even a little bit of jealousy that Tony had found someone? She'd loved him once, after all. Of course if she were honest with herself she'd realize she hadn't actually been in love with him, she'd been grateful. Tony had been her only friend and an ally against her grandmother. He'd become her escape from her life and her past. She'd been so desperate to get out of her grandmother's house and give herself a new name she agreed to marry him. It didn't take long before she realized marrying Tony wasn't going to make her happy, so she ended their engagement and left town to build a new life on her own. But their break up wasn't as amicable as she'd tried to convince herself.

Scott stopped at the edge of the street sectioned off for the band and pulled her from her thoughts. "Wanna dance?" he asked.

She stole a wary glimpse at the country-western band performing on the stage. "You're kidding, right?"

"Come on. You don't want these people to think you're a snob, do you?"

Casey made a face at him and set her elephant on the ground next to an elderly woman in a lawn chair. "Would you mind?" she asked with a sheepish smile.

"Go ahead, dear. Don't keep your man waiting," the woman answered.

Casey took Scott's hand and let him lead her into the crowd. She bit on her lip, casting a worried glance at the other couples circling the dance floor. "I'm afraid I don't really know how to two-step."

"And I thought you weren't afraid of anything," Scott said with a grin. "Don't worry. I've done this before. Here, put your left hand on my shoulder."

Casey did what she was told, willing herself to stay calm as the memory of their first embrace, and her body's reaction, leapt into her mind.

Scott pressed his right hand on her lower back. The heat of his touch radiated through the soft silk of her blouse, and she had to fight down on the knot that wanted to curl in her stomach. He took her right hand, resting it against his chest, then closed his hand over hers.

"Now, just start right foot back and follow me," he said. "No, don't look down, look at me."

Casey looked up and found herself caught in a fountain of blue. A hot wave rolled over her, settling like a shimmering ripple in her stomach. She held her breath, squeezing the air in her lungs and fisted her hand against his chest.

Scott chuckled, lowering his mouth to her ear. "Relax. This is painless."

With more grace and skill than she thought he could possess, he led her along the dance area, stepping one then two, guiding her smoothly into the dance. He kept his eyes locked on hers, a smile glowing in them. His hand slid to her lower back, pressing her closer as he circled her around the other couples.

Casey's mouth went dry, and it wasn't from the exertion of the dance. She swallowed the lump in her throat and sent him as casual a look as she could manage. "You're pretty good at this."

"Shh…don't talk to me, I'm trying to count." He flashed a smile when she laughed. "That's nice. You should do it more often."

They danced through three songs while Scott never missed a beat at the change in tune. Casey shook her head and laughed before he could sashay into another two-step.

"No more. My legs can't take it!" She took a deep breath, pressing her hand against her stomach. "That's more exercise than running."

"But a lot more fun." Scott cupped his hand at her elbow to lead her off the dance floor. "You know, you're not so bad to be around when you're off that high horse of yours," he said with a grin.

Casey glanced at him. "Is that your idea of a compliment?"

His smile was crooked and exuded a sexy charm she no longer felt immune to. "You're not too bad a dancer, either. Better be careful, Ms. Martinez, I think your Texan is starting to show."

"God, I hope not. It took years to get rid of that accent," she said with a laugh.

Scott gathered her things and handed them to her. "So, are you hungry?"

Casey shook her head with a laugh. "Why am I not surprised? Sure, I suppose I could eat something. As long as it's not deep fried or cooked on a stick."

"Well, you just take the adventure out of everything, don't you?" He took her hand and led her away from the festival. "Actually I was thinking more in the lines of a diner so we can sit for a while."

"Then I can definitely go for something to eat."

❧

They both noticed the list in Scott's jeep as soon as they reached the street where he parked.

"Son of a bitch. Sorry," he said before Casey could chastise him. He frowned at the front driver's tire. "I just bought these damn...darn tires."

"Do you have a spare?" She tossed her things into the back seat and followed him to the rear of the jeep.

"Yeah. It'll only take a minute," he said, cuffing the sleeves of his shirt.

"Want some help?" She crossed her arms at her chest when he raised his brow with an uncertain look. "I'm not as helpless as everyone seems to think I am. I do know how to take care of myself."

"Okay. Sure," he said. "Take the jack out while I get the tire."

Casey bit her lip and shifted her gaze to the back of the jeep. "Jack who?" She chuckled at Scott's sober expression and pulled out the long metal bar and stand.

It took no time at all for Scott to change the tire, though he did so through a string of curses when the lug wrench slipped, causing him to scrape his knuckles against the pavement. He picked up the flat tire and equipment, tossing them into the back of the jeep, then leaned in and rummaged around for something to wipe the grease from his hands.

"Looking for this?" Casey asked. She waved a red, worn-out bandana in front of him and snatched it back when he reached for it. "You have to

129

say *please*."

She didn't expect him to move so fast and was unprepared when he closed the distance between them in one step. She took a step back, bumping into the rear of the jeep. Scott framed his arms alongside her like two stone pylons and caged her in.

"You wouldn't want me to mess up this pretty blouse of yours now, would you? That's silk, right?" he said.

She laughed and handed him the rag. "No, no. Here." She saw the scrape on his knuckle and grabbed his hand. "You cut yourself."

Scott grinned at her concern but didn't pull his hand away. "Just a scratch, ma'am."

She looked up with a frown. "It could get infected. Where's your first aid kit?"

He nodded at the white box tucked on the side wall. His lips quirked a smile as she pulled out a wipe and gently cleaned around his wound. "Maybe you should have gone into nursing. You're good at this."

"No, that's okay. I prefer to leave all the real life gory stuff to my brother." She pulled out a bottle of antiseptic. "This might sting."

"I think I can handle it," Scott said dryly.

She smiled at him and poured the liquid over his wound. A laugh escaped her when he hissed out a string of curses. "I told you it would hurt, tough guy."

"You want a tough guy? Let me show you how tough I can be." He shot his hand out and grabbed her wrist. With one hard tug he pulled her firmly against him. The playful smile vanished. His eyes locked on hers and his fingers tensed on her wrist. His Adam's apple bobbed as if he was having trouble swallowing.

Casey's throat closed as the air lodged in her lungs. She was pressed so tightly against him that she could feel every ripple of muscle under his shirt. His eyes glinted dark and enchanting, like the deepest part of the ocean, pulling her into a whirlpool of desire. His gaze dropped to her lips. Her blood shimmered, heating to an unhealthy degree as need washed over her. It took all she had not to tremble in his arms. She swallowed hard then moistened her lips. He was so close she could almost taste him.

It was a smart woman who stepped cautiously into the unknown. She didn't want to be a smart woman just now. She closed her eyes and leaned in, prepared to go under.

A bright light flashed over them. Casey jolted back with a sharp intake of breath and blinked.

A police car pulled alongside them. "Is everything all right here?" The officer inside leaned over to see out his passenger window. "Oh, hey, Scott, didn't know that was you. Are you guys okay?"

Casey bolted to the front seat of the jeep. Scott picked up the first aid kit and placed it back in the jeep.

"Yeah. Just a little car trouble," he said.

"Yeah, okay. I'll leave you to it then." The officer said with a soft laugh.

CHAPTER SIXTEEN

It was nearly midnight when they returned to the beach house. The quick meal at the local IHOP had helped to clear the sexual tension that seemed to hang over them since they'd left the festival. In an unspoken agreement, they brushed aside the incident in the parking lot and enjoyed a quiet meal and polite conversation.

Scott was glad it was over.

"Thank you for tonight, Scott. I had a very nice time," Casey said when they stepped to the front door.

"Scott, huh?" He took the keys from her and slid it into the lock. "I think that's the first time you've actually used my name."

"It's the first time I've thought of you as human," she said with a smirk. She stepped into the house, flipped on the light switch, then tossed her bag and the stuffed elephant onto the sofa.

Scott sent her a crooked smile, moving in closer. He took her hand, his gaze roaming the length of her body. "Oh, I'm human all right," he said before dropping the keys into her palm. It did wonders for his ego to see the arousal come into her eyes, but not when it settled in him as well.

Casey swallowed and gave him a tremulous smile, taking an awkward step back toward the bedroom. "Well, it's been a pretty long day. I think I'll turn in. I guess I'll see you in the morning."

"Yeah," Scott cleared his throat and took a step back also. "I'm going to take a look around outside, make sure everything is secure before I go. The night shift will be on in about ten minutes, so you'll be okay. You...ah...sleep well." *One of us might as well.*

He whistled out a low breath as she closed the bedroom door. He could still feel her in his arms, and he wasn't at all pleased he was responding to it like a horny teenager. A cold shower, that's what he needed as soon as he got back to his apartment. Although he didn't think there was enough cold water in the world to satisfy his reaction to her.

He checked his gun in his shoulder holster before stepping back outside. He took the stairs down, making his way around to the back of the house, scanning the area for any signs of trespassers. A warm breeze blew in from the east, carrying an odor of smoke from the burning marsh. He looked at the beach, narrowing his eyes to focus on the truck parked a few yards away. He took a step forward. Pain radiated at the back of his head as a heavy object connected with his skull and dropped him to the ground.

cﾎ

Casey settled back in the tub and rested her head against the rim. Her fingers tapped in rhythm to the music floating in from her bedroom. She took a drink from the glass of wine she'd poured from the open bottle in the small refrigerator next to her bed. The lightly flavored liquid flowed warm through her body, relaxing her like a massage. She finished the drink and set the glass on the floor next to the fat candle she'd lit to lighten the room. Closing her eyes, she nestled back into the water.

She'd decided to take a warm bath before crawling into bed, hoping it would take her mind off Scott and the playful grasp he'd held her in earlier. The way his eyes had roamed over her sent an unwelcomed flash of heat through her and awakened every sense in her body. It seemed to be an all too common response to him lately, and it was getting harder to control.

She wasn't used to having that type of a reaction to a man, or the intense urge to act on those desires. She wasn't a frigid person by any means, but she also wasn't what one would call promiscuous, either. Her sexual affairs had been limited to only two men in her lifetime, and even then she wasn't quite sure what to do about them.

Her first experience had been at the age of nineteen, with the sandwich delivery boy she met at Jo's office shortly after she began working for her.

His name was Joshua Michaels and his attentive, flirtatious manner had quickly swept her off her feet and sent her hormones blazing. They dated four weeks before she gave in to her body's demands and Joshua's hot pleas. The whole sexual ordeal hadn't been as monumental as she'd anticipated, and Joshua turned out to be faster on the draw than she expected. After that night, he stopped coming by her desk during his deliveries, and Casey chalked it up to a learning experience.

Aaron's lovemaking techniques were more practiced and focused then Joshua's, which was probably why she thought she loved him. But she had obviously confused sex and love, just as she was now confusing lust with desire. After all, it had been three years since she had a man even look at her. It was only natural she would react to the first one that came near. Especially someone as ruggedly handsome as Scott. *And with those wide hands and long fingers he would certainly know how to please a woman.*

She settled back into the tub more. A sigh, like the purr of a cat, rolled from her throat. Her body felt so relaxed, it was like floating on a cloud.

Warm water sluiced over her chin. She sat up, blinking her eyes open and shook her head clear. She should probably get out of the tub or she was going to fall asleep and drown. Scott might not appreciate her drowning on his watch.

She rubbed her hands over her face before lifting herself out of the frothy water. The room shifted around her. She braced her hand against the wall to steady herself, pressing her fingers to her eyes to clear her blurry vision. *I must be more tired than I thought.*

She wrapped a towel around her and pulled in a deep breath to ease the dizziness. She opened the door and stopped. The room was cloaked in darkness. Had she forgotten to leave the lamp on?

She pushed the bathroom door open wider but the candle wasn't enough to lighten her path. She flipped up the switch behind the door but the bulb didn't flash on. It took her a moment to realize the music had stopped playing. "Great. Of all times to blow a fuse."

Picking up the candle, she cupped her hand around the flame to keep it from going out and moved into the bedroom. Her foot kicked one of the shopping bags she'd left on the floor and made her stumble. Hot wax spilled over the side of the candle, burning her fingers. She dropped the votive instantly. The flame went out.

"Shit!"

She stopped for a moment, hoping her eyes would adjust to the room. She took a cautious step toward the bed, her hand extended in front of her to feel her way, but the darkness made her feel more disoriented. She went still. A sudden uneasiness crept over her making the hair on the back of her neck spike. Before she could move, a hand clamped over her mouth and another wrapped around her waist. With a hard tug, she was pulled back against another body. Casey filled her lungs with air, her hands reaching up to grab onto the arm as the terror built inside her.

"Don't be afraid. I won't hurt you," a husky voice whispered hot against her ear. The man nuzzled her neck, inhaling her scent. "You're so beautiful. You've always been so beautiful." He took a step forward, urging her to move with him as he spoke, his hand still clamped against her mouth. "I've waited so long for you to come to me." The smell of stale whiskey lingered on his breath.

Casey struggled against him, trying desperately to pull his hand from her mouth. A sickening wave of panic surged through her, dropping like acid to her stomach. Her father's voice raced through her mind. '*I'm coming for you, Cassandra.*' She trembled, her frightened whimper muffled by the man's large hand against her mouth.

"Don't be afraid. I love you. I won't hurt you," the voice cooed.

He guided her forward, loosening his hold around her waist. Casey fought to control her rapid breaths. She had to stay calm so she could think. *Fight! Don't let the fear win.*

The corner of the comforter brushed up against her leg. Her heart slammed against her ribs. The realization of what he planned to do flooded into her. Images of her mother's butchered body flashed in her mind. *Oh God, no. Please. Don't let this happen.*

"I've waited all my life for you. I always knew we'd be together. I love you so much," he continued, one hand moving to her shoulder. "I just had to come for you. I knew you wouldn't mind." He pressed a kiss to her bare shoulder, moving his way up along her neck.

Casey's adrenaline spiked as her survival instincts took hold. Before the intruder could turn her around, she pulled back, swinging her arm up to hit him. At the same time he shifted, causing her elbow to clip his jaw. Before she could get away from him the back of his hand struck her across the face.

"I said I won't hurt you!"

Casey landed with a bounce on the thick comforter. Bright lights sparked behind her eyes. The room spun around her. The man moved closer, his breathing heavy as if trying to control his anger. She strained to focus on his face but saw only a dark silhouette arched above her.

The unsnapping of his jeans barely registered through the pounding in her skull. Fear gripped her like an icy fist. Her chest tightened, the air constricting her lungs. She willed herself to move from the bed, but her arms and legs felt heavy, as if she were drunk. But she'd only had one glass of wine.

"I've waited so long for you, Cassandra," the man said softly. "I just couldn't wait any more." He lowered to her, sliding his hands along her thigh, his breath shuddering out. "You belong to me. You've always belonged to me."

Casey squeezed her eyes shut and turned her head when he bent to kiss her. She cried out when he grabbed her chin, forcing her face back to his.

"Don't turn away from me!" he snapped, before pressing his mouth to hers with a bruising kiss.

Casey barreled her arms against his chest and pushed. He grabbed her wrists and jerked her arms over her head, pinning them down with one hand. "You don't have to pretend with me. I know you've been waiting for this. And now we can be together." His mouth dropped to assault her neck, his free hand sliding up her bare thigh. "I love you so much. You're mine now. You will always be mine."

It took all her strength to build up the scream in her throat. She howled it out, long and loud. The man jumped up, stumbling back as if he'd been punched. Before Casey could roll away from him, his hand swung down and connected with her cheek.

Scott heard the scream as he rounded the front entry. The room was dark but he knew enough of the layout to know where her bedroom was. "Casey!" He rushed forward, ramming his shoulder against the bedroom door. The lock gave on his second try. He braced against the jamb, his gun gripped between two hands. He blinked to adjust his vision, his eyes still blurred from the blow to his head.

He caught a movement near the edge of the bed and barely had time to duck behind the wall as something flew at his head. The pillow dropped at his feet with a soft plop. He crouched between the doorframe, but the figure had already bolted across the room to the open window.

"Police! Freeze!"

The figure jumped the rail on the deck and landed with a muffled thud onto the ground. Scott ran to the window as the man escaped to the beach in a fast run.

Rushing back to the bed he pressed his fingers against Casey's neck. Relief washed over him like a cold wave when he found her pulse. He pulled a flashlight from the bedside table and used the dim light to cautiously checked her for any obvious signs of injury. He lifted her eyelid to examine her pupils. They looked like two black saucers.

"Casey?" He patted her cheek lightly. "Casey. Come on, baby, it's me." The muscles that had bunched in his chest when he saw her unmoving on the bed eased as she started to stir. He sat on the bed and cupped his hand under her head, lifting her to rest in the crook of his arm. "Wake up, sweetheart," he said smoothing her hair back. "That's it, come back to me. What did you take?"

"Hmm? Nothing. A bath," she said sluggishly. She pushed his hand away as she struggled to wake up. "And some wine."

Scott grabbed the bottle she'd left on the bedside table and sniffed it. It smelled like wine.

Casey took a deep breath and rubbed her hand over her face. "What are you...?" She shot up as if the realization of what happened finally hit her. "Oh my God. Oh, God. He was in my room."

Scott wrapped his arms around her and held her against him. "You're okay. He's gone." He hesitated, then said, "Did he...?"

Casey pulled away, clutching the towel in front of her. "No. No, I don't think so. I screamed...I think. I don't know." She pressed a hand to her head to ease the lightheadedness. "I was in the bath...when I came out the lights were off....he...he came up behind..." He was leading her toward the bed. A cold chill skittered across her neck and she trembled. She took a deep breath to battle down her panic. A headache was starting to brew behind her eyes.

"It's okay. You're safe now," Scott said gently. He pulled the blanket up to wrap around her and stroked his hand over her hair. "I'm going to call this in and get you to the hospital. We'll let them check you out to be sure."

"No!" Casey grabbed his sleeve before he could rise. "You can't. Alex."

"Okay. Okay. No hospital. I'll call someone in." He carefully removed her hand and had started to rise when she stopped him again.

"Could you…just give me a minute? Just stay here for a minute?" She pressed her lips together. She hated that her voice trembled.

"Of course." He sat on the bed and eased her back into his arms. "It's okay if you want to cry," he whispered, stroking his hand over her hair.

She didn't cry. Casey told herself she wouldn't cry. Crying was for the weak and she wasn't weak.

Thirty minutes later she sat on the sofa wrapped in a thin, floor-length terry robe. Her clenched hand rested in her lap while her other arm was outstretched to allow the young female paramedic to take a blood sample.

"How's she holding up?" Captain Knowles asked as soon as he walked into the beach house.

"As well as can be expected," Scott said, meeting him at the door. It worried and surprised him that she did no more than sit quietly in his arms for ten minutes before he called the sheriff. He didn't know if it was shock or her own need to prove how brave she was that kept her from breaking down. But whichever it was, she looked wound tight and near ready to burst.

He surveyed the room, checking out the deputies who'd been called in to work the crime scene. Since the small towns along the beach were unincorporated, the county sheriff's department handled whatever violations occurred. They only employed a handful of deputies during the off season, so Scott had been allowed to phone into his own precinct for additional help. A few of the officers were assigned to the bedroom to search for trace evidence while one took a seat next to Casey and quietly asked her some questions. A middle-aged cop stepped through the room with the towel and bottle of wine secured in evidence bags.

"Send that to Fisher at the lab in Beaumont. Tell him I want the tox report on that as soon as possible," Scott said. The cop nodded and continued out.

"I guess the Feds weren't as paranoid as you thought. It's a lucky thing you were still here," the captain said, watching Casey as she calmly gave her story to the police officer.

"Yeah," Scott said. Lucky for both of them he had a hard head. He rubbed at the back of his head where he'd been hit and felt the matted patch of hair that told him blood had been drawn. *Fuck.*

"Is there anything else you remember, Ms. Martinez? Skin color? Facial hair?" the interviewing officer asked.

Casey pressed her fingers to her lips. She looked up at Scott then turned away as if ashamed. "No, no facial hair, I don't think. It was dark. I'm sorry I didn't get a very good look at him."

"You did fine, ma'am." The officer closed his notebook and stood, turning to Scott. "I'll take this in, write it up,"

"Thanks." Scott took a step toward the sofa as the paramedic closed up her case.

"Her vitals are good. She's still a little doped up with whatever sedative he used, but nothing external that I can find. You might want to take her in just to be on the safe side," she said.

"She won't go." He kept his eyes on Casey as she rose from the sofa, her fingers clutched at the neck of her robe. She stepped to the bar and leaned forward, grabbing onto the edge of the counter. Her shoulders rose with the deep breath she took and her knuckles whitened for several seconds before she eased the pressure. He wanted to go to her and hold her, help her forget what had just happened.

"Well, you should try to talk her into it," the paramedic said. She frowned when he ignored her. "Scott, I really think—"

"Thanks, Vicki," the captain interrupted. "We appreciate you coming out."

She exhaled a resigned sigh. "No problem. It's why we get paid the big bucks."She turned to leave but stopped when she glanced at Scott's shoulder. "Hey, you've got a little blood on your shirt, Scott."

"It's nothing." He brushed her hand away when she reached for the back of his head.

"If there's blood, it's something." She ignored his irritation and reached for his head, but he ducked the contact. "You never used to mind me running my fingers through your hair," she teased, shifting with him to press her fingers against his scalp.

Scott flinched and slapped her hand away. "Knock it off."

"It's a pretty nice-sized knot back there," she said, frowning. "You might have a concussion."

He scowled at her and moved away from her probing hands. "I'm fine. I'll take two aspirins and call you in the morning."

Vicki shook her head when the captain waved her off. She grabbed her medical case and left the house.

"So, where do you plan to take her tonight?" his captain asked.

"Back to my place for now."

Casey stopped mid-step on her way to the kitchen and turned around to face him. "What? No. I'm not going anywhere."

"Don't argue with me!" Scott growled.

"Uh...Captain?" A police officer appeared at the patio doors and sent a cautious look from Casey to Scott. "We found something."

Scott turned away from Casey and stormed outside to join the officer on the deck.

"Looks like he nicked himself when he jumped. We've got a little blood on the railing," the officer said, pointing to a dark red stain on the other side of the wood.

"Rush it to the crime lab and ask them to run the DNA and see if it matches up with what the Feds have on file."

"You got it."

"Well, you wanted in on this case," Captain Knowles said. "Looks like you got your wish."

"Yeah, but this isn't how I wanted it," Scott answered. He rubbed the back of his neck and squeezed his hand over the corded muscle. "Listen, Captain, if you don't need us any longer, I'd like to get Ms. Martinez back to my place so she can rest."

"Yeah, that would probably be best. If it hasn't hit her yet, it's going to soon. Bring her in if she remembers anything else. I'll let the sheriff know what's going on."

Scott nodded and went back into the house to find Casey. "Let's go." He held out his hand. Casey crossed her arms at her chest and lifter her chin with a defiant glare. "Please," he said softly. He didn't have any more fight in him.

With a resigned sigh, she took his hand and let him lead her out.

❧

He stood at the window overlooking the ghostly highway which led out of town, his chest heaving with rapid breaths. The heavy thunder of an eighteen wheeler rumbled across the overpass, vibrating through him. Sweat glistened and dripped down the tensed muscles along his back. He pressed his fists against his temples but it wasn't enough pressure to push out the sound of Casey's scream.

"Stupid. Stupid. Stupid," he hissed. Why had he been so stupid?

He gripped the windowsill and closed his eyes, taking a deep calming breath. He knew it was a bad idea to go to her. But he'd been so anxious to have her. He'd waited so long. He only needed a taste.

But then she'd screamed.

He closed his eyes and fought the pain in his heart. How could she scream like that? Didn't she know he'd never hurt her? Didn't she know how much he loved her? How he'd nearly died for her? He glanced at the thick patch of gauze affixed to his arm. The cut had stopped bleeding but the pain still radiated in the wound.

He grabbed the bottle of whiskey on the side table and guzzled it. The liquid burned a trail to his stomach, calming the ache in his chest.

It was his fault. If he'd waited like he'd planned, he wouldn't have scared her. She just wasn't expecting him, that's all. She didn't know he'd be so impatient.

He took another drink from the bottle, the warm liquid igniting his blood like a woman's touch. He'd know better next time. When the time came for them to be together, she'd open herself to him and give him everything he'd waited for.

He took another drink, liquid dribbling over his chin. He rubbed his hand over it, sliding his palm down his bare chest. His arousal built at the thought of Casey lying in wait for him.

Yes, when the time came, he would make her his.

He looked across the highway at Arthur's Pub, illuminated by the glowing streetlights, and smiled. But until then, he would have to spend his passion elsewhere.

Chapter Seventeen

Detective Juan Gomez leaned his stocky frame against the corner of Scott's desk and flipped through the small notebook in his hand. He and his partner, Jimmy LeBlanc, were now assigned to assist Scott with Casey's assault and possible stalker.

"Assuming it's the same guy, do the Feds have any clue as to why he's after her?" Gomez asked.

"Nothing they've cared to share," Scott answered. He motioned with disgust toward the file Jimmy LeBlanc held. "I had to practically pull teeth just to get that much."

LeBlanc shrugged. "Maybe he thinks she needs to be saved. All the passages he highlighted in the Bible are about honor and redemption."

Scott leaned back in his chair and scrubbed his hands over his face. He'd left Casey asleep at his apartment, certain the remains of the drug in her system would keep her knocked out until at least noon. He planned to be back by then. He'd placed a uniformed officer outside his building, though, just to be safe.

"No, I don't think Mr. Holier-Than-Thou has anything to do with this." He nodded at the file again. "Whoever is killing those women is doing it out of anger, maybe even jealousy, not redemption. They're crimes of passion. I think the guy the Feds are looking for is targeting Ms. Martinez because he wants her and knows he can't have her."

LeBlanc raised his brow as he considered the thought. "So, what? He's upped the stakes because if he can't have her, no one can?" He set the file down next to several others spread out on the desk.

"No…I don't know." Scott tapped on the assault file. "I think this guy might be someone who knows her. But I'm not altogether certain it's the same person the Feds are hunting for."

LeBlanc sent him a noncommittal shrug. "Maybe, maybe not. Of course her attack last night could also be a coincidence. Could have just been someone looking for an open window and a woman staying alone."

"But he used her full name," Gomez said. "Which means he knows who she is, and he's been lying in wait." He looked at Scott and tapped the assault file. "Maybe your guy is just someone who's developed an obsession for her because of the type of books she writes. You know, all that wild sex and stuff." A sheepish smile curved his lips. "My wife reads them. They're pretty hot."

Scott grabbed the file and leaned back in his chair. "Come on, guys. Let's use those college educations we're all so proud of. We need to search deeper. I want you to pull up everything we have that even comes close to the killer's M.O." He tossed the file on his desk and strummed his fingers on his armrest. "His DNA has got to be in the system somewhere. You don't kill this many women and not leave some sort of calling card. If both of these bastards are the same person, then we need to find him before he takes his anger out on someone else."

Gomez rose from the desk, tucking his notebook in his jacket. "Well, that's not going to be easy. The files are overflowing with sexual offenders, and the few names Ms. Martinez threw to the Feds have already checked out. It's going to be like looking for a needle in a haystack. A Texas-sized haystack."

Scott leaned on his desk and pinned him with a glare. "Then go back over the profile. Rework it if you have to. Then run it against what we pull up," he said. "If we can't find him in the Fed's database, maybe we can find him in the state's. And go back ten years. I have a feeling this guy has been killing a lot longer than they thought."

"Okay, boss. We'll get on it and let you know what we come up with," LeBlanc said. He picked up the file, tucking it under his arm and nodded to his partner to follow him.

Scott ignored the sarcasm as the men returned to their workstations.

He grabbed a thick file from under the stack on his desk and stared at the type-written name on the tab. *Alejandro Miguel Rivera.* Shifting in his seat, he tapped on the computer keyboard and pulled up the website he'd bookmarked several days before. An article from the Beaumont Enterprise newspaper archives flashed onto the screen. *Local Man Sentenced to 25 Years For Murdering His Wife.* He scrolled to read the article.

A 43-year-old Beaumont man has been sentenced to 25 years in state prison after he pleaded guilty Friday to the murder of his wife.

Authorities said Alejandro Miguel Rivera killed 31 year-old Esmeralda Delores Rivera in July 1987 by stabbing her with a hunting knife. In an interview with Brownsville police, Rivera admitted he "lost it" when his wife threatened to divorce him and take his children. The children were placed in the temporary custody of CPS and later united with their maternal grandmother, Herlinda Martinez of Rosehill, Texas

Police said Rivera repeatedly beat and raped his wife before taking her life with the knife while his children slept in another room. The investigation revealed Mrs. Rivera had over twenty-five stab wounds on her upper and lower extremities.

Rivera has been jailed at the Jefferson County Detention Center since his 1987 arrest, held in lieu of $1 million bail.

Scott closed the website and flipped open the file on his desk. According to the police report, Eduardo Morales was the first officer on the scene. He'd been the one to calm the children and had even accompanied them to the police station to wait on Children's Protective Services. Morales had retired several years ago. Scott made a note to contact him.

He took out a 4x6 black and white snapshot of Casey's father. It had been updated four years earlier. Rivera's features were gaunt, his color ashen from years of drug and alcohol abuse.

Scott saw little resemblance to Casey, but Alex shared the man's dark eyes and long regal nose. The records stated Rivera stood six feet tall and weighed two hundred twenty pounds at the time of his arrest. But twenty-five years in prison would have knocked at least fifty pounds off him.

He turned to the prison record.

Rivera had been released from prison three years ago on an early release program. His last known address was listed as Houston, Texas. Only a two-hour drive away.

Scott pressed his fingers to the bridge of his nose and eased out a tired breath. The aspirin he'd taken earlier had only dulled the headache that had been throbbing since Casey's attack. He turned back to his computer and typed *unsolved murders in the Houston area* in the search box as his desk phone rang.

"Weller."

"Hey, Scott. It's Kevin."

"Hey. How's my tire looking?" he asked, turning the next page in the file while he waited on the computer.

"It's toast, man. I don't know who you pissed off, but they sure took it out on your radials. You have so many stabs in it I'm surprised the rubber didn't crumble like confetti. And, by the way, that spare you got on, ain't gonna get you very far, either."

"Great," Scott said under his breath. "You think you can find me a replacement for both by the day's end?"

"Sure thing, buddy. I just happen to know a guy who can have you up and running right away. Shouldn't set you back too much," Kevin said with a short laugh. "You should be ready to go within the hour."

"Yeah, okay. Thanks." Scott put the phone back on its base with more force than he'd intended. He turned back to the file and pulled out another picture. Alejandro Rivera's murder weapon. A wood-handled hunting knife with an eight-inch steel blade.

"Well, well, Scott Weller. Still riding the desk, huh?" Tony Lankford stepped forward, dressed in full uniform, his hand resting on the butt of his nightstick.

Scott spared him a glance. "You could say that. I was just finishing up some work."

"Yeah, that paperwork's a bitch, huh?" Tony said. His quick smile changed into a worried frown. "I heard Cassandra had a bit of a scare last night. Is she okay?"

"She's fine."

"Good. That's good," Tony said with a pensive nod. "So, uh, you're working the case?"

"That's right."

"Well, is there anything I can do?"

Scott glanced up. He'd known Tony for a few years, but only in passing since they worked in the same station. He never made an effort to get to know him even after he learned that Tony and Alex were high school friends. There was just something about him that Scott didn't like. "Got it covered, thanks."

"Okay." Tony nodded and shifted as if he were going to leave. He paused and sent Scott an earnest look. "Cassandra's very important to me. If there's anything I can do, you let me know."

Scott sat back in his seat and studied Tony a moment. "Maybe there is something you can do," he said before Tony could leave. The best possible way to learn about a killer was to learn about his target. Right now, Tony was the only person besides Alex who could tell him about Casey. And, because he'd promised Casey, he couldn't call Alex. "What can you tell me about Casey?"

Tony pursed his lips then nodded. "What do you want to know?" He sat in the chair next to Scott's desk and made himself comfortable.

"General information. How long have you known her?"

"Oh, going on eighteen years. She was just a little thing when Alex and I started hanging out. She was quite a kid," he said, the expression on his face wistful. "Quiet and shy one minute, a spitfire the next. She and Alex used to get into some nasty arguments. Oh, nothing bad of course. Alex adored her. But she sure hated when he treated her like a child."

Scott thought about the argument they'd had less than twenty-four hours earlier. She'd accused him of treating her like a child as well. But if he had been more overprotective, she wouldn't have been attacked. *No time to second guess yourself, Weller.*

"What kind of crowd did she hang out with? Did she have a lot of friends?" he asked.

"No. Cassandra kept to herself mostly. Always felt like she didn't fit in, like people looked down on her because...well, she said it was because she's Mexican. This town doesn't have a whole lot of them, if you haven't noticed," he said with a frown. "Cassandra felt like too much of a minority, so she didn't really associate with anyone but me and Alex. It didn't help that her grandmother kept a tight rein on her. She wasn't really allowed to go anywhere or do anything. Herlinda didn't pay much attention to Alex though. Guess because he was a guy."

"Casey mentioned you two dated." The image of Tony kissing Casey at the carnival flashed in his mind and left a burning in his chest. He quickly pushed it aside.

"Yeah. We were pretty young at the time. You know, she's the first woman I ever loved," Tony answered with a soft smile. His face sobered when he looked back at Scott. "Like I said, she's important to me. I once promised her that I would always take care of her, and I won't break that promise."

"So, there's no one else Casey hung around with?" Scott asked, wanting to get away from the subject of Tony and Casey.

"No. Like I said, Herlinda kept her pretty close. She even made Cassandra clean houses with her. Said it was to remind her of what she was. To teach her to be what was expected."

"What was expected?"

"Yeah, you know, on the outside looking in. Herlinda used to tell Cassandra she would never be anything more than another man's housekeeper. But I'll tell you, Cassandra did everything she could to prove that woman wrong."

Like moving to New York and starting over, Scott thought. He glanced at the file for her father. He understood now, why Casey had changed her name. She didn't want the constant reminder of where she came from. It saddened him that she felt it necessary to change everything she was to prove a point.

"But, you know, Cassandra, she never complained," Tony continued. "I think she felt it was her duty to do right by her grandmother. Of course I don't doubt Herlinda made her feel that way. She never gave that girl enough love, in my opinion. All she needed was someone to love her."

"Where's the grandmother now?" Scott asked.

Tony sat back in the chair, adjusting his nightstick. "She died some eight years ago. You know, as badly as that woman treated her, Cassandra still cried at her funeral." He shook his head with a short laugh. "She's a special lady. Always had such a big heart. It's what made me fall head over heels in love with her. Of course, she thought she wanted different things so we didn't quite work out as I'd hoped. But then, you never know, some things are just meant." He looked at Scott with a raised brow. "You two aren't...?"

"No," Scott said quickly. Though it seemed to be all he thought about lately.

"That's good. She deserves special." Tony stared at him a moment then cleared his throat and stood. "Well, I'd better get to work before the captain tosses a desk at me. You let me know if there's anything Cassandra needs."

Scott watched him leave then rose and placed the file in his briefcase. He turned back to the computer screen and skimmed over the list that came up on his search. He clicked the print button and glanced at his watch. Barely ten. He made a mental note to pick up some food for him and Casey as one of the officer's from the beach house stepped forward, holding a file in his hand.

"Hey, Scott. Glad I caught you."

"Is that the toxicology report?" He took the folder and flipped it open.

"Yeah. The lab just faxed it over. The wine was laced with roofies."

"Rohypnol?" Scott stopped at a page to read. "That's why I didn't smell it." He looked at the officer and nodded. "Thanks."

According to the FBI file, Rohypnol was the drug of choice for their serial killer. Damn if this didn't make things worse.

CHAPTER EIGHTEEN

Steam rose like a thick fog in the closet-sized bathroom. Casey stepped under the beating spray of the shower and sighed. Her muscles were stiff and ached from tossing and turning on Scott's firm mattress. The sleep she hoped would push away the nightmare of her attack came in spurts until she finally gave up and crawled out of bed. Even now, the heat of the shower didn't wash away the memory of the night. She could still see the dark silhouette looming over her when she closed her eyes. She could feel his hot breath on her neck, smell the sour stench of whiskey on his skin. His hands were more than a rough memory on her thighs. The pressure of his lips was still hard and bruising against her own.

She pulled in a deep breath and ducked her head under the spray. She grabbed the bar of soap off the holder, lathering it in her hands and roughly scrubbed her face and mouth. After rinsing off the soap, she braced her palms against the pale yellow tile. Her chest heaved painfully with labored breaths. Her eyes burned with unshed tears. She could scrub until her skin was raw, but she would never be able to wash away the images from her head. She'd learned that early in life. Some things would always stay with you and leave you defenseless.

She slapped her hand against the tile with an angry cry, ignoring the sting that shot through her palm. Damn him for making her feel helpless!

A knock at the door shot her heart to her throat and jolted her from her thoughts.

"Casey?" Scott's muffled voice sounded from the other side. "Is everything okay?"

She closed her eyes, giving herself a moment to calm her racing pulse. "Yes. Fine," she answered. "I'll be right out." She ran the water on her face again, then grabbed the soap and finished her shower.

Scott stood at the window, staring blankly at the street when Casey opened the bathroom door.

"I hope you don't mind my using your shower," she said from behind him.

He turned to look at her. "No, of course not..." He went still as his pulse jumped and his mind went blank. She was wrapped in a large bath towel, her wet hair draped over her shoulders, soaking into the terrycloth. Droplets of water clung to her smooth skin, which was lightly flushed from the heat of the shower. Her eyes were bright, her smile slight and timid.

He swallowed, pulling in every ounce of will he could summon to speak again. "Since you didn't have time to grab some clothes from the beach house, I had one of the ladies from the station pack up some of your things." He picked up the small canvas bag beside his feet and set it on the bed. "I'll wait in the other room."

He jammed his hands in his pockets as he stepped into the living room, angry at himself for nearly swallowing his tongue. She was almost raped in her own house, and all he could think of at the moment was how much he wanted to touch her. He wasn't any better than the son of a bitch who'd attacked her.

"Is everything okay?" Casey stepped from the bedroom, her expression cautious. She'd thrown on a pair of jeans and a white cotton blouse, but her feet were still bare. The smell of his soap on her skin made every muscle in his body tense.

"Yeah, terrific," Scott snapped. He pushed his hand through his hair with a curse under his breath and moved away from her. "I put some coffee on. Want a cup?" He turned on his heel and went into the kitchen before she could answer. His body tensed when her heard her step behind him, the smell of his soap teasing his senses. He could still see her in the towel, moisture beading her bronzed skin, her wet hair falling in waves around her face. He jerked the coffee pot off the burner, splashing a drop of hot liquid on his fingers. Served him right.

She stood for several moments, her lips pressed into a thin line, her fingers twisting in front of her. After a moment she squared her shoulders and looked directly at him. "Listen, Scott," she said slowly. "I wanted to say I'm sorry."

"For what?" He didn't quite keep the bite out of his voice.

"I know I haven't been very nice to you. After last night…well, I'm sorry you were hurt trying to protect me."

"It's all part of the job." He took a drink from his coffee, hoping it would douse the heat of desire and self-disgust at war inside him.

Casey shrank back as if abashed by his words. "Of course. I'm sorry."

Scott hurled his cup in the sink, shattering the ceramic and sending shards flying onto the counter. "Goddamn it, stop saying you're sorry! You have nothing to be sorry for. You were nearly raped last night, and all I can think about right now is—" He stopped when she jerked back. The flicker of panic in her eyes tightened the knot of self-disgust in his chest.

A loud pounding resounded at the door. Scott turned on his heel and went to answer it.

"Alex—" was all Scott managed to say before Alex's fist connected with his jaw and sent him stumbling to the floor.

"*Pinche Cabròn!* Where is she?" Alex fumed. He shook his hand, flexing his fingers. He looked at the open door of the bedroom, his face darkening with anger.

Scott stood and wiped at his mouth with the back of his hand. He checked for blood, then sent Alex a deadly look.

Casey rushed into the room. "Alex?"

"Cassandra!" Alex ran to her and pulled her into a hug. He held her back at arm's length to look at her, relief washing over his face when he saw she was fully dressed. "Are you okay? Oh *hija*, your face," he said, gently touching the bruise on her cheek.

"Yes, I'm fine. It's just a little bruise," she said, slightly flinching. She shifted her gaze to Scott then back to Alex. "And, not that I didn't enjoy that, but why are you coming in swinging?"

Alex's glare followed Scott into the kitchen. "You bastard! I thought we were friends."

"We are friends, which is why I let you get away with that sucker punch," Scott answered. He pulled open the refrigerator and reached into the small icebox. He tossed a bag of frozen vegetables to Alex. "You might want to have that hand x-rayed."

"Why did I have to find out through the hospital grapevine that my sister was attacked?" Alex placed the bag on his sore knuckles, his attention caught by the blanket and pillow on the sofa.

"Oh God," Casey said wearily. "It's my fault, Alex. I made Scott promise not to tell you."

"But I found out anyway," Alex said, turning his anger toward his sister. "I had to find out from someone at the fucking police station where you were. Dammit, Cassandra! You're coming home with me. Now!"

Casey raised her brow at her brother's rampage. Alex very rarely raised his voice or lost his temper, and she'd certainly never heard him curse. But she thought it best to hide her amusement at the moment.

"No, Alex. I'm not," she said gently. "You have enough to worry about with Jennifer and the new baby. You don't need to worry about me, too."

"I've always worried about you, Cassandra, you know that. Just because you're a woman now doesn't mean I stop being a big brother."

Casey brought her hand to his face and kissed his cheek. "And I do appreciate it." She let her hand linger a moment then slid it away. "But I'm fine. Really. It wasn't nearly as bad as what you probably heard. You know how grapevines are. They're like fish stories. There's usually very little truth and they always get bigger the more they're told." She smiled at the use of the analogy, hoping it would lighten his mood. It didn't. She eased out a sigh. "Alex, I'd appreciate it if you don't mention this to Jenn. She doesn't need the worry."

"What aren't you telling me, Cassandra?" he demanded. He looked at Scott, who returned his glare with a blank stare. Alex's eyes hardened as he turned back to Casey. "Something's going on, and I want to know what it is!"

"I'm a grown woman, Alex. I don't have to report to you or anyone," Casey snapped. She took a deep breath to control her sudden resentment of her brother. Why did men always think women were so helpless? "Alex, please. Not right now. I promise to talk you later." She took his hand and held it. "Just…not right now."

Alex kept his eyes firmly on hers, a battle of wills he never won. Even when they were children.

"Okay. Okay," he said with a resigned sigh. "I'll let it go. For now." He glanced at Scott then at the bedroom door before he turned solemn brown eyes on her. "Just promise me you'll be careful."

"I'm always careful. Besides, I have a guard dog now," she said with a look at Scott. She'd seen Alex glance toward the bedroom and knew he assumed she and Scott were sleeping together. It was another amusement she thought would be best to keep to herself.

"Go on home, Alex," she said with a reassuring smile. "There's nothing here to worry about. I promise I'll talk to you soon."

"Okay," he said at length. "But I'm going to hold you to that." He turned back to Scott and tossed him the bag of vegetables. "Sorry about the jaw. It was a knee-jerk reaction."

"No problem," Scott answered as Casey walked Alex to the door. She gave him another hug before closing the door behind him.

"You lied to him," Scott said. It was bad enough he put a chink in their friendship. He didn't want to be responsible for coming between family as well.

Casey lifted her chin and returned his hard gaze. "Yes, I did. If the person last night is the same person from New York, then I don't want Alex or Jennifer caught in the crossfire. It's my decision." She watched him as he placed the frozen bag on his jaw and added, "Is your jaw okay?"

"Yeah. It was more like my ego that got bruised. I didn't know your brother had it in him." He tossed the bag back into the freezer. His jaw was going to hurt like hell later.

Casey frowned and slid a look back at the door. "He doesn't. Usually," she murmured.

"Listen, about earlier…" Scott said.

"How long will I have to stay here?"

Scott shoved his hands in his pockets and tried not to let her icy tone bother him. But whatever friendship they'd started to form the day before had stopped dead in its tracks when he'd nearly attacked her himself.

"A couple of days at least. We need to finish investigating the beach house. We can make a quick run over there and pick up whatever you need," he said.

"Good. I'll finish getting dressed."

He massaged his hand over his chin as she stalked back into the bedroom. Maybe it was better to keep her angry at him. If he allowed his personal feelings for her to get in the way, then he wouldn't be able to do his job. And that's what she was to him–a job. It would probably be in everyone's best interest if he remembered that.

CHAPTER NINETEEN

Scott stood in the bedroom of the beach house and looked around at the slight mess the investigating officers had left. Fingerprint powder still clung to the furniture and the window sill. Strips of yellow crime tape was scattered on the floor along with the shopping bags from Casey's trip to the mall. Casey had been visibly upset when he'd brought her back to get more of her things, so he told her to just grab whatever items she absolutely needed and she could get the rest another time.

After he took her back to his apartment, he called in the cleaning service, but they wouldn't make it out for another day. Not that it mattered. He wasn't going to bring Casey back. If the son of a bitch planned to go after her again, the safest place for her to be was his apartment.

He wandered to the bed, the comforter wrinkled from where she'd lain. His muscles tightened when he remembered how she had looked lying unconscious on the bed and how close she'd come to being raped.

He knelt next to the refrigerator and checked the contents inside. There was an unopened bottle of wine and several water bottles. He left them inside then sat on the edge of the bed and pulled open the drawer of the nightstand, moving aside the books and stationery Casey kept tucked inside. He didn't know what he was looking for, just satisfying his own curiosity, he supposed. There was still something that didn't sit right with him about the man who attacked Casey and the serial killer the FBI was searching for. He couldn't shake the feeling that she might have another stalker besides the killer. The declarations of love the man had whispered to her during his attack weren't typical of a serial killer. A rapist maybe, but generally not a serial killer.

A copy of the notes she'd been receiving over the years had been faxed to him and placed in her file, but they were just what she called them— pathetic rants from a sanctimonious crank. There was nothing the least bit threatening about them.

Scott pushed his hands through his hair and heaved out a breath. He hoped his theory wasn't right, because if it was, Casey was in a lot more trouble than they thought.

He opened up another drawer and pushed aside the legal pad she used for her book outline. Buried underneath the pad were several typewritten notes.

"Dammit, Casey," he muttered. He should have expected this from her.

He pulled out his handkerchief, picked up the letters, and placed them on the bed. There were three of them, each typed on a standard sheet of notebook paper. The first one was a short paragraph declaring the man's love, the second, a badly written poem. Though none of the notes were the least bit threatening, the third one seemed a little more anxious. As if the man thought Casey wanted him to come for her.

Scott cursed under his breath while he carefully wrapped his handkerchief around the papers. With any luck, Casey didn't ruin any of the prints, and he wouldn't have to strangle her himself. He found a paper bag in the kitchen and tucked the notes inside as his phone rang.

"Weller."

"Hey, Scott." Gomez's voice sounded at the other end. "We just got a call about a body. Might be from our guy. LeBlanc and I are heading there now."

"Where?" He waited as Gomez gave him the address. "I'm on my way."

He disconnected the call then phoned the patrol car stationed in front of his apartment, giving the officer orders to stay put until he returned. As he rounded the bottom of the stairs, he kicked over the small vase of flowers Casey had gotten the week before. The petals were singed black as if they'd been set on fire. Sprinkled over the soil were several ripped pages from a book.

"Shit."

As he carefully lifted the vase another note fluttered out from underneath. He carefully placed everything into the bag and continued to his jeep.

❧

The Best Western, located off the main highway, was swarming with police and curious onlookers when Scott pulled into the parking lot. Gomez stood outside the room speaking to a small Hispanic woman dressed in a beige housekeeping uniform. Her hands fluttered wildly as she spoke, and she made the sign of the cross with each pause. Gomez spotted him as soon as he reached the top floor. He thanked the woman and dismissed her.

"What do we have?" Scott asked, peering into the room. The coroner stood against the far wall writing in a notebook with a stoic detachment. Two uniformed officers had been assigned to the room to gather the evidence; one was snapping pictures, the other scrutinizing the areas around the bed.

"The room isn't registered to anyone, and according to the manager it was supposed to be vacant. There's no sign of forced entry, but the lock looks like it's been picked." Gomez flipped through his notepad. "Our vic's name is Amanda Ortiz. According to her ID she lives in north Beaumont. We're still trying to contact her family.

"She was found this morning by housekeeping when one of the maids noticed the door was unlocked. The poor woman about had a heart attack. She ran to get the manager then quit right on the spot." He laid his hand on Scott's arm, stopping him from entering the room. "It's pretty messy."

Scott clenched his teeth, bracing himself for the too-familiar stench of death. But no amount of preparation would ever ready him for the violence he found in the room.

Face down in the center of the bed was the nude body of a woman. Her legs were spread out, her arms bent at the elbows with her hands tucked under her. The sheets and pillows were saturated with blood. Spatters stained the walls, and a small pool had formed on the floor. Tattered clothing was strewn around the room as if the garments had been ripped from her body.

Scott pulled on a pair of latex gloves. He stepped to the side of the bed and carefully moved a strand of matted hair to look at the woman's face. His stomach coiled. "Jesus!" he hissed. He turned away to catch his breath. There was nothing left of her face.

"Someone was pretty pissed off," the coroner said. He closed his notebook and tucked it under his arm. "There aren't any defensive wounds so I'm guessing the first strike is what killed her. She has a collection of stab wounds in her chest. Her insides probably look like coleslaw. The mess to her face was after death, and I'm assuming because her killer was very angry. The cuts are deep and jagged, like he lost control."

"Was she raped?"

"She definitely had sex, but there's no tearing so it's hard to say. I'll have to wait until I get her on the table to give you anything conclusive."

"Thanks. And I'll need the tox screen as soon as possible." He stepped out of the room, inhaling a deep breath of the humid air outside. He'd seen a lot of bodies in his career but nothing like the mess in that room.

The parking lot had filled with more spectators and a couple of news vans. Several cameras zeroed in on them. He turned his back to them. "Any witnesses?" he asked Gomez.

"Not so far. The rooms on both sides were empty. The guests downstairs checked out a few hours ago—a family of five on their way to San Antonio. Manager said they didn't complain about anything, but we have their contact info and San Antonio P.D. is going to talk to them." He hesitated as if preparing himself to say something he didn't want to say. "There's one more thing."

Scott braced at the grim tone in his friend's voice. His gaze dropped to the piece of paper Gomez held out. For a brief second his heart stopped. On the page was a photo copy of the woman's ID.

She looked a lot like Casey.

CHAPTER TWENTY

Scott's apartment was located on the bottom floor of a two-story unit near downtown Rosehill. It consisted of one large room which fed into a small kitchenette and one bedroom barely large enough to house the queen-sized, wrought iron bed. The carpet on the floor was faded and worn, and he'd tried to dress it up with various throw rugs. A black leather sofa and love seat were placed in the center of the living room, taking up most of the space. A wooden chest, much like a footlocker, filled in as a coffee table.

On the plain white walls were various police citations and commendations in oak frames. A United States flag, encased in a mahogany triangle frame, sat atop a small shelf between two photographs of uniformed police officers. The only plant in the room was a large fern in a terra cotta vase shoved in the corner next to a bay window.

Arms locked across her chest, Casey paced the meager space of the living room like a panther in a cage. She'd been locked up in the cramped apartment for three days and was beginning to understand the term cabin fever.

The first couple of days hadn't bothered her so much since she'd used the time alone to snoop around Scott's apartment, hoping to learn a little more about him. If he thought he could lock her up there and not expect her to snoop then he had another think coming. She was a writer after all and research was part of the job. However, she made sure to put everything back exactly as she found it. She'd researched enough law enforcement personnel to know they would see the telltale signs of someone looking through their things.

She'd found his yearbook tucked in the corner of his closet along with a small shoe box of family photos. Even as a teenager he'd had that lazy, self-confident and sexy smile. The pages of his yearbook were covered with enamored love notes from most of the female students in his class, and nearly all had been signed with cutesy little hearts.

Casey shoved her hands in her pockets. To her annoyance she didn't find much else of Scott in his apartment. He was either very private or very good at hiding the pieces of himself.

"But he sure is nosy when it comes to my life," she muttered.

She stopped her pacing and glanced at her laptop sitting untouched on the coffee table. She hadn't been able to write since bringing it from the beach house. The writer's block had come down like a six-inch thick steel wall crushing any and all ideas for the manuscript she'd been working on. She felt frustrated, irritated and in desperate need of a cigarette. She hadn't smoked in over three days because in her rush to pack she forgot to grab them. Plus, Scott had made a point to tell her he didn't allow anyone to smoke in his apartment. She'd planned to quit anyway and had even been weaning herself from them since leaving New York. But all that was beside the point. Who the hell did Scott Weller think he was to tell her what she could and could not do?

She stalked to the stereo on the built-in bookshelf and turned it on. George Strait filtered through the large speakers, singing about his Exes in Texas. Appropriate, she thought sourly. She quickly turned the knob, grimacing at the high-pitched squeal of Dolly Parton. She hissed a string of curses, twisting the dial roughly, tuning in and out various country stations.

Scott walked into his apartment carrying a plain brown shopping bag. He stopped short and glared at her. "You're going to break that."

"Don't you people listen to real music around here?" Casey snapped as she continued to twist the knob. Songs and tunes jumbled together in a montage of high frequency static.

Scott set the bag on the kitchen counter and moved behind her to push a button on the receiver. Aerosmith screamed through the speakers.

"Better?" he said.

"No, it's not better!" Casey spun around, the anger a fierce spark in her eyes. "I've been locked up in this dump for three days. I want to get out of here."

Scott squared his shoulders as he returned to the kitchen. His place might be small, but it wasn't a dump. "That's not a good idea right now," he said removing small cartons of Chinese food from the bags.

"Why not?" Casey moved in behind him when he turned to get plates. "You can't keep me here like a prisoner while you and that psycho get to run around free."

Scott struggled to hold his temper as he reached into the cupboard. He'd been at the police station for the last eight hours with Gomez and LeBlanc, buried under paperwork, trying to find a substantial lead in Casey's attack. At the moment, his mood wasn't any better than hers.

So far, they hadn't been able to find anything on the blood from the deck railing and only Casey's prints had been on the wine bottle. No prints turned up on the notes from her nightstand or the note he'd found with the dead flowers. And that note wasn't one of undying love but a threat that read, *I warned you.* It was an idle threat, but a threat nonetheless. And now, they had another body, which they weren't even sure was a part of the investigation at hand.

"That's exactly the reason you aren't leaving," he said through clenched teeth. He thought he had been doing her a favor by giving her the privacy she'd fought for since their first meeting. He also needed a little time away from her himself. It hadn't been easy sleeping on his pullout sofa, knowing she was in the next room. His room. His bed. "We don't have any leads as to who this guy is or why he wants to kill you. And until we do, you're not going to leave this house." He set the plates on the counter with a snap. It was an old argument that he had grown weary of, but his frustration and anger had put him in just the right mood for a fight.

"You can't tell me what to do. If I want to leave, I will," Casey snapped.

She turned on her heel to storm from the room. Scott grabbed her arm. To his surprise her fisted hand came up and swung around. He managed to dodge the blow before it connected dead on with his nose. With a snarl he latched onto her wrists and pinned her against the wall.

"Better watch it, darlin'," he said in a tight voice. "You come out swinging, I'm liable to hit back."

A flicker of reluctance crossed her face before she lifted her chin and stared at him. "I'm hardly afraid of you," she countered.

Beneath his grip her pulse hammered. He couldn't tell if the look in her eyes was in defiance or a dare, but it made his blood rage. The longing he'd worked hard to control rose to the surface like a geyser. She wasn't his type any more than he was hers, but that didn't seem to matter just now. He lowered his eyes to her full, sexy mouth. All the warning bells sounded in his head. He chose to ignore them.

"Maybe you should be," he murmured before he crushed his mouth to hers.

The low growl in Scott's voice sent a ripple of excitement through Casey's body, which both surprised and terrified her. She'd always considered herself a careful person when it came to men, which was why she rarely kept one around. But she didn't want to be careful now. She tasted Scott's frustration as acutely as her own. Need built like a fire ready to consume her.

What the hell. She leaned in and welcomed his kiss with an urgency of her own.

Scott let go of her arms when she pressed against him. His hands came up to tangle in her hair, gathering her closer as desire built to an ache inside him. It took every ounce of strength he had to pull back and gather his breath. "I've waited a long time to do that."

"I think I have, too," Casey said, her breath as labored as his.

Scott smiled. "I'm going to have to do it again."

"Yes, definitely." She gripped his shirt and yanked him against her.

Scott seized her mouth with the hunger of a starving man, his need to consume excruciating and near impossible to satisfy. His heart hammered. The air thickened his lungs. He moved his hands over her body, searching for somewhere to hold on to. She was destroying him with her taste, casting an intoxicating spell that threatened to overpower him.

"I want you, Casey," he said as he moved anxiously to her neck. "God, I want you so bad I can't breathe."

"Yes."

Her breathy whisper kicked his libido into overdrive. He lifted her up, allowing her to wrap her legs around his waist, and carried her to the bedroom. He stopped when he reached the side of the bed.

Casey gripped his shoulder. "What? What's wrong?"

Scott flashed a smile and set her down to stand beside the bed. "Nothing. I just want to enjoy this." He moved his hands to the buttons of her blouse and slowly unfastened them. "It's been keeping me awake at night wondering what you look like under all these fancy shirts you wear."

He peeled the shirt away, roaming his gaze over her golden tan flesh. She was a vision of soft curves and sculpted angles. The air backed up in his lungs and every muscle in his body tightened. He was definitely going to burn this into his memory.

"Oh yeah, much better than my imagination," he murmured on a slow breath.

He scooped her from the floor and placed her in the center of the bed. He slid his fingers through her hair, fanning the strands out against the white cotton sheets. The need to touch and take pulsed through his hands, and he had to force himself to move slowly. He'd dreamt about this for far too long. He planned to enjoy every minute of it.

Casey trembled, her body throbbing with anticipation. The desire in Scott's eyes burned through her, turning her blood into a river of fire. She never had a man look at her with such longing. It made her feel more alive than she'd ever felt before.

Scott lowered to kiss her, sliding his hands around her back to unhook her lacy bra. He tossed it aside, gliding kisses along her jaw line to the curve of her neck. He slid his hand over the soft mound of her breast, his thumb brushing over the hardening tip, his shallow breaths falling in sync with her own.

She groaned and curled her fingers into the sheets when he took her in his mouth. His tongue flicked over her tip as he continued the erotic assault on her breast while one hand slid over the curve of her hip to explore her body. A delicious shudder shot through her as his hand slid down the sensitive area of her inner thigh. His teeth scraped her nipple, biting gently as his hand cupped her through the fabric of her slacks, sending her body into exhilarating convulsions.

She had expected a quick, almost passionless jump into bed, but his movements were slow and lazy, his tongue taunting her until she thought she would die from the ache of pleasure. She could only close her eyes and indulge in the euphoric sensations coursing through her.

Scott lingered at her breasts, the pleasure for him as much as Casey. He tasted the subtle scent of jasmine she always wore. It filled him with a passion he never would have believed existed. He rose long enough to strip off his shirt, needing to feel her bare against him. She arched up, pressing against him, her hand sliding around his neck to pull him into a kiss.

He shifted to unfasten her slacks, caressing along the flat of her stomach, down to the smooth skin of her thighs while he guided the pants down. She bowed up with a gasp when he moved his hand between her legs and pressed on her center. He stroked his fingers over the thin lace she wore, the fabric moist and hot. He slipped his hand under the elastic band and gently rubbed the bud of her arousal. Her soft whimper of pleasure made his head spin with delirium.

He nipped her lower lip then traveled down her neck biting kisses into her flesh. Her back arched, as if willing him to take her deeper when he closed his mouth over her breast. He obliged and took the nipple between his teeth savoring the taste of her. She writhed beneath him, urging him to move faster. Too bad for her he planned to take his time.

He traveled the length of her body, using tongue and teeth. Her breath hitched when he reached the cleft between her legs and teased his tongue over the silky fabric she still wore. Easing a finger under the elastic, he stroked the slick bud of her arousal, then slid his finger inside. Her hips curved up. He accepted the invitation and closed his mouth over her. A heavy groan rolled from her chest as he pleasured her with his tongue, the cry nearly pushing him over the edge.

He told himself he would move slowly, but he didn't think he could manage it any longer. He returned to her mouth, crushing his lips against hers. She reached out to fumble for the snap of his jeans. He closed his hand over hers.

"Just a minute," he said. His voice sounded like sandpaper on brick. He rose and stripped off the jeans. His whole body went taut when her hand closed around him, making him harder than he ever imaged.

"Now. I want you now," she said, her voice a husky whisper.

Scott stopped and eased back, cursing under his breath.

"What?" Casey said, with an exasperated look.

"I don't have anything," he said.

The relief on Casey's face was almost comical. "That's okay. I'm on the pill." She stared at him when his brow arched. "You seriously don't want to have that conversation right now, do you?"

Scott grinned and shook his head. "No."

He positioned himself over her to let her guide him in. Her warmth enveloped him, welcoming him home. His muscles quivered as he struggled to keep a slow rhythmic pace. He knew she was close, and he wanted to take the leap with her. He braced above her, one hand scooping up her leg to hook around his arm. A strangled cry escaped her lips as she opened up to him. Every nerve in his body screamed with pleasure.

"Open your eyes, Casey," he said. "Look at me."

Casey's eyes fluttered open and met his dark gaze. Her hands slid down to grip his arms. "Now!"

The cry caught in her throat when she rounded up to meet him. The release was explosive, their bodies shuddering as Scott followed her over and reclaimed her mouth.

Casey closed her eyes and savored the tremors in her body from her orgasm. So, that's what it felt like? She thought she knew what great sex was, she wrote about it enough in her books. But she never dreamed—even with her very animated imagination—that she would ever experience those unobtainable crests she put on paper. With a cat-like purr, she smiled and stretched her arms over her head. Her body had never felt so relaxed, so sated. Her impressions of Scott were right. He was a very attentive lover.

She floated her hands down to rest on his back and grazed her nails down his shoulders, following a path down to his waist. She marveled in the feel of his skin and the thickness of his muscles.

"I felt that, so I guess I'm not dead," Scott murmured, his head still nuzzled in her neck. "But I think I'm paralyzed."

Casey touched her tongue along his neck then bit him on the shoulder.

"Hey." He pushed up and looked down at her.

"Hallelujah, it's a miracle."

Scott rolled to his side and propped himself up on his elbow to look at her. A wide, satisfied grin curved his lips. "It certainly was," he said. "I think I can honestly say I saw God. Maybe we should fight more often."

"That wasn't a fight, it was more of a disagreement," Casey said, the rush of heat warming her face. She reached for the blanket to cover herself, suddenly feeling awkward lying naked beside him. Scott held tight to the blanket, a flicker of amusement in his eyes. She pressed her lips together, biting back a sigh. She'd better face this sudden turn of events head on if she wanted to stay in control.

"Look, Scott, we both know this only happened because we were feeling a little frustrated and, yes, a bit angry. I don't make it a habit to jump into bed with just anyone. We're adults here and I think we have the makings of a friendship. And I won't deny I've been attracted to you." She hated that she sounded prim, but she had to make a point. It would only make things more complicated if they tried to make the situation more than it was. She wouldn't risk her heart or her life on a man. "This was a result of that attraction as well as a way to release all the pent-up emotions we've been feeling for the past week," she said.

Scott grinned, pulling at the blanket again. "Been thinking about that long?"

She lifted her chin with an indignant frown. "I just want to make sure we both agree to the rules, that's all. Sex is a very natural thing among consenting adults. We're hardly each other's type after all, so there's no reason to make this more than it is. Especially if we decide to—"

"Release more of our pent-up emotions?" Scott answered for her.

Casey jerked on the blanket and tried to keep her dignity. "Don't make fun of me."

"Sorry, I've just never had a woman actually tell me in so many words that she only wanted me for my body."

Casey tried not to smile at the foolishness of her words. "And do you have a problem with that?"

Scott rolled her on top of him, his smile widening. "Not in this lifetime," he said before pulling her into a kiss.

Chapter Twenty-one

Alejandro let himself into the beach house and looked around the tidy living room. It had been cleaned two days earlier. He saw the workers come and go. He'd waited on the beach to see if Cassandra would return. She had to be expecting him. He'd sent her enough messages. But the house stayed empty.

Probably with that cop, he thought with disgust. He sniffed, wiping his nose on his sleeve. The hit he took earlier was starting to wear off. Worthless shit. He should have known that fucking whore he took it from wouldn't carry the good stuff. Now he was going to have to go out and buy his own. And, the damn shit was expensive. He scanned the cabin, eyeing the stereo on the wall. Not that it mattered anymore. He had a rich daughter now. And according to the good book, daughters must honor their fathers. As her father, it was his job to make sure Cassandra didn't stray from that commandment again.

He wandered to the bar and searched the cabinets, hissing out a disgusted breath when he found them empty. He spotted the paperback book on the corner of the bar and grabbed it, his lip curling into a snarl when he read the cover. *Casey Martinez.*

"Fucking whore. You think you're too good for my name? I should have put you in your place a long time ago." He wiped his mouth with the back of his hand and tossed the book into the garbage can.

He wandered into the bedroom, stopping to stare at the queen-sized bed. He pictured his daughter there, her legs spread for the man who'd climbed into her window a few nights ago. He'd watched from the marsh, heard the scream and saw the man jump from the deck. Just like a whore to cry rape when the man gets a little rough.

He turned away from the bed and continued to check out the room. He found another book on the dresser. Casey's smile stared up at him from the back cover, sending a flutter to his stomach reserved for the *putas* he found in Houston. He grabbed the book and turned it over to look at the title. *Embittered Salvation*. Her first book. He'd found a copy in the prison library one night when he'd been assigned to clean the room. He had recognized her face immediately and knew it was a sign. One he knew he shouldn't ignore.

He tucked the book in the waist of his pants and stepped to the mini refrigerator by the bed. His lips spread into a smile when he found the bottle of wine. Maybe his daughter *was* expecting him.

He pulled out the bottle and lifted it up like a sacrament. "The blood of Christ." He pulled out the cork and took a deep drink.

He had all his signs now. It wasn't too late to show his daughter the way to salvation. Only he could do it. It was his duty. He was still her father, after all.

❧

Agent Simms thumbed through the paperback book then tossed it on his desk and pressed his fingers over his eyes. It was the fifth book he'd read by Casey Martinez in the past week, and he still wasn't any closer to tying her work in with their serial killer.

"Still think this has to do with what she writes?" Hawthorne stepped into the office and passed Simms one of the cups of coffee he carried.

"Hell, I don't know." Simms rubbed his hands over his face, exhaling a heavy sigh. "But it's definitely about her. Otherwise, why leave the books and why leave them so damaged?"

"And why disfigure the girls after killing them?" Hawthorne took a seat next to the desk. "You know, maybe we should be looking at this another way."

"What do you mean?"

"These murders are crimes of passion. The rape. The ripped up books. Whoever is killing these women, disfiguring them, has to be doing so out of jealousy. Maybe we should start looking at her competition."

"What, you think maybe Stephen King wants to kill her because she bumped him off the bestseller's list?" Simms said.

"I'm not talking about someone that big. I'm thinking more in the lines of someone who hasn't quite made it as far. Besides, King is a man and doesn't write romance."

Simms shifted in his seat, considering the thought. "You're thinking a woman did this?"

"It's not out of the realm of possibilities. We've had woman serial killers before. And let's face it…there *are* ways for a woman to rape another woman."

Simms shook his head before the image planted itself in his mind. "Okay, so assuming it is a woman, any suggestions on who to look at?"

"Well, Ms. Martinez belongs to a romance writer's organization. Unfortunately, they have over eight thousand members which will make it difficult to narrow down. But, I called the president of the group, and she's going to go through their membership and see if there's anything that might help. She did mention something though."

"What?"

"Seems about three years ago, Ms. Martinez was in a lawsuit with another writer over plagiarism."

"Plagiarism?"

"The woman's name is Camella Stamper. She said Ms. Martinez stole her book after they both attended an online workshop. There was no proof to the claim, and Ms. Martinez countersued for libel. The woman ended up settling, but not before she tried to ruin Ms. Martinez's career with bad reviews."

"Who knew romance writing could be so cut-throat," Simms said. He pressed his fingers to the bridge of his nose, trying to force back the headache starting to brew. He'd had too much coffee and too little sleep since he began working on the Paperback Murder case. "As disturbing as it is, let's check with the coroner and see if she can discern between real and fake before we bring Ms. Stamper in."

"Excuse me, Agent Simms?" A young woman stepped into the room holding out a thin sheet of paper. "This fax just came in."

Hawthorne stepped forward to take the paper, dismissing the woman with a nod. He scanned the fax then looked up. "Shit! He's on the move again."

Simms gripped the cup of coffee he forgot he held and looked at the fax in his partner's hand. "Where?"

"Texas," he said, passing him the fax. "Rosehill Police Department ran a blood sample that matched up with the DNA on the hair."

"Rosehill?" Simms furrowed his brow trying to wrap his mind around the familiarity of the town's name. His eyes widened when recognition set in. "Ms. Martinez. The son of a bitch found her!" He set the cup down hard on his desk. Coffee spilled out over his blotter but he ignored it. "Find out where the hell Rosehill is, then contact the local bureau and put them on alert. Let them know I'm heading to Texas."

Hawthorne nodded and rushed from the room.

Simms grabbed the phone off his desk and prepared to make the arrangements for his trip. If their guy stayed on his usual pattern, it meant they had less than two weeks left before he struck again. With any luck they would have him before that victim was Ms. Martinez.

cᴀᴏ

Casey lay propped up on her elbow, her fingers tracing over the smoothness of Scott's skin. *He really does have an incredible body.* She stole a peek at his face. His eyes were closed, his breathing steady. A shimmer of excitement coursed through her as she thought about how he'd made love to her throughout the night. He certainly had stamina. She smiled wondering how difficult it would be to wake him for another round.

It was a strange kind of excitement to lie in a man's arms and think about sex first thing in the morning. She never thought she'd enjoy having such a satisfying physical relationship. In her meager experience, the excitement of sex never lasted more than a couple of days. She didn't even mind anymore that she was locked up in his small apartment.

They'd become closer over the last two nights, almost like real friends, which was another surprise to her. Aside from Jo and Tony, she'd never had any real friends.

She grazed her hand over the flat of his stomach and swirled her fingers through the dusting of hair around his navel. She worked her hand up, exploring the toned muscles of his chest. Her hand touched the scar and stopped. Scott's hand came up and closed over hers. She snatched her hand away. "I'm sorry, I didn't mean—"

Scott kissed her to stop her words then smiled. "Good morning."

"Good morning," she said, returning his smile. She looked at the scar again and cautiously ran her finger down the healed skin. "This looks pretty ugly."

"Yeah, well...I survived."

She looked up when he shrugged. "Just part of the job?"

"I knew what I was signing on for," he answered. He shifted to his side, propping up on his elbow to face her. "Just like my father and grandfather each knew." He slid his hand over her shoulder, following the length of her arm down to the curve of her hip. The heat of her skin radiated through the tips of his fingers.

"Are they still on the force?"

"No. They were both killed in the line of duty."

"I'm sorry," she said. "I know how hard that must have been for you."

Scott had intended to leave the conversation at that but the concern in her eyes stopped him. He knew she had searched through his apartment the first couple of days she was there. He'd seen the subtle signs and her conscientious attempts to return everything to its proper place. It had annoyed him at first, even though he knew she wouldn't find anything. He'd always been a private person and never discussed his personal life with anyone, especially someone he was dating. It helped keep the relationship less complicated. Any personal items he had were kept in a storage locker in his mother's attic. But it felt different with Casey. There was something about her that made him want to share that part of himself with her.

"It was a long time ago," he said. "I barely remember my grandfather. I was ten when my father died. He was shot during a so-called peaceful protest. My father took the bullet meant for the main speaker, but he managed to tag the shooter before he went down." He paused, swallowing the anger that always came with that memory. "My mother had family in Dallas so we moved there for a while."

"What brought you to Rosehill?" she asked.

"Burying my father was the hardest thing my mother ever had to do. But she was a strong woman and she managed to get through it." He remembered her fierce determination to keep their life as normal as possible. His mother worked two jobs to make ends meet and never once complained. He had a profound respect for her no person could ever measure up to.

"She wasn't too happy when I joined the force," he continued. "So instead of putting her through that worry, I transferred to Rosehill where it was less likely I'd be killed in the line of duty." He saw Casey's gaze return to his scar and sighed. "I guess if it's going to happen, it's going to happen."

"Fate?"

He sent her a noncommittal shrug and continued to skim his hands along her body as if she were a priceless gift.

Casey thought about his words. She'd never believed in fate. She preferred to think a person made their own life decisions and there was no predetermined path mapped out for them. Because if it were true, then God was in desperate need of a GPS.

"So, what about you? What sent you running to New York?" he asked.

"I didn't run," Casey said. She heard the irritation in her voice and paused to gather her thoughts. It was a simple question and deserved a simple answer. She rolled onto her back, settling into the comfort of the bed and his lazy strokes. "I wanted a better life and I didn't see that happening here."

"But you were engaged to Tony. What happened?"

Casey looked up at him and narrowed her eyes. There was something about the tone of his voice that made her bristle. "Is this an interrogation, Detective?"

"Just a simple question," he said, continuing his soft caresses as if knowing it would put her at ease. "I can't imagine Tony breaking your engagement. I mean, he seemed really happy to see you at the festival the other night."

Casey thought about the embrace Tony had given her. It *had* been a little more intimate than she'd expected.

"I've known Tony since I was ten. He and Alex were the best of friends all through high school. He was like part of the family," she said. "It seemed natural that we would start dating. It was almost like it was expected."

Scott stopped his soft strokes and looked at her. "But you didn't want to date him?"

"No, it wasn't like that. I really liked Tony. He was a great guy and actually the first man to ever show any kind of interest in me. My grandmother didn't allow me to date, much less leave the house. She didn't like the idea of Tony coming around either, but since he and Alex were friends she tolerated him. Tony knew how she felt about him so I think he made a point to hang around, just to irritate her," she said with short laugh. "Anyway, Tony was always very nice and very attentive, so he kind of became my boyfriend. And since we had something in common, I thought, 'okay ...he's my boyfriend.'"

"What did you have in common?" Scott asked.

"We both lost our mothers at a young age," Casey said. "The only difference was Tony's mom walked out on him and his father, whereas my mother didn't. Tony always kept open the hope that she'd return one day. While I knew I'd never see my mother again."

"Not really a basis for a relationship," Scott said.

"I know. And deep down Tony knew, too. But we were both very lonely people. When he asked me to marry him, I jumped at it simply as a way to escape my grandmother's house." Though they had both moved on with their lives, she still felt guilty for leading him on.

"But you didn't marry," Scott prompted.

"No, we didn't. I realized it wouldn't have worked and that I was only using him. So instead of going through with the wedding, I packed my bags and headed to New York to find a new life for myself. And I never looked back." She shifted in the bed, fixing her eyes on the ceiling. A few weeks after she left, she'd taken the coward's way out and phoned Tony to let him know she wasn't coming back. She could still hear the pain in his voice as he begged her to come home and the relieved pleasure when she'd lied and said she would.

"Sometimes I wonder if it was all worth it," she said under her breath. She sighed, easing the breath out slowly. *Closure.* She would never find it with Tony unless she faced him, and she wasn't sure when she would be ready to do that again.

The cell phone vibrated on the end table. Scott reached behind him to pick it up.

"Weller. Yes, sir. Be right there." He hung up and placed the phone back on the table. "The captain wants to see us."

"Us?" Casey sat up. "Did they catch the guy?"

"They brought someone in. He wants to see if you can ID him. You don't have to do this if you don't want to."

"I want to. Give me ten minutes." She pushed off the bed and rushed to the bathroom.

✦

The police station was larger than Casey expected and cleaner than most of the ones she'd been to. The squad room was located on the third floor and made up of one large room about the size of a high school gymnasium. The large picture frame windows were covered with wide vinyl blinds which were open to let in the late morning sun. A line of metal desks were arranged like a horseshoe in the center of the room. Most of the seats were occupied by uniformed officers who glanced up, acknowledging Scott when he walked in.

He walked her toward the back of the room and down an extended hallway. They stopped in front of a wooden door, and Scott knocked before he led her inside.

It was a moderate-sized office with dark paneling and a wide picture window overlooking the main street. Several bookshelves and metal file cabinets lined one wall while citations and framed photos lined another.

This must be where Scott gets his decorating tips.

A large man stepped from behind the desk, extending his hand to Casey. "Ms. Martinez. I'm Captain Knowles. We met the other night."

"Yes. I remember," she said taking his hand. She spotted Agent Simms standing at the back of the room when Scott closed the door. "Agent Simms? I didn't know you were in town."

"I've actually just arrived," he said, sending her a warm smile. His expression sobered. "I heard about your incident. Are you okay?"

"Yes. I'm fine. Thank you."

Captain Knowles returned to his desk and waved his hand toward Scott. "Agent Simms, this is Detective Scott Weller. He's lead on this case and is assigned to keep watch over Ms. Martinez."

Agent Simms raked his gaze over Scott before he extended his hand. "Detective Weller."

Scott accepted the brief handshake but didn't bother to hide his contempt. "Agent Simms. To what do we owe the honor?"

"DNA," the agent said with a thin smile. "The blood you ran matched up with a hair we found on our last victim. Our man is in town."

He spoke with a manner of arrogance that Scott found more amusing than annoying. He returned the man's smile and crossed his hands over his chest. "Could have saved you a trip since we already knew that. We have another victim."

"What? You didn't tell me that," Casey said.

"You didn't need to know." Scott spared her a glance and turned his attention back to the agent. "It was about thirty miles out of town. It came across the wire a few days ago. Looks like the same MO, but a little more frenzied. The knife wounds on the victim appear to be the same as the ones found on your last vic in New York, and I wouldn't be surprised if it were the same knife that turned my tire into confetti." He felt Casey's glare, but continued to ignore it.

"Your tire?" Simms glanced at Casey's angry reaction but kept his face sober and pinned his eyes on Scott. Scott returned the knowing look with his own arrogant smile.

"We moved Ms. Martinez to a secured location and added an extra patrol car to the beach just in case the guy was still watching there," Captain Knowles said. He pushed a file with Casey's name typed on the tab toward the agent and sat down.

Simms picked up the file and flipped through the report. "Any leads on the latest victim?"

"Not yet," the captain said. "But we've just picked up someone lurking around the beach house where Ms. Martinez was staying. He's with LeBlanc and Gomez in interrogation."

"I want to see him," Casey said, sending Scott a cutting look.

The captain nodded. "Detective Weller will take you."

Scott opened the door to a small dimly lit room and stepped back to let Casey in. It was the size of a walk-in closet and smelled of stale coffee. The walls were painted dull gray and there was a large pane-glass window in the center. On the other side of the glass, hunched over the wood table, sat an elderly man. He was smoking a cigarette, pulling from the filter as if it was his lifeline. His hand flexed open and closed on the table while his leg bounced nervously underneath. He wore dark slacks and a light-blue cotton shirt. His hair was thick and silver and he had a neatly trimmed mustache of the same color. He looked pale, nearly ashen in color, the skin under his eyes sagging with age.

Officers Gomez and LeBlanc were in the room with him. Gomez was sitting on the corner of the table, while LeBlanc leaned against the wall. Gomez appeared to be asking the questions. In his hands was a paperback book.

Casey pressed a hand to her stomach. Her face was slightly pale.

Scott turned off the speaker in the room so they couldn't hear the conversation on the other side of the glass. He glanced at Casey, wondering if she would recognize her father sitting in the chair.

Casey swallowed before she spoke but there was a slight tremor in her voice. "Is that him?" she asked. "Is he the one that attacked me?"

The man looked at the mirror and spoke, but they couldn't read his lips. Scott placed his hand on her shoulder. "We don't know just yet. Do you know him?"

Casey stepped closer to the glass to study the man. There was a vague recognition, but nothing she could put her mind to. She'd met a lot of people in her life and Rosehill was a small town. It was likely she'd passed this man in the street or maybe even signed a book for him.

She shook her head and looked at Scott. "No. No, I don't."

Scott tapped on the glass. The detective rose from the table and left the room, followed by his partner. The man sneered at their backs then looked into the mirror as if he could see right through the glass.

Scott cupped his hand under Casey's arm and felt her shudder before he led her out of the room. He gestured her toward the squad room. "I'll be a minute. Why don't you go wait for me at my desk?"

Casey stopped, pulling her arm out of his hold. She narrowed her eyes with an icy glare. "I don't like secrets, Scott. Especially when they're about me."

"Just a minute, okay? Then I'll tell you what you need to know." He kissed her forehead and ushered her toward his desk.

"What's his story?" he asked Gomez as soon as the two detectives stepped to him.

"His name's Alejandro Rivera. Says he's a relative. The guy's a bit jumpy though if you ask me," Gomez said. "Looks like he needs a fix."

"Probably does," Scott said with disgust. He'd read the man's file and knew the kind of candy he preferred. "What was he doing at the beach house?"

"Says he heard Ms. Martinez had been harassed and he wanted to make sure she was okay," LeBlanc answered. "He lives in Houston and works as a stocker at a home improvement store. He has a record, but says he's been clean for the past six years. Claims to have found God while he was in lockup."

"Don't they all," Gomez put in. "The looney keeps spouting Psalms like he's a televangelist. I think he was hoping she'd hear him on the other side of the glass."

"I turned off the monitor," Scott said.

"We're checking with Houston P.D. to make sure he's clean, but right now we've got nothing on him. Did you want to talk to him?" LeBlanc said when Scott glanced toward the room.

"No, that's okay. Hold him as long as you can, though," he said. "See if you can get a DNA sample from his file and run it with what we have on our guy. I'm going to work from home so give me a call on my cell if anything comes up." He turned to leave then stopped with a resigned sigh. "You may want to fill in the Fed. Looks like he's going to be sticking around for a while. But make sure he knows he's here to assist. This is still our case."

"Will do," LeBlanc answered "Oh, and one more thing. A couple of reporters have been staked out at the beach. Word's gotten out about Ms. Martinez's attack and the Feds' involvement in the case. You might want to go out the back before they start migrating here."

The men went back into the interrogation room as Scott made his way back to Casey.

"Well?" Casey asked, rising up from his desk chair.

"Not our guy. Just someone interested in the case." He didn't think it was necessary to let her know who the man was just yet. Since she didn't recognize her father, he figured it was something she'd worked hard to do. And he wasn't going to remind her about a man she wanted to forget.

"What are you going to do with him?" she asked. She turned and caught a glimpse of the man as the detectives ushered him down the hallway.

"We'll hold him as long as we can, see if there are any outstanding warrants." Scott took her hand and turned her toward him. "Let's get out of here before the press show up."

"The press?"

"Somehow, your name has been released. They've been camping out at the beach house waiting for a story. Right now, only a handful of people know you're staying at my place. I'd like to keep it that way."

CHAPTER TWENTY-TWO

Casey remained quiet during the drive back to Scott's apartment. He could tell by the firm set of her jaw that she was upset about something. He wasn't sure if she wanted to talk and he didn't quite know how to ask, so he kept quiet too. She was visibly angry when they reached his front door, but he was too distracted by the white florist's box leaning against the wall.

"What did you mean by *need to know?*" she asked.

"What?" He opened the door to let her inside then pulled out his handkerchief, using it to carefully pick up the box. It was the third flower delivery that week, although the other two had been left at the beach house. Each box was unmarked and contained a charred bouquet of flowers and a type-written note threatening to kill Casey.

He'd checked with the local flower shop after he found the first box lying on the deck. According to the florist the boxes and flowers had been taken from the dumpsters, so there was no point of sale. No one had witnessed the pickups and no prints were found on the envelopes or the floral boxes. He didn't like that the flowers had been delivered to his home. It meant whoever was after Casey now knew she was there.

"At the station you said you'd tell me what I need to know." Casey fisted her hands on her hips, turning to face him. "What gives you the right to decide what I need to know?"

"I'm the detective in charge of this case. I'll decide what information I share with you or anyone else. And what I don't," he answered, passing over her irritation. He carried the box to the kitchen counter and used a letter opener to slowly lift the lid. Inside were several long-stemmed lilies. The battered petals were singed, but not completely burnt, as if someone had set them on fire then immediately stomped them out. He'd managed to keep the delivery of the other flowers from Casey, but now he had no choice but to show her what was delivered. He poured the lilies onto the counter and carefully separated them with the letter opener.

"Why, you arrogant son of a...I am not just anyone!" Casey stalked next to him, more furious that he was ignoring her. She pushed at his shoulder to get his attention. "What you don't seem to understand is that this case is about me and I have just as much right to know what's going on as you do. More, actually."

"And what you don't seem to understand is that this isn't just some foolish fantasy playing out in this guy's head," Scott fumed. He flipped a small piece of paper onto the counter with the words 'burn in Hell' typed on the page. He swept the lilies onto the floor and grabbed her by the shoulders. "It's real. And he's dangerous."

"And I can take care of myself," Casey finished. She slid a look at the note and swallowed hard.

Scott jerked her closer to keep her from looking at the note too long. "Not as long as I'm around," he growled.

"Well, you aren't always going to be around, are you?" Casey snapped. She pushed him back, breaking away from his grip. "This is *my* life, Detective, and I won't allow anyone to run it for me. Especially you."

Scott shoved his hands in his pockets. Her words were like a punch to his gut, but he didn't want to think about why they stung. "I'm not trying to run your life. I'm trying to let you continue to live it," he returned with the same fury in his voice. Although he wasn't sure who he was angry at. He took a calming breath and stepped toward her. "Casey, we don't know who or what we're dealing with. This man has killed thirteen women that we know of in the last five years and now he's fixed his obsession on you." He placed his hands on her shoulders, pinning his gaze firmly on her. "I won't chance having anything happen to you."

"How can anything happen to me when I'm locked away in this apartment?" She pushed away again and stormed to the refrigerator. She snatched a water bottle from inside the door. When she turned back to look at him, her eyes were blazing. "You're treating me like a victim, Scott. And I don't like to be treated like a victim. This bastard has forced me to leave my home. He's locked me away in this apartment. And he has me jumping every time the phone rings. I don't like that, Scott. I don't like to be treated like a helpless female."

Scott saw the fire in her eyes and the fight in her stance. He didn't want to fight with her and he knew if he were in the same position, he would want to know everything about the case as well. "Okay, you're right," he said with a heavy sigh. "You have a right to know what's going on so you can be better prepared for days like today."

Casey watched him with narrowed eyes. "Then do you promise to tell me everything that's going on?"

"I promise to tell you what I can."

"That's not good enough!" She crossed her arms tightly at her chest. "I want to know everything you know. I don't like secrets, and I don't need a knight in shining armor."

"Casey, it's the best I can do right now," he said, trying to keep his building anger in check. He didn't know why the knight-in-shining-armor comment made him mad.

She slammed the unopened water bottle onto the counter. "Then I'll go to Agent Simms! This is his case anyway."

Scott tensed, his teeth clenching tight enough to strain his jaw. "Fine! You do that if you want. He'll tell you even less than I have!" He stormed to the refrigerator and grabbed a beer before slamming the door shut again. The loose bottles inside jangled. *Dammit!*

He gripped the neck of the bottle and took a moment to garner control before he turned back around. "Look, I can promise not to treat you like a victim, but I won't keep you on edge with worry," he said. "When we get a break in the case, then I'll let you know. But until that happens, you're just going to have to trust me."

Casey blew out a resigned sigh and stepped to him. "I do trust you." She laid her hand on his arm. "I wouldn't be here otherwise. And as long as you promise to treat me with that same respect you give your fellow officers, then we won't have a problem."

"I have nothing but respect for you," he said softly. He took her hand and pressed a kiss on her palm. "And from now on, what I know about this case, you will know." He saw the acceptance in her eyes and thought about her father. He still didn't think it was necessary to tell her who the suspect at the station was, since it was likely Alejandro Rivera wasn't the man they were after. He wasn't keeping a secret. He was only protecting her. Of course she probably wouldn't see it that way. *That'll just have to be a fight for another day.*

With a boyish grin he slid his arm around her waist and pulled her against him. "So, are you still mad at me?"

Casey's lips twitched as she bit back a smile. "I'm still a little annoyed, yes."

"A little is good." He brushed his mouth over hers with a gentle kiss. "But, maybe I can make it up to you. I've heard make-up sex is amazing."

Casey sent him a wry smile. "You've heard that, huh? Well, it's an awful lot to make up. I was pretty angry."

"Yeah, I noticed." He moved his kiss to the curve of her neck and felt her pulse jump. "And you're very sexy when you're angry." His hands moved to the buttons on her blouse and slowly unfastened each one.

"Does that line work often?" she asked, tilting her head to give him easier access.

He slid the shirt off and pressed a kiss to her shoulder, his hand skimming down to cup her breast. "You tell me." He lowered and twirled his tongue over the tip of her breast.

"Works for me," she said with a heavy sigh.

Scott returned to her mouth, circling his arms around her to lift her from the floor. He carried her to the sofa, deepening the kiss as he skillfully removed her slacks.

Casey lay back, resting her hands over her head as Scott explored her body. He took her nipple between his teeth, sucking softly until he felt her pulse quicken. His hand moved between her legs to stroke her center and felt her muscles quiver.

"You are definitely good at make-up sex," she said with a satisfied moan.

Scott continued his sultry journey, searing a path down her stomach, exploring the silky bronze flesh with his tongue. Passion radiated from the soft core of her body. Her taste was even more intoxicating than the first time they'd made love. His heart pounded in his chest as he stroked his fingers between her legs, awed by her wet response to his touch.

"God, you're incredible," he murmured before he closed his mouth over her with a passionate kiss.

Casey's fingers gripped the cushions, her body arching up as he pleasured her with his tongue. He eased a finger inside and heard her sharp intake of breath. A strangled cry escaped her throat and her body convulsed with the orgasm.

Scott rose and stripped off his clothes with a satisfied grin. "That's just one. Let's make it two." He scooped her up and lowered her on top of him, a heavy groan rolling from his chest as she closed around him.

❧

His anger rose as he watched them through the tinted windows on his truck. She betrayed him! She gave herself to another when she should have been saving herself for him. It was like a knife in his gut to see her straddle Scott.

Her back arched. The smile of pleasure on her lips. Her body glowing with passion. She lowered her head to take his mouth, her long, dark hair falling in a wavy curtain around her face.

"Whore!" He fisted his hand in his lap, his heart beating wildly in his chest. It couldn't be true! It was a trick. Yes, his mind was only playing a trick. Maybe if he closed his eyes it would be over. But she was so beautiful, he couldn't stop watching. It was as if she had hypnotized him, forcing him to see the powers she held.

His arousal grew with the heat of his anger. He unsnapped his jeans to free the pressure. It should be him underneath her glorious body. He should be the one touching and tasting her every inch.

His breath quickened when Casey arched again. He watched Scott's hands close over her breasts as she bowed back, her fingers combing through her hair in a sultry pose.

No! She belonged to him! He'd waited too long to lose her now. They were meant to be together. She promised him!

He struggled to control his breathing and grabbed the book lying in the seat next to him. Her picture smiled back at him, the warmth of it filling him.

She would be his again, just as he'd planned.

He pressed his mouth to the photo on the back and shuddered in release. In his mind's eye, Casey surrendered herself to him.

Chapter Twenty-three

Scott spotted Agent Simms at his desk the minute he entered the police station. "This is my desk. You're set up in the back conference room." He pulled open a drawer and took out a legal pad.

"I didn't think you'd need it while you're staying with Ms. Martinez," The agent replied. "Where is she, away?"

"At the apartment. I have a car on her." Scott motioned to Detectives Gomez and LeBlanc who were sitting at their own desks, to follow them.

They entered the conference room, each taking a seat at the eight foot table in the center of the room, while Agent Simms took his spot at the front of the room. Stacked along the wall were several file boxes, each marked with a victim's name and case number. A map mounted to the wall contained different colored pushpins marking several states.

"I had copies of the files sent. Since we're working together, I thought I should catch you up on where we are right now," Simms said. He stepped to the map and used his pen as a pointer. "Each of these pins marks where a body had been found. These red pins are victims who lived in the states where Ms. Martinez set her books. The white represent the states where Ms. Martinez lived. The green are places she never lived or set a book, but she visited during her book tours or a conference."

"So you're certain she's your connection to the murders, then?" LeBlanc asked.

"As certain as we can be. These murders have been personal," Agent Simms said. "These women aren't killed because of who they are or what they do. They're killed because of who they look like. The killer is definitely fixated on Ms. Martinez. We just haven't figured out why."

"Okay, so let's say this guy has been seeking her out at these places and killing the women because he thinks they're her," Gomez said. "How did he know Ms. Martinez would be there?"

"Her website. It lists her appearances."

"That's one relentless son of a bitch," Gomez said.

Scott moved to the map to study the pins. Nine states in five years. Two murders a year, which means two trips a year for their killer.

"This guy has to have some major frequent flyer miles. He's doing an awful lot of traveling. Even on my salary I can't afford two out of state trips a year. Maybe we should check with the airlines or train stations. He has to be making quick trips in order to keep his everyday life normal." He turned around to look at the agent. "Is there any way to get a passenger list from the airlines for the dates of the murders?"

Agent Simms raised his brow. "Maybe not all of them, but it's worth a try. I'll get my people on it." He offered Scott an appreciative nod then picked up a box from the floor and proceeded to fill them in on the rest of the investigation.

❦

Casey sat at the small kitchen table, tapping the keys on her laptop. She'd risen just before sunrise and pulled on one of Scott's shirts and snuck out of the bedroom so as not to wake him. She hadn't been able to write since she'd moved into his apartment. The words she'd lived on for the past seven years of her life were lost to her. Until recently, she thought with a smile. Scott sure knew how to get rid of writer's block.

"You're up early," he said as he stepped from the bedroom. He wore a pair of jeans and a Rosehill P.D. T-shirt. His hair was wet and he smelled sinfully of soap.

"I wanted to work on my book," she said with a shrug.

He stepped behind her, laying his hands on her shoulders. "Anything I can do to help?" he asked, leaning over to kiss her neck.

The soft touch of his lips made her heart stutter and sent a wave of desire shimmering to her stomach. She stood and turned to wrap her arms around his neck.

"Mmm, you know, I am writing a scene you might be able to help me research," she said with a slow smile. "You see, research is an important element in writing. There's so much you need to learn before you work your plot or bring your characters together."

She pressed a kiss along his neck and shoulder, nipping softly. His scent absorbed into her, warming her blood. "The hows and whys. Lots of hows," she continued, speaking as if she were a teacher lecturing a student.

Scott stood transfixed, hypnotized by the seductive flow of her voice. He concentrated on breathing as she planted kisses along his jaw and down to his neck. Her long, elegant fingers grazed over his shoulders, her mouth following the movement and sending blazing sparks through him.

Casey continued her journey over his chest, skimming her hands over the rippled muscles of his stomach. She stopped to rest at the clasp of his jeans, smiling when he tensed. "After all," she continued, watching him through her lowered lashes. "You want to make sure all the information you have is correct so it's believable to the reader. They need to be able to see and feel as you do."

She slipped her hands into the front of his jeans and found him hard and ready for her. She looked at him, a pleased smile curving her lips. "So, sometimes you have to search really hard to make sure you have just the right amount of information and, of course, that you're using said information correctly."

Scott swallowed against the knot in his throat as Casey slid down his body and freed him from the jeans. Every muscle in his body tensed and locked when she closed her mouth over him. Passion surged through him, a tempest boiling over as she worked tongue and teeth along his shaft. He drew in a breath as a hot ache settled in his chest. His heart pounded with an explosive rush of pleasure.

He braced his hand on the table as he sought to find his balance in the storm of sensations coursing through him. He'd never had a woman give him as much or take him as far as Casey did.

Afraid his legs would buckle if he didn't stop her soon, he gripped her shoulders and pulled her up and set her on the table. "Oh, I'm real good at research," he said.

"I was hoping you were," she said before he ravaged her mouth.

Scott pushed his hands roughly over her thighs, snaking them under the shirt to claim her bare breasts. He'd only whet his appetite before, now his hunger for her was stronger and much more demanding. He wrapped her hair around his fist, pulling her head back and attacking her neck with fanatic urgency. With less grace and more impatience, he stripped off her shirt and hungrily took her breasts. He was nearly desperate to taste, to devour every inch of her luscious skin. It was as if he was a starving man and she was his nourishment.

Using his teeth and tongue along her rosy crests, he suckled and nipped until her gasps became more labored. When he could no longer control his own breathing, he grasped her legs and spread them apart. His blood raged, ringing in his ears.

"Let go for me, Cassandra," he said in a rough voice. "I want all of you." He gripped her hips, pulling her forward and entering her with one impatient thrust.

Casey groaned, her body going liquid at his touch. She locked her fingers onto his shoulders and wrapped her legs around his waist to pull him deeper inside. Her nails bored into his skin, her breath pumping in ragged gasps as if she were holding on for dear life.

Scott lifted her from the table assaulting her mouth, absorbing her husky groans as she surrendered her body to him. He'd been with a lot of women over the years and always walked away knowing their time together had been pleasurable. He was afraid he wouldn't be able to walk away this time.

I want all of you.

The finality of his words clung to his mind as he let go and filled her. The realization that he had waited all his life for Casey slammed into him and left him more than staggered.

Scott sat on the sofa looking through the police file on Casey's assault. He'd managed to talk her into a nap after lunch, but he'd been unable to sleep or relax since he and Casey had made love on his kitchen table. His blood warmed when he glanced at the small oak set.

He was in love with her. What the hell was he supposed to do about that?

His attention shifted to the file in his lap and the picture of their last victim, Amanda Ortiz. He would do the only thing he could do. Find the son of a bitch who was after her and give Casey her life back.

A life that wouldn't include him.

He'd always known she would return to New York once the case was closed. It was where her life was. Where she really belonged. He had no right to want more.

He rubbed his hand over his face and slapped the file closed. But he did want more, dammit. For the first time in his life he wanted more.

His phone chimed, jolting him from his reverie. "Yeah?"

"Hey Scott," Gomez said. "We just got the DNA back on Rivera. It wasn't a match."

"Yeah, I didn't think it would be. Was there anything on him from Houston?"

"He's wanted for questioning in an assault with a hooker and he's in violation of his parole. He isn't even supposed to be anywhere near town."

"Great. Ship him out."

"Already done."

"Good. Anything else?"

"Well, we've narrowed the list of names for sex offenders. We're down to two hundred."

"Well, that's something," Scott murmured. He pinched the bridge of his nose and sighed. "Keep me posted." He disconnected the call and pulled out the photo again. A knot twisted in his stomach. Amanda Ortiz's murder had been during an act of violent rage but the fact that she looked a lot like Casey was what worried him more. Their killer not only wanted her dead, he wanted her destroyed.

He pulled out the list of names Casey had given to Agent Simms. So far, all but one checked out. Aaron Taylor. He'd been out of town for the past two weeks and was due back yesterday.

He looked over the names again. Casey said she had given them the names of every man she'd ever been associated with but there was one name she didn't give them.

Scott managed to keep from jolting when Casey stepped behind him and curled her arms around his neck. Her hair was wet and the musky smell of his soap floated on her skin. It uncoiled the knot in his stomach and turned it into a ball of heat.

"Hey. What are you working on?"

He slipped the papers back into the file and tucked it back into his briefcase. "Nothing. Are you hungry? I can cook up a quick dinner." He rose from the sofa and walked to the kitchen.

Casey looked at the briefcase then back at him, her eyes narrowed. "I thought we talked about this, Scott. You promised you would share your leads on my case."

He pulled a canister from the cupboard and began to make coffee. "Yeah, and there are no leads just yet. We're still going through the list of possible suspects, but so far we've had no hits."

"Then why does it seem like you're hiding something from me?" she asked.

Scott started the coffee then turned around, keeping his expression steady. "Tell me about Tony."

Casey's brow furrowed, confused about the change in subject. "I already told you about Tony. What does he...? Wait a minute." She looked back at the briefcase then at him. "You don't seriously think he has anything to do with this, do you?"

Scott crossed his arms and leaned against the counter while the coffee sputtered and dripped behind him. "Why didn't you mention him to the Feds?"

Casey blinked, her brow creasing with a bewildered stare. "Are you serious? I didn't mention him because I didn't think it was necessary. Aside from the fact that I've known Tony since I was a child, he would never do something like this. He would never hurt me. He would never hurt anybody."

"How can you be so sure about that?"

"He's a cop, for Christ's sake!" she snapped. "You know him. You work with him."

"I work with him, but I don't know him."

The professional detachment in his voice fueled her anger. "Well, I do! And I say he would never do this. Tony is a wonderful man. The best person I know." She stepped into the kitchen and glared at him. "You leave him alone, Scott. He's not a part of this. Just because you don't like him—"

"What makes you think I don't like him?" he asked.

Casey sent him a dark look. "I'm not an idiot."

"Okay, you're right. I don't like him. But that has nothing to do with this."

"It has everything to do with this," she countered. "Leave him alone, Scott. I won't let you ruin him like I—" she stopped, the anger dying out of her words. "He's a good man. Leave him alone."

Scott stepped to her, placing his hands on her shoulders. He saw the shame in her eyes and it stirred the guilt in him. Maybe he was jealous. After all, Tony had been an important part of her life once and it was something he knew he would never have the chance to be.

"I'm sorry. I wasn't trying to start a fight. This damn case is just so frustrating sometimes." He pulled her against him, pressing a kiss to her forehead.

"I know. It's frustrating for me, too." She wrapped her arms around his waist and rested her head against his chest. "But Tony isn't a part of this. I just know he isn't, and I don't want him to think...Please, Scott. Promise me you'll keep him out of this."

Scott closed his eyes with a heavy sigh. It was becoming easier to promise her anything, which is what made it so damn hard. "I promise."

"Thank you." She eased back and offered him a smile. "But don't think this means you're getting make-up sex because I'm hungry and don't have the energy."

He laughed and kissed her. "Then I'll just have to settle for after-dinner sex."

They settled on the sofa to eat. Scott had whipped up ham and cheese omelets and pan-fried potatoes, while Casey prepared their coffee.

"I thought you and Alex were supposed to play racquetball this afternoon," she said before biting into the potatoes.

She realized her mistake when he sent her a questioning look. He'd never mentioned his weekly games to her but they were marked in his daily planner, which she'd likely found during her search of his apartment. He and Alex set aside two hours every week without fail.

"We've canceled them for a while. It's not exactly the time," he said. It bothered him that he and Alex hadn't even spoken since their last encounter, the morning after Casey's attack.

Casey dropped her fork onto her plate with a clatter. "I hate this, you know. Having to stop our lives because of this psycho running around."

"You're not stopping your life. You're just being cautious," Scott said.

"No, I'm running scared. And I don't run scared, Scott. Not anymore." She set her plate on the coffee table and stood up to pace. "I won't let this guy run my life. If I continue to stay locked up in this apartment, then he wins."

"If he gets his hands on you, he wins. Staying locked up is going to keep him from crossing that line." He watched her as he sipped his coffee. He understood what she said, as well as what she felt, but he wouldn't chance losing her at the hands of a madman. "Casey, it's not forever. Sooner or later he's going to make a mistake, and we're going to catch him."

"And if you don't? Damn it, Scott! I'm not going to stay locked up anymore. I've wasted too much of my life being afraid. I'm not going to do that anymore." She turned to him, her gaze steady. "You of all people should know you can't let fear run your life."

And because he did, he knew she was right. She had overcome so much in her young life. He couldn't let that determination die because of some deranged lunatic's desires. He could keep her safe and still let her enjoy the life she deserved. "Okay," he said. "What is it you want to do?"

Casey smiled, though there was not the least bit of smugness in it. "Dinner."

Scott laughed and stood to take the plates to the kitchen. "Didn't we just do that?"

"I mean tomorrow. I think it's time to let Alex know what's going on. Some of it, at least. I know he's worried and probably has Jenn on edge."

"Okay. It's your choice." He turned when she walked into the kitchen and stood in front of him as if braced for a fight.

"I want to tell them what I choose to tell them. No more, no less," she said.

He placed the dishes in the sink and nodded. He wasn't sure what affect Casey's story would have on his friendship with Alex or what would happen when Alex found out he and Casey were sleeping together. But it was her choice now. It had been taken away from her before and now he was handing it back. He hoped to hell he wasn't making a mistake.

Casey wrapped her arms around him and kissed his cheek. "Thank you. I'll go make the reservations, then call Alex," she said with a wide smile. She hurried into the bedroom to search for the phonebook.

He rubbed a hand over his chin and frowned. Maybe he should bring an ice pack, just to be safe.

CHAPTER TWENTY-FOUR

Casey chose an elegant restaurant built on the top floor of the First Interstate Bank in downtown Rosehill. Alex and Jennifer were waiting in the lobby when they arrived. Jennifer greeted them both with a kiss.

"Wow, Scott, I don't think I've ever seen you in anything but jeans. You clean up nice," she said with a laugh.

Scott resisted the urge to fidget in the linen jacket Casey made him wear. He wore a pale blue dress shirt underneath and dark slacks. He had argued with her over wearing a tie and was thankful he won that battle.

"You look beautiful, Jenn. Pregnancy agrees with you," he said, leaning over to kiss her cheek. He extended his hand to Alex and noted he chose to wear a tie. Somehow it looked much more dashing on him. "Alex."

"Martinez, party of four?" A young woman in black formal wear stepped around the corner. "This way, please."

She led them through a large dining room with crystal chandeliers and small intimate tables draped in white linen. A soft, melodious tune drifted from somewhere in the room. The clink of silverware on china chimed from the occupied tables amid hushed conversations.

The hostess sat them at a table near the window overlooking the Rosehill skyline. A young waiter appeared out of nowhere and enthusiastically announced the dinner specials. He took their drink orders along with their dinner order then quickly disappeared.

"Nice place," Scott said, adjusting his jacket with obvious discomfort.

Casey smiled and shrugged. "I was in the mood for elegant. Not that the meals you cook aren't good."

"The food here is wonderful. Alex and I came here last year for our anniversary," Jennifer said. She laid her hand over Alex's, giving him a curious look. "We even sat at this same table so we could watch the sunset. It's so beautiful when it drops below the buildings."

"The sunsets in New York are just breathtaking. My apartment has a great view of the Hudson. Some days I'll sit out on the terrace just to watch the sun go down. It's very inspiring, too. I've written some of my best scenes at dusk," Casey said. As long as she kept a conversation going she could avoid the real reason they were there.

"Have you decided when you're going back?" Alex asked.

"No, not yet. Why? Are you trying to get rid of me already?"

"If I had my way, you'd be moving back here permanently."

"Lucky for me, it's not your decision," Casey said as the waiter brought their drinks to the table.

Scott picked up the bourbon he ordered and tossed back half the liquid as his phone rang. "Excuse me," he said tightly.

"Is he okay?" Jennifer asked when Scott moved away from the table to answer his phone.

Casey shrugged and sipped her wine. She had enough to worry about tonight without having to try and figure out Scott.

They made it through dinner with limited, but polite, conversation. Casey could feel the tension rise in Alex as they were served coffee after their meals.

"Well, that was really good. Anyone up for dessert? I could really use some chocolate. Jennifer? I'm sure you at least want to indulge," she said with a smile.

"What's going on, Cassandra?" Alex asked. He glanced at Scott then back to her.

Casey eased out a sigh. "Alex. Don't go big brother on me, okay? I promised I would talk to you and I will...am. Just keep your head."

"Casey, are you in trouble?" Jennifer laid her hand on Casey's with a worried frown.

"No. Not really. Look, the reason I came back to town...the reason I'm here...." She swallowed and glanced at Scott. This was not going to be as easy as she'd practiced.

"Someone has been stalking Casey for the past few months, so the authorities thought it would be best if she left town for a while," Scott said. He played it down as Casey had asked but he would have a hard time lying if they asked him a direct question. He didn't lie to his friends and he still considered Alex his friend.

"Oh my God. Casey, are you okay?" Jennifer grasped Casey's hand.

"Yes, I'm fine," she answered quickly. "It's really nothing to worry about."

"Do they have any idea who it is?" Jennifer asked, her grip tightening on Casey's hand.

"No. Not yet," Scott answered. "We pulled someone in for questioning but he didn't fit the profile so we released him." He stole a glance at Casey to see if she had made the connection to her father. She watched him with a mixture of gratitude and relief, so he continued. "The Feds have been going over the list of names Casey gave them, and they've just ruled out another person of interest. An Aaron Taylor." He looked at Casey again and wondered if she still had feelings for the man.

"Aaron? Really?" Smug pleasure lit her eyes. "I would have liked to have been there when they dragged him downtown. Must have been humiliating." She sipped her wine with an amused grin.

Scott tried not to let his relief show. *I guess she's over him.*

"Where do you fit into this?" Alex pinned his gaze on Scott.

"Jo pulled some very large strings before I left New York and had Scott assigned as my bodyguard," Casey said. "After the incident at the beach house and with the press hovering all over it, we decided I should stay at his apartment for a while."

"What incident at the beach house?" Jennifer asked.

"It was nothing," Casey said quickly.

"So that day I found you at his place, he was just doing his job?" Guilt passed over Alex's face.

"Yes, Alex. He was only doing his job," Casey said. "Look, I know I should have told you about all of this sooner, but I didn't want you to worry. As it is, I've only made you worry more."

"Casey, you should come stay with us," Jennifer said.

"No." Casey pulled her hand back, resisting the urge to shake it out. Jennifer had the grip of a wrestler. "I don't want you two to get in the middle of this. If this guy turns out to be dangerous—"

"Dangerous?" Jennifer said.

Scott exchanged a look with Casey and sat back in his chair. "It's always a possibility with stalkers." He looked at Alex, his expression firm. "Right now, Casey is safer by my side. I won't let anything happen to her. You can trust me on that."

"We *are* trusting you with that," Alex said.

✌

Casey slipped out of her shoes the minute they stepped into Scott's apartment. "Well, that went well, I think," she said.

"Yeah and thank God it's over so I can finally get out of this." He shrugged out of the jacket and loosened another button on his shirt.

"Yes, but Jennifer was right. You do clean up nice, Detective," Casey said. She wrapped her arms around his neck and nipped at his ear.

Scott brushed his lips against hers then pulled away. "Yeah, well, don't get too used to it. Unless I have a wedding or a funeral to go to, this thing stays packed away."

Casey eyed him as he tossed his jacket over the back of the sofa. "Something wrong?"

"No. Long night." Scott dropped onto the sofa and rubbed his hands over his face. Casey didn't mention their relationship to Alex and Jennifer. He wondered now why he had expected her to. He knew he wasn't the type of man she preferred, and she proved it with the restaurant she chose tonight. She even picked up the tab, which grated more on his pride than anything else.

Throughout dinner she'd spoken nonstop about New York and how anxious she was to get back to her apartment in Yonkers. It was like a stake to the heart. She would go back to New York because nothing had changed for her. It was his own damn fault that it had changed for him.

Casey stepped behind him, her arms curling around his neck. "Are you ready for bed, then?" she asked in a low, seductive voice.

Scott felt the heat pulse through him, blending with the ache. What they had together was just sex. Pure and simple. A physical relationship between two consenting adults, with no strings attached. Those were the rules they set. But dammit, he didn't want the rules anymore. He wanted her.

She stepped around the sofa to take his hand and pull him from the sofa.

All he had to do was convince her that he was what she wanted as well. *Right. That shouldn't be too hard.*

Chapter Twenty-five

Casey leaned over the counter in Scott's kitchen and scribbled on a strip of paper. She wore one of his cotton shirts, though the hem barely reached mid-thigh.

She had talked him into a day at the gym, and after they returned home and showered, he talked her back into bed. Both workouts had given her quite an appetite.

"You want me to go to the grocery store?" Scott asked, his brow arched skeptically. "So you can cook."

Casey looked up with a haughty smile. "I'll have you know, I've been known to cook without emergency assistance needed." She stepped to him and tucked the strip of paper into his shirt pocket as he slipped on a light jacket to cover his shoulder holster.

"I do live alone after all. At least I did. I can't afford takeout every night. I'd be more than happy to go myself if you'd let me out of here," she said with a beseeching smile.

"I'll go. I'll go," Scott said. He pulled the list from his pocket and studied the neat handwriting. "You're going to make enchiladas?"

"What can I say? I love Mexican," she said with a playful shrug.

Scott pulled her against him, snaking his hand under the shirt to rest on her butt. "I'm pretty partial to it myself."

His soft kiss made Casey's knees go weak. Her hands instinctively went around his neck to pull him closer. She couldn't seem to get enough of him or he of her. It was a sensation that baffled her.

Scott had to force himself to pull back. "Are you sure you don't want to order in?"

Casey laughed and turned him toward the door. "No, not really."

"Don't get dressed," he said. He kissed her again then pulled open the door. The woman on the other side of the door yelped, her hand raised in the air mid-knock. Scott braced, shoving his hand into his jacket to grip around his gun.

The woman's green eyes went wide and locked on him, her hand was pressed to her chest. She wore a dark pinstriped business suit, her neat auburn hair pinned back from her face. *Definitely not a serial killer.*

Scott relaxed his hand, removing it from his jacket. "Can I help you?"

"I hope so. I'm looking for Casey Martinez. I was told she may be here," the woman said, looking him over as if he were an ax-murderer.

"Jo? What are you doing here?" Casey squealed when she spotted the woman at the door.

Jo pushed past Scott and grabbed Casey in a hug. The worried frown quickly changed to a relieved smile. "Casey! Oh, sweetheart, are you okay?" She pushed Casey out to arm's length to study her.

Scott closed the door, watching with amused interest as the petite woman fussed over Casey.

"I'm fine," Casey said, pulling Jo into a hug. "I've missed you so much. What are you doing here?"

"I've been trying to reach you for days and was so worried I came down to check on you myself. That FBI agent said I would find you here." She leaned back and studied Casey again. "Where are your clothes? Why aren't you dressed? And who is this?" She placed her body in front of Casey like a protective mother and sent Scott a suspicious glare.

Scott attempted a smile, trying not to flinch under her steely gaze. Why did he suddenly feel like he was in high school and had just been caught with this woman's sixteen-year-old daughter?

"This is Scott Weller. The bodyguard," Casey said. "Scott, this is Josephine Landry, my agent and dearest friend in the world."

"Detective Scott Weller, ma'am. Rosehill P.D. It's nice to meet you." He extended his hand then shoved it in his pocket when she blinked at him.

"I was just heading out, so you two will have some time to catch up," he said. He leaned over to Casey and kissed her on the forehead. "I guess this means you're getting dressed," he murmured, with a frown. He nodded his goodbye to Jo and let himself out of his apartment.

Jo turned from the door when it closed and sent Casey a prim frown. "So, I guess this bodyguard thing is working out."

Casey bit her lip with a sheepish smile and started toward the bedroom. "I'll go get dressed."

"Yes and then you can tell me just what the devil has been going on," Jo said as Casey rushed from the room.

⚬❧

"Are you sure you're okay?" Jo asked after Casey told her about the assault at the beach house and the incident while shopping with Jennifer. She set the glass of wine Casey poured for her onto the coffee table and laid her hand across Casey's arm.

"Yes, I'm fine. A little shaken up at first, but you know me, I bounce back pretty easily," Casey said. She pulled her legs up on the sofa and crossed them underneath her. She'd put on a pair of khaki slacks under Scott's shirt and had pulled her hair back into a ponytail.

Jo cocked her head and studied Casey suspiciously. "And what's the story with this detective?"

Casey resisted the urge to squirm. "Scott? He's lead detective on the case and the officer originally assigned to me, which is why I'm here."

"That's not what I mean, Casey. You're about to cook dinner for the man, right? You haven't cooked dinner for a man since Aaron Taylor."

Casey dropped her gaze to the pink liquid in her wineglass. "Your point?"

"My point is, you thought you were in love with Aaron until you found out yours wasn't the only salsa he was taste-testing." Jo took Casey's hand and squeezed. "Sweetheart, are you in love with the cop?"

Casey's head came up, the question sending a rush of panic through her. No, she wasn't in love. She couldn't be. She didn't know how to love. The two times she'd committed to the word had been disasters. The first time she had only been sixteen and desperate to find any emotion. The second time she was just plain lonely.

"No, don't be ridiculous. It's not like that between us. We're just enjoying ourselves right now. Heat of the moment stuff, you know? Summer fling, or spring fling, whatever the season is," she said with a tremulous smile. She sighed because she knew she'd spoken too fast. She always spoke too fast when she felt cornered. "We're two adults, having an adult relationship. That's all. We're hardly each other's type, anyway." Casey twirled her glass, watching absently as the wine rippled and swirled. "Besides, it isn't what he wants. Once this is over we'll both go back to our own lives. His here–"

"And yours?" Jo asked.

"Wherever the next story takes me."

Before Jo could comment, Scott entered the apartment carrying two grocery bags. Casey jumped up from the sofa to help him, grateful for the interruption.

"Do the FBI have any leads yet as to who this person is that's after Casey?" Jo asked when she and Casey settled back on the sofa after dinner. She was both surprised and pleased when Scott volunteered to cook so Casey would have more time to visit. Her first impression of him had been wary at best and not because he nearly pulled his gun on her. She was wary of anyone who wanted to get close to Casey, especially now when she was most vulnerable. However, she had watched him throughout dinner and saw the quiet looks and subtle touches when he and Casey were close. It pleased her to know Scott's feelings were real, and she had to admit, he looked right for Casey.

"They only recently arrived in town, but we've been working together," Scott said stretching his legs out from the love seat he was lounging on.

Jo turned to Casey and placed a hand on her arm. "Maybe your coming here wasn't such a good idea. You should come back to New York. You can stay with me. My apartment has great security."

"I'm sure it does, but I can't very well keep moving from state to state and hope that maybe that nut-job will get as tired of traveling as I would,"

Casey answered. "Besides, in a town this small, he can't hide out forever. They'll catch him eventually."

"It's the eventually I'm worried about. You're not safe here. For heaven's sake, you couldn't even go shopping without someone trying to hurt you—" She stopped when Casey shook her head and tried to wave her off the subject. But it was too late.

Scott bolted to his feet. "What? You didn't tell me something happened at the mall when you and Jenn were shopping."

"I didn't?" Casey bit her lip and shifted her gaze to Jo.

"No! You didn't! God dammit, Casey! I don't fucking believe this!" Scott pushed his hands through his hair and paced the room. "I put up with your bitching and moaning for days about wanting some space, and the first time I give it to you, something happens that you don't even have the decency to tell me about! Just like the damn notes."

"Stop cursing at me," Casey snapped. Damn, she'd forgotten about the notes.

Scott turned to look at her, his eyes dark with fury. "I haven't even begun to curse you. Why didn't you tell me? What the hell else are you hiding from me, Cassandra?"

"*Casey!* And I'm not the one hiding anything! Nothing even happened! And the reason I didn't mention it was because when I came home that night you jumped down my throat, and I was too pissed off at you to think about it!"

Scott raked his hand through his hair with a string of curses under his breath. He stopped and spun around to look at her. "My God, was Jennifer hurt? Did she see anything?"

"No, she wasn't hurt. And she didn't see anything, either." Casey sprang from the couch to stand nose to nose with him. "Christ! Do you think I want her to get involved in this mess? Why do you think I've been avoiding her for so long? I don't want her in harm's way any more than you do." She pushed at his chest and tried to step around him.

Scott grabbed her arms and turned her to face him. "Of course not. But dammit, Casey, you should have told me about this."

"Oh right, like you've been so forthcoming with all your information," she shot back.

Scott clenched his teeth and made an effort to keep his grip on her arm light. "That's different."

"Why? Because you say so? Because I'm on a need-to-know basis, and you don't think I need to know?" She pushed away from him and stormed to the kitchen.

"No."

Casey spun around and glared at him. "Who the hell do you think you are? What makes you think you have a right to run my life?"

He closed the distance in one step and grabbed her by the shoulders. "I have every right. I'm in love with you, dammit!"

Casey jerked loose from his hold and staggered back. He didn't mistake the flicker of panic in her eyes. "What?"

Scott snapped to attention. His body went cold. It was the first time he'd ever said those words to a woman, and she was looking at him as if he'd threatened to kill her. "You heard me."

Behind him Jo cleared her throat. "I think it's time I was on my way. I have an early flight out in the morning." She stepped to Casey and placed a hand on her arm. "Casey, please be careful, and call me when you get the chance." She pulled her into a hug and kissed her cheek before turning to look at Scott. "Mr. Weller. Take care of my girl. She means the world to me." She gave his shoulder a gentle pat and let herself out of the apartment.

Casey linked her fingers and stared at him. Her panicked expression had been replaced by a deep sadness. She bit her lip, swallowing hard before she spoke. "I don't know what to say."

Her words sliced through his heart like the cold steel of a knife. He didn't think he had the will to hide his pain, but he managed. "You don't have to say anything. I know I'm not the type of man you'd fall in love with. I'll survive," he said. The cold inflection of his voice surprised him. He walked into the kitchen and pulled a beer from the refrigerator. He twisted off the cap and took a deep drink. It didn't help wash away the ache in his throat.

Casey stepped behind him, laying her hand on his back. His body tensed. He focused on breathing.

"I'm sorry," she whispered.

"Don't be." *Some things just aren't meant to be.* His mother always told him that.

"No, I'm sorry I'm handling this so badly. I've never been in love before, and I'm not sure how I'm supposed to feel." She stepped in front of him, tentatively placing her hand on his chest. His heart pounded against the warmth of her palm. "But I do know I've never wanted to be with someone as much as I want to be with you. Can we make that enough for now?" She pressed her lips together and swallowed. "Please?"

Scott lowered his gaze to look at her. He stroked his thumb over her cheek, wiping away the tear that spilled over. His heart stumbled over the hope of her words, but his chest was thick with the pain of knowing it would never be.

"Yes. It can be enough for now," he said. He placed his hand under her chin, lifting her mouth up to his. He would have to make it enough.

CHAPTER TWENTY-SIX

"**A**re you sure you'll be okay by yourself for a while?" Scott asked as he put on his jacket. It had been two days since he gave her his heart and though she never repeated the words to him, he felt them in her touch when they made love. She needed time was all, and he was willing to give it to her if it meant she would tell him what he wanted to hear.

"Yes, I'm fine. I think I can handle a few hours alone. And I could use the time to get some work done."

"Okay. I'll call you and let you know what time I'll be home. And don't open the door to anyone."

"Don't worry, I'm perfectly safe with one of Rosehill's finest sitting across the street." She smiled and waved to the officer in the unmarked police car when Scott opened the front door.

"Okay. I'll see you in a couple of hours." He lifted his hand to rest against her cheek and kissed her, lingering a moment before he pulled away.

Casey watched him turn to leave. She knew he waited to hear the words she was afraid to say, but she wanted to mean them when she said them.

She laid her hand on his arm and sent him a warm smile. "I'll be here when you get back."

❧

Scott arrived at the police station twenty minutes later and found Agent

Simms sitting at his desk punching numbers on the telephone. He returned the phone to its receiver and stood when he spotted Scott.

"Detective. I was just about to call you. We have a possible witness to the Amanda Ortiz murder."

"Where?"

"She's in room one." Simms motioned toward the interrogation rooms and followed Scott down the long hallway. "Her name is Danette Schultz. She was a friend of the deceased." He stopped at a metal door and opened it, following Scott inside.

The room was small with dull gray walls and a wooden table placed in the middle. On the center of the table were a Styrofoam pitcher and a stack of paper cups.

A middle-aged woman with cropped red hair sat in one of the wooden chairs, the crushed remains of a tissue clutched in her hands. Detective Gomez sat across from her. He stood when Scott entered the room.

"Miss Schultz, this is Detective Weller. He's one of the officers on this case."

"Miss Schultz, anything you can tell us will help us find whoever did this to your friend," Scott said. He pulled out one of the chairs and sat next to her.

The woman sniffed, blotting at her red, swollen eyes. "Amanda was such a sweet girl. She never hurt anyone. I don't understand why someone would do this to her."

"Were you with her the night she disappeared?" Scott asked, handing her another tissue.

"Yes. I was just telling the detectives, we had met a few friends for dinner after work. We're dental hygienists downtown," she said. "One of the girls in the office was having a birthday, so we went to dinner at Joe's Crab Shack. Afterwards we went over to Arthur's Pub—no one wanted to go home right away." She wiped her eyes again then took a deep breath to settle herself.

"Did she meet anyone at the pub? Or was there anyone who tried to pick her up?"

"Amanda was a beautiful woman. Men were always trying to pick her up. Most of the time she would ignore them or maybe just let them buy her a few drinks," she said. Her eyes widened, and she searched Scott's face as if she thought he might disapprove. "She wasn't promiscuous or anything. She just liked men and enjoyed having fun. She was so young, you know. You don't think about something like this happening when you're young."

"Can you remember any of the men who approached her that night?" Agent Simms asked.

The woman flinched at the deep command of his voice. Scott sent him an annoyed look.

"There were a few who bought her drinks and asked her to dance. No one she spent more than a few minutes with. Except for one guy. She met him when we went up to the bar to order some drinks for our table. He was just sitting there, looking so sad. He was holding a book, not reading it, just holding it and staring at it."

"A book?" Scott shifted in his seat as a knot of uneasiness formed in his stomach.

"Yes. That's what caught Amanda's attention because it was the same book she'd picked up at the mall last week. She even had the author sign it for her."

"Casey Martinez's book?" Scott' asked.

"Yes, I think so. Amanda asked him about it, then they just started talking so I didn't bother to stick around. After a while she came and told me she was leaving. I asked her if she wanted a ride, but she said she was going to leave with her new friend. He seemed so nice I didn't think there was anything to be worried about." Danette's eyes filled, and she shifted her gaze back and forth between the men. "I couldn't have stopped her. She's a grown woman."

"No, you couldn't," Scott said gently. "Do you remember what the man looked like or if he mentioned his name?

Danette took in a slow breath, furrowing her brow. "He sat most of the time, but he looked tall. About your height, maybe. He was a nice-looking man, thin, but in shape, like he worked out. His hair was short, sort of like a military cut only longer. Brown, maybe black. He didn't say his name, or I just can't remember."

"What about his car? Did you happen to see what kind of car they climbed into?" Agent Simms asked.

"It was a truck. I don't know what kind. They all look the same to me. It was parked in the corner, so I couldn't tell the color. Black, maybe blue.

I'm sorry. I'm really no help at all." She choked out a sob and squeezed her hand around the battered tissue.

"You're doing fine, ma'am," Scott said. He paused to give her a moment to calm and handed her another tissue. "I'd like you to work with one of our artists, see if maybe you can come up with a picture of the guy."

She sent him a grateful smile, blotting her face. "Yes, of course. I can try."

Scott stood and nodded to Gomez. "Thank you, Miss Schultz. You've been a great help. Detective Gomez will take care of you from here." He left the room, followed by Agent Simms.

"Looks like we're back to square one," Simms said as Scott returned to his desk.

"At least we're a step closer to two. I think once she calms down, she'll remember a little more. I'll have LeBlanc pull out the pictures of the offenders we've pulled. It's amazing how many used the same MO with rape and murder in the last ten years. We've narrowed it down to about a hundred fifty, but maybe someone will strike a chord."

Simms cocked his brow, his expression sober. "Sounds like you've been working on my case for a while."

Scott sent him a careless shrug then picked up the phone and punched in his phone number. He glanced at his watch as the phone rang, unanswered, on the other end. Casey was probably in the shower. He hung up and waited while Danette Schultz spoke to the police artist.

⚘

Casey pulled on her robe and scrubbed a towel over her hair before she stepped out of the bathroom. The hot shower was just what she needed to work out the stiffness of her muscles and clear her head. She'd put in a couple of hours work at the computer, the story flowing from her mind without hesitation. When she noticed she'd written Scott's name in place of her lead character, Jordan, she forced herself to stop and take a break.

She sat on the bed as she pulled the brush through the wet knots in her hair. She had been writing the climatic love scene between Jordan and his love interest, Rebecca Hightower, when she noticed the words 'I love you, Scott' in her dialogue. It took a moment for the words to register in her brain, but it was like a punch in the stomach when they did.

Had the words she typed been a subconscious message from her heart to her head? Was she really in love with Scott? He'd been on her mind all morning. He was everywhere she turned. His smell was in her skin, his taste still lingered on her tongue. Even now, just the thought of him sent a rush of pleasure through her. She pressed her hand against the flutter in her stomach and took a breath. A smile curved the corners of her mouth.

Yes, she was in love and damn, did it feel wonderful.

"You've always had such a breathtaking smile, Cassandra."

Casey leapt up from the bed, dropping the brush on the floor. Tony's large frame stood dominant in the doorway, his thumbs hooked in the pockets of his jeans. She pulled the top of her robe closed and tightened the belt. "Tony, you scared me. What are you doing here? How did you get in?"

"I'm sorry, sugar," he said with a contrite smile. "I knocked, but you didn't answer and the door was open."

Casey glanced toward the front room. She remembered locking the door when Scott left, or at least she thought she did. She sent Tony a polite smile, keeping her voice pleasant as a chill shivered across her neck. "Is there something you needed?"

"I've come to take care of you. I know I'm a little late, but I'll make it up to you." He moved into the room, frowning when Casey stepped back.

"I don't understand. Did Scott send you? Is he going to be working late or something?"

"You don't need Scott anymore. I'm here to take care of you now. Just like I always promised I would. Come with me, Cassandra," he said, offering her his hand.

A nervous flutter shimmered through her, twisting like barbed wire in her stomach. She swallowed the panic before it could build and stepped around him to the front room. "You shouldn't be here. I think you need to leave."

Tony frowned and grabbed her arm as she stepped past him. "I'm not going anywhere without you, Cassandra."

Casey whirled around and connected her fist with his jaw. She bolted for the front door when he staggered back and let her go. Tony recovered quick and lunged for her. He grasped her by the shoulder and wheeled her around. The back of his hand struck her across the cheek. Bright sparks of pain flashed in her eyes and shot through her head as she slammed against the door.

Scott was her last thought before everything went black.

Scott tried his number again, tapping his fingers on his desk as the phone rang. "Dammit, Casey, pick up," he muttered.

"Something wrong?" Agent Simms asked. He stepped to the desk and offered Scott a cup of coffee.

"She's ignoring the phone." He dropped the handset back on the base and took the coffee, nodding his thanks. "She does that when she's working sometimes. She gets so engrossed in what she's doing that she's oblivious to everything around her."

"I take it you and Ms. Martinez have become good friends?" Simms asked, taking a seat in the chair next to Scott's desk.

"You could say that." Scott sipped from the cup, watching the agent over the rim. Though it had sounded more like a statement than a question, he heard the disapproving tone.

"Do you really think it's such a good idea to get mixed up with the person you're assigned to watch?"

Scott set his coffee aside and sent the agent an even stare. "I'm not exactly mixed up. I'm in love with her."

Agent Simms pursed his lips and nodded. "I see."

"No, I don't think you do. But I don't really care, either. I've got more important things to worry about than you taking the moral high ground with me."

Simms took a drink of his coffee, but couldn't hide his grin. "Can't say I've ever been accused of that before. But I'll keep my opinions to myself if you wish."

Scott glanced at his watch. It was nearly five o'clock. "I'm going to head home. Have Gomez give me a ring if Miss Schultz comes up with anything."

"Will do."

Scott knew something was wrong the minute he walked into his apartment. The room looked as it did when he left, but there was a sense of uneasiness and an emptiness to the place. He pulled his gun from its holster and listened through the silence.

"Casey?"

Her laptop sat on the table, closed up for the night. Sitting next to it was an empty wineglass. The door to his bedroom was open. He took a guarded step toward it, his muscles tensed.

He raised his gun at the ready and peered around the frame before taking a step inside. He found the brush on the floor and picked it up, scanning the room.

"Casey!" he called again. But he already knew she was gone.

⟡

She felt something cool on her face and the soft wind of a fan blowing above her. Pillows were propped under her head. She was on a bed.

Scott? His name lay unspoken on her tongue.

A headache pounded against her temples like a sledgehammer. She heard the groan whisper from her lips and struggled to pull herself out of the fog and cobwebs clouding her mind.

"You're going to be okay, my love." Someone spoke and pressed a kiss to her forehead. "Just rest. I'll be back soon."

The mattress shifted with the release of his weight. The hinges on the door creaked before it clicked shut.

I'll be here when you get back. The words echoed in her mind as she drifted off again.

⟡

Scott waited, watching from his living room while the forensics team spread their powder around looking for prints. He doubted they'd find any other than his and Casey's, but it was part of their job, just as his job had been to protect Casey. And he failed.

He glanced up when the young officer he'd assigned to watch the apartment walked in. He didn't think about what he was doing when he lunged for the man and pinned him against the wall. "Where the hell were you?"

Agent Simms and several of the officers close by wrestled him away from the stunned officer.

"Jesus, Scott. What the hell's wrong with you?" The officer staggered back and adjusted his shirt.

"Where were you? You had orders to sit until I returned." Scott jerked loose from the other officers and glared at them. "I'm good," he said. He turned back to the other officer. "Why did you leave your post?"

"What are you talking about? You sent Lankford to relieve me."

"Lankford? Tony Lankford was here?" Panic iced its way to Scott's gut. His conversation with Tony flashed through his mind.

She's the first woman I ever loved...I made a promise that I would always take care of her, and I won't break that promise. It's what made me fall head over heels in love with her...Of course, she thought she wanted different things. But then, you never know, some things are just meant.

"Yeah. He said it was his job to take care of Ms. Martinez, and I wasn't needed anymore. What's going on?" His last words were barely heard as Scott bolted for the door.

❧

Scott stood in Tony's living room, his hands jammed in his pockets. He didn't expect to find them there, but a part of him had still hoped.

The apartment was noticeably larger than his own, the furniture more rustic. There were several pictures and trophies of fish and wild game hanging on the walls. Tony was the outdoors type.

On the mantel above the mock fireplace was a picture of Tony and Casey. They were dressed in formalwear though the smile on Casey's face didn't quite reach her eyes.

"When was the last time you saw him?" Scott asked turning to the landlord standing behind him. He was a short, stocky man in his mid sixties, with thinning gray hair. His eyes were pink and glazed; the stale odor of alcohol lingered on his breath. Scott took a subtle step back, biting back his annoyance when the man stepped with him.

"He was here early this morning. Had a fight with his girlfriend around breakfast time, and she stormed out," the landlord said. His eyes, lit with excitement—or alcohol, Scott couldn't be sure—followed the police officers as they rifled through the room. "Mr. Lankford didn't seem to care none though because he didn't go after her. Is he in trouble or something?"

"We just need to talk to him. Thank you for your time. We'll be in touch if we need you for anything else," Scott said, dismissing him with a nod.

The man stepped back with a disappointed frown. "Okay then. Just give me a call. I'm always here." He took one more look around the room then hurried away.

Scott walked around the apartment, his steps rigid and tense. Several officers were searching the bedroom when he wandered in. The drawers on the dresser were hanging open, clothing draped over the sides after the other officers' search. He spotted a silver frame underneath a T-shirt and pulled it out. Matted behind the glass was a wedding invitation dated ten years earlier to the day. Embossed in gold letters were Casey's and Tony's names.

A knot coiled in his chest.

Casey had mentioned she and Tony were engaged once. She just didn't mention how much engaged. A part of him wondered if maybe she had gone with him voluntarily. There hadn't been any signs of a struggle, after all.

"There's no sign that either Ms. Martinez or Mr. Lankford have been here." Agent Simms stepped behind him. "But he obviously has her somewhere." He glanced at the wedding invitation as Scott meticulously set it down.

Scott slammed his hand on the dresser, rattling the pictures. "I shouldn't have listened to her. I should have gone after him when I had the chance."

"He slipped by us too, Detective," Simms said. "No one likes to think this could happen in their own back yard."

"Detective Weller. I think we found something."

Scott turned as a young officer carried a large cardboard file box from the closet. He pushed away from the dresser and joined the office near the bed.

Inside the box were various snapshots of bloodied and mutilated bodies.

"Son of a bitch!" Agent Simms hissed. He pulled out the pictures and sifted through them. "These look like they were taken before the bodies were even found."

Scott rummaged through the box, pulling out a stack of vinyl notebooks.

"Looks like he even kept a journal."

Simms dropped the pictures on the bed and grabbed one of the books. "They're date books," he said thumbing through a page. "Our murders started about five years ago. I have a feeling these books are going to connect Mr. Lankford to them."

Scott flipped through the pages of the top book. He stopped at April, scanning the dates. "He was in California in April, five years ago. At a pharmaceutical convention with his girlfriend," he said, his voice sounding hollow to himself.

"Our first known victim was a prostitute from L.A. Murdered five years ago," Simms said. He stopped at a page in the notebook he held and read over the dates. "He was in New York around the time Michelle Castillo's body was found." He closed the book, tossing it back in the box, his expression grave. "I think we've found our guy," he said.

Scott tossed his notebook back into the box and walked out of the room. Simms nodded to the officer to take the boxes then followed Scott into the living room. He looked around at the various deer and boar mounts lining the walls.

"The guy sure likes his outdoors sports. Unfortunately, he made rape and mutilation one of them." He winced and turned to Scott. "I'm sorry. I didn't mean—"

"Fishing," Scott said.

"Excuse me?"

"He fishes. He has a fishing cabin up near the Woodlands. It's just over two hours north of here." Scott rushed for the door without looking to see if the agent was behind him.

"Do you know how to get there?" Simms asked as they reached the street.

"No. But her brother does," Scott said. And he wasn't looking forward to giving Alex the news about his sister.

Chapter Twenty-seven

The lights were dim, the drapes on the windows drawn when Casey finally managed to open her eyes. She was on a large four-post bed in a room she didn't recognize. On the far wall was a six-foot blue-green marlin affixed to a large mahogany wood frame. Its wide eyes were rolled back, its mouth open as if ready to grab onto a baited hook. The other walls were covered with mounted deer heads, their dead, black eyes staring at her. A cold shiver skittered down her spine.

She pushed herself up to a sitting position and gave herself a moment to wave off the dizziness before easing off the bed. She pressed her hand to her head to push back the insistent pounding. Nausea churned in her stomach, rising to burn her throat. She swallowed hard to try and quell it.

She took a cautious step to the dresser. A groan escaped her throat when she saw her reflection. The left side of her face along her cheek was a brilliant shade of purple. Her eyes looked glazed and dark circles colored the skin underneath. She gently pressed her fingers against her face and winced.

Had she been in an accident? How did she get into this room?

She pressed her fingers to her temples, trying to bring back the memory of the night. She was in Scott's bedroom—she remembered that— and she had just come out of the shower. Then Tony walked in. Had Scott sent him?

"You're awake."

Casey spun around at the sound of Tony's voice, her heart jumping to her throat.

He smiled at her as he entered the room carrying a bed tray. "I brought you some soup. It should make you feel better. It was quite a nasty spill you took." He placed the tray on the end table and poured hot water into a teacup.

Casey took a steady breath, moving carefully to the edge of the bed. "What's going on? Where am I?" A wave of dizziness washed over her. She grabbed onto the bedpost to steady herself.

"Why, you're with me now, sweetheart. Just like you're supposed to be. Now, come on, have some soup. I made it special for you." Tony extended his hand, frowning when she didn't make a move toward him. "Now, Cassandra, you need to eat something. You're going to need your strength for the ceremony. I can't have you fainting dead away before we say our vows."

"What?" Casey froze, her fingers tightening on the bedpost. "What are you talking about?"

Tony stepped to her and placed his hands on her shoulders with a bright smile. "It's our wedding day, sweetheart. Don't you remember?" He stroked his hand over her hair, his eyes glazing with a dreamy look. "I've waited a long time for this day. When Alex told me you were coming back…well, I just knew it was time. I never gave up hope that you'd come back to me and be my wife."

Casey pushed away from him. "You're crazy."

Tony's hand shot out and struck her across the face. She fell to the ground like a rag doll.

"Don't call me that!" Tony stood over her, a warning look in his eye. "I told you once, I'd never hurt you. But it looks like I'm going to have to teach you a little respect for your husband," he said in a low voice.

Casey pressed her hand against the fire in her cheek, swallowing hard against the tears constricting her throat. The attack at the beach cabin flashed in her mind. The husky whisper, the warm breath on her neck. It was Tony. He'd been the one in her bedroom. An icy fear stabbed her chest. She bit her lip to fight it. If she wanted to survive this night, she had to stay calm and do her best to placate him.

"I'm sorry," she said hoarsely.

Tony smiled and bent to help her from the floor. He circled an arm around her waist and pulled her against him. "You're going to make me the happiest man in the world, Cassandra." He cupped her face in his hands and pressed a kiss to her mouth.

Casey barreled her arms against his chest and pushed, breaking the contact. He sent her a thin smile, his eyes dark.

"Right. There's plenty of time for that later." He laced his fingers in her hair and watched it cascade over her shoulders. "Your dress is in the closet," he said. "I'll give you a couple of hours to make yourself pretty."

Casey glanced at the door, judging the distance. If she could just make it past the bedroom door, she could outrun him. Tony's hand tightened around her hair and jerked her head back. She cried out against the pain, panic surging to tighten her chest.

"I can help you get dressed, if you'd like," he said, clenching his teeth. "But I won't guarantee I'll get that far."

"No," Casey managed. "I'll be fine."

He smiled, dropping his hand from her hair. "Good. I'd like to keep you pure until our honeymoon." He kissed her cheek then left the room.

Casey's breath quickened as the lock clicked. She swallowed dryly trying to quell the sickening wave of terror welling up from her stomach. She pressed her hand over her mouth and, with a shuddering rush of breath, gave in to the tears.

❦

"Why the hell weren't you with her?" Alex shoved Scott against the living room wall, his fingers curled around the collar of Scott's jacket.

"Alex, stop it!" Jennifer pulled at his arm, her eyes bright with tears.

Agent Simms grabbed Alex's arm and yanked him back. "Mr. Rivera, you need to calm down. This won't help your sister," he said.

Scott straightened his jacket as he watched his friend try to control his anger. It was the second time in the five years they'd known each other that Alex had taken a swing at him. He didn't blame him in the least and knew it would be a long time before their friendship was repaired.

"You're right. I should have been there," he said, his voice thick with controlled emotion.

Jennifer stepped to Alex, laying her hand on his back. She looked at Scott and reached out to take his hand. "You don't think Tony would hurt her, do you? He's always loved Casey. He could never hurt her. He could never hurt anyone."

Scott looked down at her hand in his. It was a show of family unity he had always wanted with them, but no longer felt he deserved. He dropped Jennifer's hand and took a step back.

"At the moment we don't know what he would do. But we need to find him just to be safe," Agent Simms answered.

"Oh God, Cassandra," Alex said.

Scott shoved his hands in his pockets as Alex dropped onto the sofa, his hands pressed over his face. He wanted to tell him something to put him at ease, but as hard as it was, he had to be all business now.

"I need to know how to get to his cabin. The one he uses when he fishes. It's possible he may have taken her there," he said.

"I have the directions on the refrigerator. I'll go get them." Jennifer rushed from the room.

Alex stood and stepped in front of Scott, his hands fisted at his side. "I'm going with you."

"No. You're not. You need to stay here with your wife."

They stared at each other like two enraged animals, each waiting for the other to charge. Scott knew he could subdue Alex if he had to. He just hoped he wouldn't have to.

Alex's eyes blazed with fury and he took a step closer to Scott. "Then you'd better bring her home safe."

"She will be. I'll see to it," Scott answered.

✣

The cabin was located off Interstate 45 on the north side of Houston in the middle of a thicket. Scott made good time on the beltway with his siren blaring, but he didn't make it before the sun set.

He parked Agent Simms's unmarked car at the end of the dirt road that led to the cabin. Scott had been there once with Alex and remembered that it was a half-mile walk from the main road. However, it would be trickier in the dark.

He jumped out of the car and scanned the entrance to the woods. He checked the magazine in his gun then shoved two more in his back pocket.

Agent Simms moved beside him and grabbed his arm. "We need to wait for backup."

"Then wait." Scott shook off the agent's arm and charged down the dirt road.

Agent Simms cursed under his breath and grabbed a shotgun from the backseat of the car. He knew he should have called in backup sooner instead of allowing Scott go off half-cocked. But he understood the man's need to get to Casey first.

He sent a wary gaze to the trail Scott had taken. The area was thick with trees, so they would at least have a momentary element of surprise. He just hoped he didn't get lost in the unfamiliar and very dark woods.

⁂

Casey tried the windows only to find them nailed shut. She searched the room, looking for a weapon or a way out but found nothing. Standing in front of the dark pine dresser, she slapped her hands on the lacquered top then drew in a deep breath to control her frustration. She had given into the tears, but only briefly. Now, she needed to stay calm so she could figure out a way to escape. The simple white gown Tony chose for her would be easy to maneuver in if she made it through the front door. She would just have to bide her time until she could.

Casey glanced at her reflection in the mirror and frowned. The bodice of the dress was low cut and fit snug around her waist. The skirt flowed over her hips and down to her ankles. Though it was a lovely dress, the bright, white fabric only enhanced the bruises coloring her face.

She pushed her hair back with her fingers, then clipped it at the sides with the combs Tony had left on the dresser. She bypassed the makeup except for the copper colored lipstick. He might get angry if she didn't at least try to fix herself up, so she wouldn't take the chance.

She heard the lock click on the door and turned around with a strained smile. Tony entered the room dressed in a black tuxedo. He stepped to her and placed his hands on her shoulders to study her at arm's length. Pleasure lit his eyes. "You look beautiful, Cassandra." He frowned and titled her chin up when she dropped her gaze. "Now, sweetheart, I know you wanted a big wedding but we can always go back and do it again with our friends and family." He took her hand and wrapped it snugly around his arm. "Tonight is just for us," he said as he led her out of the bedroom.

He stopped outside the threshold to give her a minute to take in the room. The lights were dimmed and various sized tapered candles were scattered along the floor and end tables. The tiny flames flickered and danced to the soft strings of Mozart, which drifted into the room from the small stereo in the corner. Vases of carnations and daisies dotted the length of the wall. The pine rafters were draped with ribbons of white tulle. Large paper wedding bells dangled from the fabric. A fire blazed in the stone fireplace, and he'd placed two large pillows on the hearth. Two crystal goblets sat beside an urn of chilling champagne.

Tony leaned down to whisper in her ear. "This is all for you, sweetheart."

Casey's heart picked up speed, hammering violently against her chest as she scanned the room. She forced herself to stay calm as the panic threatened to choke her.

"We've still got a little time. Let's have some champagne," Tony said. He coaxed her in the direction of the fireplace, chuckling at her hesitation. "It's okay to be nervous, honey. I hear all women are nervous on their wedding day." He circled his arms around her waist, drawing her against him. "I love you so much, Cassandra," he said.

"No, Tony. You're confused. You love Alicia. She's the one you want, not me," Casey said in as steady a voice as she could manage.

"No, Cassandra. It's you I love. Alicia was just a pleasant distraction. She could never hold my heart like you have. There's never been anyone for me but you, sweetheart. You've always known that. And now you've come back to me. Just like you promised." He brushed his lips over her face with soft kisses. "Tell me how much you love me," he murmured.

Casey closed her eyes, forcing herself to breathe.

Tony pressed a kiss to the curve of her neck following a trail to her ear. "Tell me, Cassandra. I need to hear you say it," he whispered.

"I can't. I'm sorry, Tony, but I don't love you. I never have." She winced when he pushed her back, his fingers biting into her arms.

"But you will. You will love me, Cassandra. Just as you were meant to." He yanked her forward and crushed her lips with a bruising kiss.

Casey struggled, pushing against him. His fingers gripped tighter as he deepened the kiss. She pulled away to take a breath and bit his lip. She tasted blood.

Tony jerked back, his eyes wild and crazed. He drew his hand back and hit her across the face. Casey crumpled to the floor, her hands scraping against the wood as she tried to catch herself. Her ears rang, and she tasted her own blood.

Tony wiped his lip then looked at her with a wicked smile. "You always were a feisty one, Cassandra. I'm going to really enjoy making love to you."

Casey scrambled off the floor and made a dash for the door. The dress tangled around her legs and sent her stumbling to the ground. A scream pealed from her throat when Tony grabbed her around the waist and yanked her off the floor. He hugged her against him, pinning her arms behind her.

"Where are you going, sweetheart? It's our wedding day," he said with an amused grin. His eyes darkened as he pulled her toward the pillows. "Maybe we should do the honeymoon first. It'll help you relax more."

The fear Casey tried to control burst through, crashing over her like an icy wave. Her heart slammed against her ribs, pounding as if trying to break free. She twisted in a feeble attempt to loosen his hold on her arms.

"Tony, no. Please. Don't do this." He voice hitched on the edge of hysteria. Tears blurred her vision. Her body trembled uncontrollably.

Tony stopped and blinked at her, his brow furrowed. He let her go and gently wiped his thumb over her cheek to catch the tear spilling over. "Don't cry, sugar. I'm not going to hurt you. The first time is always the scariest."

Casey took an unsteady step back, her chest heaving painfully as she tried to control her laborious breaths. *Oh God, he is crazy.*

"Come here. Let me show you," Tony said gently. He put his hand out and reached for her. She took another step back. "Now, Cassandra," he said with tense patience. "I've had about enough of this. You are my wife. You will do as I say." He closed the distance in one step and locked his fingers around her arm.

Scott's voice called to her from outside seconds before the door exploded open. Splinters of wood flew into the room like confetti as he charged in with his gun drawn.

Tony wrapped his hand around Casey's throat and yanked her tightly against him. She instinctively brought her hands up to loosen his grip. Scott's name came out on a choking sob.

"Let her go, Tony." Scott locked onto Casey. His heart pounded like fists against his chest. It took more than he had to fight the fear gripping him.

Tony took a step back with Casey in front of him and grabbed a knife from the fireplace mantel. He slipped it out of the leather sheath and held it point out, like a sword.

"Now I don't recall inviting you to our wedding, Scotty boy."

"Put the knife down, Tony, and let her go," Scott said. His heart had nearly stopped when he heard Casey cry out to him. She looked at him with a glassy stare, tears shimmering in her eyes. A dark bruise colored her right cheek and her bottom lip was split. The blood from a small gash on her forehead had already caked and dried.

She's alive. It was the one thing he tried to focus on.

Tony shook his head with a short laugh. "Now, I can't do that, Scott. See…she's mine. She always has been."

Scott raised his gun higher. His hand whitened on the grip. He didn't have a clear shot, not with Casey pressed against Tony. "I don't want to kill you, Tony. Now, let her go," he said between clenched teeth.

Tony laughed then narrowed his eyes to two thin slits, his lip curling into a snarl. "You want her, don't you, Scott? Yeah, I saw you two together. On your couch. Making love," he said, spitting out the words like venom. "That's just like a woman, though. Spreads her legs for just about anyone with a dick." His hand squeezed on Casey's throat. She gasped, pulling at his fingers. Tony spared her a look then loosened his fingers enough for her to catch her breath.

"But see, Cassandra wasn't like those other women. She was special. She was supposed to be saving herself for me." He pressed the point of the knife at Casey's throat. His lips curled. "But you couldn't do that, could you, sweetheart?"

Scott's heart pounded in his ears when Casey cried out. A drop of blood trickled down her neck. He took a small step forward, his hand gripped tighter on the gun.

"Don't do it, Tony," he said, surprised his voice didn't betray the fear he felt for Casey.

"Sorry, buddy, but she's mine. Till death we do part and all that." Tony took another step back toward the bedroom. He pointed the knife at Scott and waved at the door. His mouth curved into a wicked smile. "Now if you would please excuse us, we have things to do."

Tony's hand came off Casey's throat to allow her a gulp of air. Scott took another step, his gun aimed high. He still didn't have a clear enough shot, and he wouldn't risk a shot that could hit Casey.

"You don't need to hurt her, Tony. Just send her to me and we'll talk about this."

Tony stopped in the threshold of the bedroom and sent Scott a baffled look. "Hurt her? I'd never hurt Cassandra. She's my wife," he said. "We belong together. We always have." He placed the knife on the lamp table and shifted her slightly to look at him. "You will always be mine," he whispered. "And I won't let anyone else have you."

Tony reached behind the table with one hand while his other hand cupped Casey's chin and turn her mouth up to his. Casey set her feet and waited for Tony to kiss her. As he leaned in, she bent her right arm and swung it back, ramming her elbow into Tony's stomach. He whooshed out a lungful of air and staggered back. His hand came up from behind the table. Light glinted off his gun.

"No!" Casey broke away and lunged toward Scott.

"No, Cassandra!" Tony reached out as Scott charged forward to pull Casey away. A shot echoed, the burnt smell of gunpowder filling the room. Casey stumbled, falling into Scott's arms. Scott pressed the trigger on his gun as they dropped to the floor. Two shots hit Tony in the center of his chest and sent him flying back into the bedroom.

"Weller!" Agent Simms charged into the room, the shotgun raised against his shoulder. He spotted Tony sprawled in the bedroom doorway before looking at Scott. "You're bleeding. Are you hit?"

"Oh God, Casey," Scott said. The back of the shoulder of the white dress slowly turned red.

"I'm okay. I'm okay," she said, her voice barely audible.

Scott lowered her to the floor and ripped at the dress to expose her back. The bullet had gone straight through the top of her shoulder. A clean wound.

"Yeah, you're okay," he said. He grabbed the handkerchief from his pocket and pressed it to her shoulder. He pulled her up against him, struggling to control his racing heart.

"Cassandra." Tony's voice rasped from the doorway, his hand was extended toward her. "How could you betray me? I'd never hurt you. I love you. I've always loved you." He coughed, blood gurgling from his chest. "I thought you loved me. Why didn't you love me?" He wheezed in a breath, then he went quiet.

Casey turned to look at Tony. Her voice hitched as she spoke, but the only word Scott could make out was 'sorry'. She grasped Scott's shirt and buried her face in his chest. Her body convulsed with sobs.

Scott pulled her closer as his own war with guilt rushed through him.

CHAPTER TWENTY-EIGHT

Scott paced the tiled floor in the emergency room lobby while the doctors examined Casey and tended to her wound. Blood stained his jacket and the front of his shirt. It was Casey's blood and a reminder to him that he'd almost lost her because of his job. He'd avoided love his whole life because he didn't think it was fair to put someone through that kind of fear. He understood it now more than he ever had before.

"Scott, come sit down. You're making me nervous," Jennifer said. She stepped beside him, placing her hand on his shoulder.

Scott attempted a smile and took her hand. "She's okay, you know," he said, squeezing her hand.

"Yes, I know. And Alex is in there with her right now, so we know she's in good hands." She ushered him to a row of plastic chairs. She took the seat beside him and rested her hand on his back.

He hunched over, pressing his head into the palms of his hands, exhaling a heavy breath. His mind flashed back to the scene at the cabin. Casey falling into his arms. The shock in her eyes when she'd been hit. The blood on his hands.

His heart lurched.

"You really love her, don't you?" Jennifer asked.

Scott glanced at her, then looked outside through the double glass doors that exited the hospital. The streetlight on the corner was burned out. The traffic light blinked red, reflecting off the quiet pavement. The town seemed as empty as he felt.

"Yeah," he said, his voice rough with emotion.

Jennifer rested her head on his shoulder. "I thought so."

They looked up as Alex stepped through the automatic double doors. He wore a surgical gown over his clothes. It was stained with blood.

Jennifer jumped from her seat and rushed to meet him. Scott stood and braced as he waited to hear what Alex had to say.

"Is Casey all right?" Jennifer asked.

Alex wrapped his arms around his wife and buried his face in her neck. He held on a moment before taking a deep breath and pulling back. "Yes. She's going to be fine. The bullet went straight through and didn't tear any muscle or ligaments. It'll take some time to heal, but she'll be okay," he said with a relieved breath. He noticed Scott standing by the chairs. His arm tightened on Jennifer's shoulder. His expression hardened. "She's refusing to stay the night, so I'm taking her home with me."

Scott swallowed the knot in his throat. His heart battered against his ribcage, and his lungs felt as if they were going to burst, but he managed to keep the emotion from his voice.

"Good. That's good," he said. "She's going to need to come downtown as soon as she's able and give a formal statement...when she's up to it."

"I'll bring her when she's ready," Alex answered.

Scott nodded and rubbed absently at his chest. He'd heard the final break in their friendship when he called Alex from the ambulance. Losing Casey too was only fitting.

❧

Casey sat propped up on the narrow metal bed, staring at the tiles in the ceiling of the cramped trauma room. The medication the nurse had given her finally kicked in, and she could no longer feel the hot pain from the bullet hole in her shoulder. She wondered if it was the same type of pain Scott felt when he'd been shot and wheeled into the emergency room.

Scott. He'd almost died trying to protect her.

Images of the night fixed to her mind like a video that had been looped to play the same scene over and over. She knew the bullet that went through her shoulder had been meant for Scott. She'd seen it in Tony's eyes.

She couldn't let Scott die for her. Not like the others did. And not like Tony.

She pulled in a breath and rubbed her hand over her face. The pain medication flowed through her with a cloudy sensation, making her feel weightless.

She told the doctors she wanted to go home, but she wasn't sure where home was. Was it New York? Or the beach house she rented? Was it Alex's house or maybe Scott's? She thought maybe she had finally found a place to belong with Scott, and she couldn't help but laugh at the irony in that.

She heard the door open and looked over. She masked her disappointment when Alex stepped inside. "Hi," she said, attempting a smile.

"Hey. How are you feeling?"

"Like I've just been shot," she said, failing her attempt at humor.

"God, Cassandra. I thought I'd almost lost you."

Her voice hitched but she didn't try to blink back the tears. "I'm sorry, Alex."

He rushed to the bed and pulled her into his arms. He shuddered as he struggled to control his own tears.

"I'm okay, Alex. I'm really okay," Casey murmured. She let herself be held for a moment then gently eased him back. She glanced at the door then back at her brother. "Where's Scott?"

"He's gone."

"Oh," she said, biting her lip. His job was done. He didn't want to see her anymore.

"Cassandra, about Scott," Alex started.

"He was doing his job, Alex. He isn't the one to blame for what happened." She pressed her lips together and dropped her gaze to her hands in her lap.

Alex lifted her face to look at him, his eyes narrowed. "What? You think you are?"

"Tony died because of me. And Scott almost died. Because of me, Alex. They always die because of me," she said. She pushed away the tears rolling down her cheeks.

"What are you talking about? No one has died because of you. Tony was crazy, and it had nothing to do with you." Alex took her chin in his hand when she tried to turn away. "He was messed up long before you two got together. Don't blame yourself for him."

"I have to blame myself. It's my fault," she said. Her voice hitched again, and she took a breath to calm herself.

"Cassandra, none of this is your fault," he said, taking her hand. "You should try to get some rest. I'm going to go sign you out so you can come home. You'll feel better once I get you home."

"No. Don't you see?" Casey grabbed his arm before he could leave. "He never would have killed her if it weren't for me."

"Killed who?"

Casey moved her hand to her brow, brushing it over the rough fabric of the bandage. Her head felt as if it was floating ten feet above her body. She closed her eyes, leaning back against the pillow. "I could have helped her," she said. She barely recognized the faint, distant voice as her own. She wasn't even sure if it was really her voice, but she had to tell him. Alex needed to know what she did. "I could have done something to help her. But I didn't. I didn't do anything but hide."

Alex rested his hand against her cheek. "Cassandra, what are you talking about?"

She opened her eyes to look at him. He watched her with such care and concern, it broke her heart. Would he still feel the same once she told him?

She took a deep breath and forced the words from her mouth. "I killed our mother, Alex. It was my fault she died."

"What? Casey, no. Why would you say such a thing?" Alex grabbed her hand and squeezed.

Casey clenched her hands in her lap and shifted her gaze to the ceiling. Tears spilled out of her eyes, burning a trail down her cheeks. "He came into my room that night. Momma found him and they had a fight. I was so scared Alex," she said, her voice breaking. "I thought...I thought he was going to hurt me."

"Oh God, Cassandra. No," Alex said hoarsely.

"It was my fault, Alex. He killed her because of me." Casey shuddered in a breath and let the tears fall. "I didn't want Tony to die. Why couldn't I love him? If I had just loved him..."

Alex wrapped his arms around her, holding on as she wept. "I'm so sorry, Cassandra. I'm so sorry."

❧

Scott considered stopping at the local cop hangout to drink until he passed out but decided to stop and grab a bottle to take home instead. He much preferred drinking alone.

"Detective Weller. How's Ms. Martinez doing?" Agent Simms stepped behind him as he moved to the checkout counter to pay for the three bottles of Southern Comfort he'd grabbed.

Scott spared him a glance, tossing his money on the counter. "Following me, Agent Simms?" He grabbed the bottles and walked out to his jeep parked at the curb.

"Well…yeah. I thought you might be heading this route when you left the hospital. I spoke to your friend. He was royally pissed."

Scott ripped the seal from one of the bottles and took a deep drink. He hissed out his breath as the liquor singed his throat. "Yeah well, I nearly killed his sister. I think I'd be royally pissed too." He offered the bottle to the agent, shrugging when he waved it off.

"No. You saved his sister," the agent said. "And who knows how many other women. The knife Mr. Lankford had on him was the same one used on our latest victim. And we're pretty sure on the rest of them, as well. He fit the profile to a T, Detective. And Miss Schultz identified him as the young man Amanda Ortiz left the bar with. You should be celebrating this one, not drowning your sorrows."

"Well, forgive me if I don't feel like celebrating. I just feel like getting piss-faced drunk." He tossed his keys to the agent and climbed into the passenger side of his jeep.

❧

"Well, you certainly look like shit," Alan Broussard sneered as he approached Scott's desk.

Scott glanced up from the file he was looking through. The remains of the headache he thought he'd finally gotten rid of moved between his eyes, sparking like a strobe light. *The price you paid for a two-day bender.*

"What the hell do you want?" He dropped his gaze back to the file though at the moment he couldn't read two words of it.

"Don't worry, I'm not here about you. Not directly, anyway. I just wanted to ask you some questions about Officer Lankford."

"He's dead. What else do you want to know?" Scott said.

"I'm aware of that."

"Look, Broussard. There's nothing I can or will say about Officer Lankford to you or anyone else in your slimy little world. So you can forget about trying to make yourself into a hero by turning him into a crooked cop. He's dead now, let him rest in peace," Scott said.

"Officer Lankford has been named as a prime suspect in a series of violent murders, Detective. I don't think the families of the victims would give a shit if he ever rested in peace," Broussard returned. "You worked with Lankford. I'm sure you've socialized with him. I think you owe it to the families, as well as this department to tell them what you know. Or is there something you're trying to hide?" he said with a sneer.

Scott didn't think about what he was doing when he bolted from his seat. The quick movement sent his chair tumbling on its side. He grabbed onto the investigator's tie and jerked him forward until their noses nearly touched. "I didn't know a damn thing about Tony Lankford," he said, his voice low and dangerous. "We weren't partners, and we weren't friends. You can dig up all the garbage you want, but don't you even think you're going to pull me down with him. Now, get the fuck away from me before I do something I won't regret." He let go of the tie and pushed the stunned man away from him.

Broussard recovered quickly and stole a look at the other officers in the room. They each pretended they were unaware of the confrontation. He adjusted his jacket and glared at Scott. "We'll do this later. When you aren't so hung over," he said with disgust.

Scott watched him leave then picked up his chair and set it back at his desk. He dropped into the seat, scrubbing his hands over his face. He never liked to lose his temper, even if it was on someone like Alan Broussard.

He turned back to the file on his desk pulling out the reports on Amanda Ortiz. Something about her case bothered him. There was just something about it that didn't feel right. The Feds wanted to believe Ortiz was another Paperback victim, but there hadn't been a book with the body.

"But the knife wounds match the wounds on the other victims," he murmured.

He grabbed an older file and pulled out the coroner's report, laying it beside the report for Amanda Ortiz. He rubbed his eyes clear before scanning the pages. The autopsies revealed the women had all been brutally raped. The person appeared to have worn a condom because there was no trace of semen, just a small trace of latex.

Scott looked at the coroner's report for Amanda Ortiz again. No vaginal tearing like the rest of the women and no traces of semen. However spermicide, a lubricant commonly found on condoms, had been found on her. Tony was fingered as the person she left the bar with that night, so it stood to reason he was the one who raped her. Or, just had sex with her.

He sat back in his chair, rubbing absently at his chest. But did Tony kill her? Or did someone else? A jealous boyfriend? No, she hadn't been seeing anyone seriously for a while.

He pushed his hands through his hair and blew out a frustrated breath. He was grasping at straws because he didn't want to believe Tony was the killer. He didn't want to believe it because of Casey. She had loved Tony once. He needed to make it right for her.

He pulled out the statement Casey had given to Agent Simms. He'd been on the second day of his binge and skipped the meeting. It was going to have to be a clean break if he wanted to get over her.

He tried to distance himself as he read over the report, but the ache was still there. He leaned on his desk, pressing his fists to his temple and continued to study the file.

Before he died, Tony told Casey he loved her. But if Tony loved her as he claimed to, why did he shoot her?

"Because he was aiming for me," he said.

"What's that?" Gomez asked. He stepped up to the desk, giving Scott a worried look.

"Nothing. Just talking to myself," Scott said.

Gomez nodded. Scott knew he recognized the signs of a hangover, having felt the need to overindulge himself a few times over the years.

"I just wanted to see if you'd like to pitch in some money to help Alicia out," Gomez said. "I know she and Tony weren't married, but she was with the man for a long time and rumor had it they were planning to be. Anyway, we wanted to get her a little something from us here at the station. She was a really nice lady. She didn't deserve this."

"Yeah, sure." Scott took out his wallet and grabbed the bills, passing them across his desk. Casey wasn't the only one he would have to make it right for. Alicia grieved now, as well.

He closed up the files and shoved them in his briefcase as Gomez made his way through the rest of the squad room.

He needed a drink.

❧

Scott took a long drink from his beer and scanned the reports he'd spread out on his kitchen table. He rubbed at his chest, turning to look at the notes he set on the counter. There was something he wasn't seeing. What was he missing?

A knock sounded at his door. He set his beer down and went to answer it. He braced, fisting his hands at his side when he found Alex on his doorstep.

"Alex," he said in hard voice. "If you're here to fight, I've got to warn you I won't hold back."

"No." Alex held up his hands in surrender. "I just want to talk."

Scott turned around and wandered back to the table. He grabbed his beer and swallowed half the liquid. "So talk," he said.

Alex stepped into the apartment, closing the door behind him. He glanced around at the disarray in the living room. Strips of yellow police tape lay crumpled on the floor. The residue from the powder used to dust for prints lingered on the walls and doorknobs. Several empty bottles of Southern Comfort were strewn around the small space of the living room.

Scott didn't look any better. He wore his usual faded jeans with a Rosehill P.D. T-shirt and his shoulder holster. His hair was uncombed, his eyes shadowed. He looked as though he hadn't shaved or showered in days.

"Have a party?" Alex said.

Scott turned to look at him, his eyes cold and distant. "What do you want, Alex?"

Alex shoved his hands in his pockets and sighed. He'd gotten the riot act from Jennifer about how badly he'd treated Scott. She even went as far as to tell him that Scott was in love with Casey. Since he'd known Scott for several years, he found that hard to believe. But when Jennifer threatened to leave him if he didn't make things right with Scott, even though it was a bit extreme, Alex decided that maybe he should see for himself.

He stepped farther into the room and crossed his arms at his chest. "So...how are you doing?" This is why men never apologize, he thought sourly.

Scott tipped back his bottle, letting the warm liquid slide down his throat, though he could no longer taste anything. "I've been better."

"Look, Scott. I just wanted to apologize," Alex said. "I was out of line at the hospital...and all those other times. It's just...Cassandra is my sister. And I love her very much."

"Casey is going to be fine now, Alex. She'll go back to New York and put her life back together. She's a strong woman. I don't think she's going to have any residual effects from her ordeal. You have nothing to worry about." He returned to the table and gathered up the files.

"I know you love her, Scott," Alex said quickly.

Scott tensed, his hands briefly stopping on the files before he began to gather them again. "Yeah, well you don't have to worry about that either."

"I'm sorry, man. For everything. I've been a jerk, I know that. But it was always my job to take care of Cassandra, and I failed. I guess it was easier to blame you than myself."

Scott stepped to the refrigerator and took out two beers.

"You can't be blamed for being a protective big brother. Casey is lucky to have you." He tossed a bottle to Alex. He caught it at his chest with an understanding nod. And that was that, Scott thought. Their friendship would eventually survive.

"She's at the beach house," Alex said. "She wanted some time alone before her friend, Jo, came in to take her home. I just thought you'd want to know that."

Scott didn't say anything and instead turned back to stare at the notes on the counter. Alex stepped beside him, placing his beer on the bar. He looked at the notes and frowned.

"I've known Tony for eighteen years. I still can't believe he would do something like this. I always believed he would die for Cassandra. I never thought he would kill for her as well." He shook his head and sighed. "It's like these notes were written by two entirely different people." He placed his hand on Scott's shoulder and squeezed. "I've got to run. Thanks…for the beer."

Scott watched him leave and took a deep breath, rubbing his hand over his scar. For the first time in years he noticed it was there. *It was hard not to be a friend to someone who had their hands in your chest.* He always thought that.

He turned back to the notes lining his counter. He had separated them into three groups. The first set were copies of the notes Jo turned over to the police in New York. Agent Simms said the prints on the Bibles belonged to Casey's father, so he'd been the person who sent the notes. Scott guessed they were his twisted attempt to insert himself back into her life. Fortunately for Casey and Alex, Alejandro Rivera was now back in Huntsville serving ten years for the assault in Houston, as well as the breaking and entering at the beach house.

The second group of notes was more cryptic than the sanctimonious rants of the first set. This group spoke more of undying and everlasting love. Scott had no doubt that they were written by Tony. But if Tony was so much in love with Casey, why would he disfigure the women who looked so much like her?

He looked at the third set of notes, focusing on the words typed across the pages. These were the ones that puzzled him. They were more threatening and hateful. The exact opposite of Tony's other notes.

Alex's words played back in his mind. *It's like these notes were written by two entirely different people.*

He picked up the file box they'd found at Tony's apartment. He'd been granted permission to check them out for forty-eight hours and he was running out of time.

He pulled out each of the books and laid them on the table. He opened them to the month of April, scanning the appointments written on the pages. His heart tripped. He swept his hand over the pages of each book, stopping at the month of June. Panic twisted the muscles in his chest as he scanned the appointments marking the first two weeks. He grabbed the files of the killer's victims and compared the dates.

"Son of a bitch!" he hissed.

Tony might have been in each of the cities during the time of the Paperback Murders but according to the entries, he hadn't been traveling alone.

Scott grabbed his jacket and bolted for the door.

CHAPTER TWENTY-NINE

Casey stood at the window in her bedroom, watching the waves roll onshore. The beach was quiet, the overcast sky leaving the coast empty for most of the morning. A man and his young son stood waist-deep in the water, casting their fishing lines against the wind and waves. A flock of seagulls hovered over them, as if milling around a buffet line.

Casey closed her eyes, taking in the breeze. She had told Alex she needed to be alone for a while, and though he'd been hesitant to let her out of his sight, she was grateful he agreed. She had expected him to be angry with her once she told him how she was to blame for their mother's death. But he'd pulled her into his arms and held her until she'd fallen asleep. When she'd awakened the next morning in his guest bedroom, he was still there. Holding vigil in a chair he'd placed next to the bed.

"I would never blame you for something you had no control over," he'd said. "You can't let what happened destroy your life, Cassandra. Momma loved you very much. She wouldn't want you to blame yourself. She would want you to go on. To survive."

Casey wiped at the tear on her cheek. That's all she could do, now. Survive.

She rubbed at her arm, which was hanging in a blue sleeve draped around her neck. The pain in her shoulder couldn't compare to the pain in her heart.

She had expected to see Scott at the hospital or at least at the police station when she went in to give her statement, but he hadn't been around. She knew it was for the best. They wouldn't have worked out anyway. They were two entirely different people who wanted entirely different things. They came from two different worlds.

He had told her he loved her. But, a man like Scott Weller probably said that to a lot of women just to get them into bed. She could be grateful she never repeated the words to him.

She leaned against the window and eased out a sigh. If only she could stop feeling it.

"You should never have come here," a voice said behind her.

Casey spun around and found herself face to face with Alicia. Gripped in the woman's hand was a small revolver. "Alicia. What are you doing here?"

"You fucking bitch! You should have stayed away. You ruined everything!" Her voice broke as she waved the gun at Casey.

"I'm sorry. I'm so sorry about Tony," Casey said. Tears filled her eyes, but she didn't try to blink them back.

"Don't say his name!" Alicia shrieked. "He thought he loved you. That you were supposed to be together. But he was wrong. It was him and me!" She moved farther into the room, waving the gun to emphasize her words.

Casey took a cautious step back. "No, he was mixed up—"

"You nearly killed him with your selfishness. I put him back together. Me! Not you! It was my love he needed. But he was so full of you I never had a chance." Her eyes darkened, her words spitting out like venom. "I should have killed you a long time ago when I first saw you in California. But then that would have just made you a martyr in his eyes, and he never would have forgotten you."

Casey swallowed her panic, holding her hand out cautiously. "Alicia…please…let's just—"

"I did everything for him." Alicia slowed her steps. Her eyes became glazed and unfocused. "I thought maybe if I could just show him how much I loved him, he'd forget about you. But he couldn't. Everywhere we looked, there you were!" She threw a ripped copy of Casey's book onto the floor and shot a hole into the binding.

Casey jumped, ramming her shoulder against the window. The pain shot through her body like fire. She bit her lip, trying to keep her voice calm. "No, Alicia. He didn't love me. He was sick. He was sick and confused," she said.

Alicia pointed the gun at her and sneered. "I told him what a whore you were and how you'd never be his. But he wouldn't believe me. He just threw my love away just as carelessly as you did him." She edged closer, her steps slow and guarded like a cat cornering its prey. Her eyes brightened, as if she had a secret she couldn't wait to tell.

"He thought maybe he could find you in all those other women. Stupid little whores, just like you," she said with a short laugh. "I had to kill them. It was only right. Tony had to be taught a lesson, you know. That's why I used his knife, planted his hair on that last whore in New York. I enjoyed doing her the most because she looked so much like you!"

Casey's heart jolted. Her blood froze in her veins. The agents were wrong. Tony hadn't killed anyone. It was Alicia.

"Oh my God. Why? How could you do such a thing?" Her voice rasped, unsteady and barely audible.

"He betrayed me! He never should have betrayed me!" Alicia's voice hitched with the tears she tried to blink back. She used her fist to scrub at her eyes, then raised the gun to Casey's chest. "You should have left us alone. You should have disappeared a long time ago. We could have been happy. I would have made Tony happy! But now he's gone, and it's all your fault. You killed him!" She lifted the gun, extending her hand to arm's length.

Casey braced, her eyes locked on to the menacing barrel. Her heart pounded, the blood rushing like a freight train in her ears.

"Put it down, Alicia. It's over." Scott took a cautious step into the room, his gun raised and steady in his hand.

Alicia wheeled around and fired. Scott dove to the floor and fired. Three bullets hit Alicia in the chest, throwing her against the bed. She bounced off the mattress and landed in a crumpled heap onto the floor.

Scott jumped up and rushed to Casey. Her face was pale as if every ounce of blood had been drained from her. She stared at Alicia's body, her eyes glazed, her body trembling.

"Casey? Look at me. Are you hurt?" His heart raced wildly as he ran his hands along her arms to check for injuries. "Oh God, I thought I'd lost you again." He pulled her against him then crushed his lips to hers. His grief and anguish surged through the kiss.

Casey wrapped her arm around his neck and held on tight. "Scott," she said breathlessly. "It was her. It was Alicia."

"I know, sweetheart. I know. You're safe now. She can't hurt you. Come on. Come with me." He led her from the bedroom, closing the door behind them. "Just sit here. I'll be right back." He sat her on the sofa and went to the kitchen to call the sheriff. He never took his eyes off of her.

Casey gave her statement to the sheriff's deputy who responded to the call. Scott watched her from the kitchen while she sat calmly through the questions and answers session.

It didn't take long to get her statement or place Alicia's lifeless body into the coroner's wagon. When it was over, Scott walked the officer out and told him he would be in later to file his report.

He shoved his hands in his pockets as he stepped back into the beach house. Now that they were alone, he wasn't sure what to do.

Casey walked into the kitchen and took a water bottle from the refrigerator. She would have preferred something stronger, but with the pain medication she was on she didn't want to take a chance. The click of Scott's boots broke the silence as he edged into the room.

"When is Jo supposed to be here?" he asked.

"Tomorrow," Casey said. The grip on her heart tightened at the indifference in his voice.

"Good. It'll be good for you to get back to your normal routine. Move on. Try and forget about everything that's happened."

Casey turned around to look at him. *Bastard.* How dare he allow her to fall in love with him then tell her to forget it even happened? "You want me to forget *everything*," she said, anger adding an edge to her voice.

Scott crossed his hands over his chest, regarding her with an even expression. "I think that would be the best thing for you, yes."

Casey set her bottle down with a deliberate snap and moved to stand in front of him. She lifted her chin, pinning him with a glare. She'd felt the passion in his kiss. Why would he push her away now?

"I see," she said through clenched teeth. "And again, you seem to think you know what's best for me."

Scott squared his shoulders not bothering to hide the annoyance in his voice. "I know it would be better if you went on with your life in New York. Staying here isn't the type of life you deserve," he said. *Of all times for her to want to fight.*

"Since when have you ever had a say in what type of life I deserve?" Casey snapped. She glared at him, pushing her finger against his chest as she spoke. "I've always taken care of myself and made my own decisions without help from anyone else. And I plan to continue to do that whether you want to be a part of it or not."

Scott's heart stumbled at her words. He grabbed her wrist to stop her one handed assault and narrowed his eyes. "And what's that supposed to mean?"

Casey pulled her hand back, lifting her chin with a challenging look. "It means I love you, Scott. It's taken me a lifetime to find someone I could truly feel that way about. But I won't hold you to it if it's not what you want."

Scott moved closer. Her defiant look shot heat straight through him. "If it's not what I want," he repeated. He cupped her face in his hands. "It's what I've wanted since the first time I saw you. I've never *stopped* wanting you, Casey." He rested his head against her forehead and felt the pain in his heart fading. "I love you. More than my own life. But I can't ask you to give up your life in New York for me. It's who you are. Where you belong."

Casey lifted her hand to his face and looked at him, her eyes soft. "I don't have a life in New York. And you are who I want and where I want to be."

The certainty of her words flowed over him, the warmth settling in his heart. He took her hand and placed it against his chest. "You don't know what you're getting yourself into being with a cop."

She looked at their joined hands then lifted her eyes to his. "I know exactly what I'm signing on for, and I'm not the least bit afraid of it," she said.

She spoke with such fearlessness he couldn't help but grin. "Then neither am I."

He buried his hands in her hair and pulled her into a kiss.

~ABOUT THE AUTHOR~

Terri Molina is a native Texan, born and raised in Southeast Texas. She is an active member of the Romance Writers of America including the Northwest Houston Chapter and Desert Rose Chapter in Phoenix, Arizona. She writes multicultural romantic suspense, blending in the flavor of the Southwest with her Mexican heritage. After years of living a nomadic life with her Coast Guard husband, she now resides in Southeast Arizona with her husband, four children and a dog. When she's not writing she enjoys reading, singing karaoke with the kids and spending time with family and friends.

www.terrimolina.com

Made in the USA
Middletown, DE
20 April 2015